Good in Theory

The Funny You Should Ask Series

Cori Wamsley

Aurora Corialis
Publishing
Pittsburgh, PA

Good in Theory

Copyright © 2025 By Cori Wamsley

Paperback ISBN: 978-1-958481-42-4

Ebook ISBN: 978-1-958481-43-1

Printed in the United States of America

Cover illustrated by Pierre at Fiverr

Edited by Allison Hrip, Aurora Corialis Publishing

Other Books by Cori Wamsley

Praise for Good in Theory

"This inspiring story showcases the power of resilience, perseverance, and the indomitable spirit of a woman in science. With unwavering determination and a brilliant mind, she faces her self-doubt and fear amidst a web of deceit and treachery. Get ready for a thrilling adventure that celebrates the triumph of knowledge over darkness and the unyielding spirit of a true heroine."

~ Em S. A'cor
Author of *Twitter Crush* and *Twitter Flames*
EmSAcorBooks.com
IronedWordsProductions.com

***

"A wonderful tale of growing up, acceptance, and recovering from the past. Lacey's smart, witty, and overall goofy approach to her life and the strange things happening at her job were engaging and kept the pages turning—and I certainly can't complain about the little sprinkling of romance throughout!"

~ Sarah McKnight

Author of *A Journey of Love and Painted Wings*

Twitter: @mcknight_writes

Facebook: Sarah McKnight - Author

Instagram and TikTok: @sarahmcknightwrites

***

I throw on joggers and a tee with a comic book drawing of a woman in a lab coat, holding two beakers, saying, "I have all the solutions." If I didn't laugh at the all the science jokes, who would?

"Lacey, a researcher who studies gut bacteria in salmon, feels stuck in her life and career. But everything changes when the lab she works in suddenly shuts down for mysterious reasons, and her curiosity pulls her into a dangerous and secret investigation, where she uncovers a nefarious scandal. In the process, she rekindles old friendships, discovers new love, and finally finds purpose in her life.

"*Good in Theory* is a well-crafted, rollicking story filled with humor and romance. It is especially sure to please mystery-lovers, readers who appreciate a strong female protagonist, and anyone who laughs at science jokes.

"I enjoyed it from beginning to end."

~Ann K. Howley

Author of *The Memory of Cotton*

@annkhowley for FB, IG, Threads

www.annkhowley.com

***

"Cori Wamsley's *Good in Theory* captures the audience with a riveting storyline. Lacey finds herself in the most exciting part of her career that is soaring into a crescendo. Yet, in one quick moment, Lacey finds everything changes rapidly all around her, which is scary and even exhilarating. Readers will discover the intrigue of deceit, family relationships rekindled, old memories flooding through Lacey, and much more as a mystery unfolds around her. *Good in Theory* is beautifully written, quite suspenseful and intriguing.

"Additionally, Cori is a gifted book writing coach and editor who helps other authors find their authenticity in their own stories to share with the world."

~ Sue E. Fattibene,

Life Coach, *Author of The Day the Angel Sat Beside Me*, Motivational Speaker

www.suefattibene.com

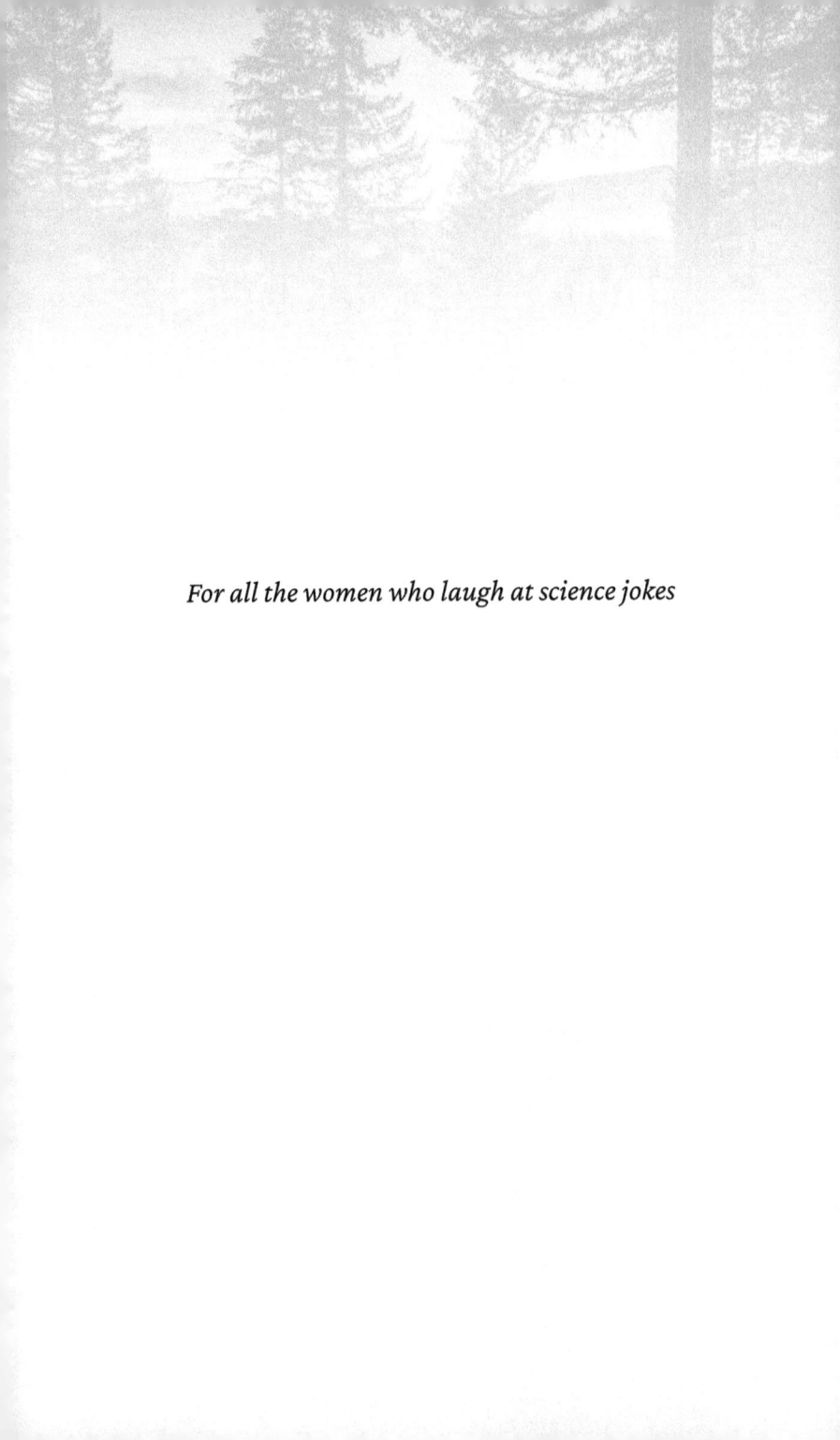

For all the women who laugh at science jokes

Author's Note

T hough my books always have happy endings, I do tackle some difficult topics because I want to give background to how my characters are reacting to the world around them. If you don't mind a mild spoiler and would like to be prepared for the tougher content, please read the note below. I do, however, try to write in a way that reduces the chance of triggering the reader.

This book contains a brief mention of a drug overdose and death (side character), as well as discussion of a past cancer diagnosis and treatment (main character). There is also a difficult boss and a shady ex, who is mixed up in something questionable.

Chapter One

T he lab is unusually quiet today, aside from the tap of fingers on keys.

We're done. At least with this set of experiments.

For the past year, our group has been researching the microbiome of sockeye salmon in natural waters in the Seattle region. Our goal was to compare our results to tests performed in the region every five years. We have lists and levels of microorganisms present in the gut and on the skin of salmon dating as far back as the 1960s. Some of this testing was performed by scientists who have long since retired: a cool legacy project.

Our results are both exciting and disappointing.

Disappointing because, obviously, the levels have changed drastically due to climate change. Some parasites that were present in earlier tests and even seemed to be thriving in recent years have completely dropped off in this year's data. Like they don't exist at all anymore. We could be seeing the start of an extinction event, wiping out the most fragile and least adaptable creatures first. Yikes.

Exciting because ... this is my jam. I love that I get to study fish, especially salmon because it allows me to stay close to home. I grew up running through the fields and creeks of Issaquah, east of Seattle. I loved frogs and fish. I'd go fishing with my dad and my cousin Blaise while my sisters went shopping or baked cookies with Mom. Incidentally, I can catch a catfish and pan fry it over an open fire, but I can't make a batch of chocolate chip cookies from the tube without burning them. It's best to eat the dough from the tube with a spoon anyway, right?

The rivers, streams, and winding waterways in the northwestern part of Washington State are teeming with fish, hundreds of species, and I managed to stumble on important research on one of them when I was doing my job search a couple years ago, fresh from my doctoral work on bacteria in chum salmon.

I lucked into an internship at Northwestern Laboratory for Biological Studies (NLBS) because my mentor Dr. Tataro is friends with the chief research officer of the lab, Dr. Cuervo, and he recommended me for the opening with the salmon group. So the wilds of Washington and my retired parents are only half an hour away now. I get the mountains and wildflowers and Snoqualmie Falls anytime I want. It's kind of a dream. I managed to keep the position due to "brilliant work" or as I like to call it, keeping my head against the glass of the fume hood or my eye glued to a microscope. I've done little other than work to get to this point since I was eighteen.

It's easy to forget about everything else going on in the world when your own world grows so small. You forget to call your dad and don't even realize that your parents sent a care package that your roommate left for you on the counter. I'm glad the most recent one didn't have cheese in it, especially since I no longer have a roommate. They learned.

I tend to be hyper-focused. It's not a bad thing. And thanks to my laser focus, this is the moment I've been preparing for.

"Lace, did you submit your abstract for the Parasitic Research Symposium yet?"

I give a sour look and a nostril flare to my lab mate, Luke, who knows I hate being called "Lace."

Even "Lacey" is hard sometimes. Try being a scientist, living in a virtual men's world, and be taken seriously when you have a cutesy girly name like "Lacey." My work is usually credited as "L.S. Sturm," which is fine. Most people assume I'm a "Lucas" (head nod to Luke over there) or "Lawrence" or "Liam." I tried out going by "L. Sutton Sturm" in college to sound more serious, but when Dr. Cartwright thought he was being funny and called me "Sudden Storm," it led to "Stormy" as a nickname, and I about died.

It's definitely a fairy name. That's the opposite of serious.

Even without a name that sounds flimsy and frivolous, being taken seriously as a woman in science is incredibly hard. Then try being five foot eleven with red hair. I'm just a bundle of contradictions.

Luke ignores the look, then prods me in his *professional voice*. "Dr. Sturm ..."

"Dr. Davis," I answer with snark. I smack the mouse button, clicking "send" on my screen. "Yes, just sent it."

"*Did you?*" Twyla squeals. "I'm so happy for you. You *deserve* to present about this." She places a hand on her heart and sighs dreamily. "We've all had our moments at the Parasitic Research Symposium. I remember the first time I presented ... 'Impact of Iprodione Runoff on *Actinobacteria* and *Proteobacteria in Wild Salmon Populations in Port Orchard and Commencement Bay.*' That was a great study. I was fresh out of school. Did I tell you that's how I met my husband?"

"We know, Twyla," Luke winks at me, and I grin. Twyla's love story is pretty cute, but she brings it up a lot.

"Luke, what were you asking about?" He never said *why* he wanted to know if I sent it, and a fresh wave of nerves washes over me. Did he have a correction to the results that I should have added before I hit send?

"Just checking that you had." Luke leans back in his desk chair and rocks. "I'm with Twyla. I'm hoping you get that one."

"What did you submit to?" I ask.

"Ichthyology Association of America. God, I love a good fish studies event! Their conference is in July. This year they are in—" he drumrolls on the table— "Costa Rica."

"Why do they hold the conference out of the country?" I ask. That makes no sense when all the members are here.

"Why not?" Luke flashes a big dopey grin. "It's an excuse to travel. See a new place. Meet new people. Talk about fish and drink like a fish." He weighs the two thoughts like his hands are a scale.

"You are a permanent frat boy," I respond.

"Who's a permanent frat boy?" Dan asks. He strolls into the lab with a pile of papers fresh from the printer, likely for applications that require printed copies of the research and our paper.

"It's you, Dan," Violet says. Typically quiet, Violet waits for opportunities to zing us.

Dan chuckles. "Of course." We just had his sixtieth birthday celebration last month, and the thought of Dan doing a keg stand suddenly makes me snort.

"I can only imagine." I return to my desk, sliding the handful of notes from the recent *Firmicutes* cultures into a file in the drawer.

"Lacey, I didn't see that canister outside that should have gone to Parsons & Brewster," Dan began. "I'm guessing someone got it."

"Yes, the lab number was the same, just the wrong building. I told supplies to send it to the geologic research building, and they picked it up after lunch." I glance at the clock just over Dan's shoulder and realize it's time to head home. It seems a little anti-climactic, considering we all just finished submitting this research to organizations and journals across the globe, at least the ones that are accepting submissions right now. We missed a couple journals that I really wanted us to submit to because of a frozen pipe that delayed some of our findings. (It's weird. Don't ask.) But we can always submit later this summer for the next edition. "I'll see you guys tomorrow. There is a seafood linguini in the fridge calling my name." I cooked last night and made enough for leftovers. My life is pretty exciting, obviously, since I'm looking forward to reheating it tonight.

"That sounds so good," Violet says. "Nadia is cooking tonight. Not sure what we're having. I'm hoping for fish tacos—."

"You know," Luke interrupts, "we could all go to Los Amigos Cantina for dinner and margaritas, *ladies*." He says that like he's thinking Dan would go regardless, but the rest of us would *only* go for the margaritas. Personally, I could devour like three or four fish tacos myself. And maybe a pitcher of margaritas. Oh, and the company would be nice too.

"Honestly, we *should* celebrate our submissions, send them off in style," Twyla agrees.

"Really? You aren't in a hurry to rush home to your honey?" I tease.

"I know I should be, but this is special." Twyla's face breaks into a grin that crinkles her eyes. That expression brings me such joy. It's lovely working with someone so positive and supportive and ... well, happy. She shakes her ash blonde hair from its claw and pats Dan on the shoulder. "What do you think? Or will Sandy be expecting you?"

"I can let her know I'll be late," Dan nods, twitching his salt-and-pepper mustache when he grins. "This is a night to celebrate, and I can't let Luke be in charge of the debauchery or I may not have a lab team to come back to tomorrow."

"Aw, come on." Luke waves him off. "I'll make the reservation." He pulls his phone from his jeans pocket and starts tapping at the screen. Crossing one long leg over the other, he leans back in his chair again, casually rocking.

"I have to get my car, so I'll probably be later than you guys." My car is in the employee garage behind the apartments, which are reserved for people who work at the Exploration Research Plateau—"the Plateau," because no one has time for all those syllables. I didn't name it, so don't blame me. The best part of living here is that I can walk to work, and with the sun finally out and an April-miracle high of sixty-three, I couldn't resist. Since everyone else drove, their cars are all clustered outside NLBS.

The Lab is comprised of several departments, studying many different aspects of the living world all in one building. The next building over, building B, is Guttmann (pronounced "goot-men") Pharmaceuticals, so lots of researchers there too. We also have a geological research group, Parsons & Brewster, on the other side of the pharmaceuticals facility, building C, so there are tons of people working in a small area.

I jog inside my apartment to drop off my bags and change. I've been in the same long-sleeve cotton shirt since seven a.m., so I'd love something a little breezier. I throw on a sleeveless floral silk watercolor blouse in cream and grab my chocolate brown biker jacket. The jeans will do, but I swap my tennis shoes for red ballet flats. With my purse on my arm, I clatter down the stairs to the breezeway to the garage where my blue Corolla—named Lizzie—is in spot 4L. I slide in and drive the ten minutes to Los Amigos Cantina.

When I enter, I spot my lab mates at a table already, in the back corner under the huge painting of a young woman in full *Dia de Los Muertos* regalia, where we often go for our lab lunches. Violet is there, playing with her glossy black curls as she listens to something Luke is saying, so I guess Nadia gave her a pass. They're newlyweds, but they do need time apart.

As I'm reveling in the aroma of steak fajitas from a nearby table, I hear Luke raise his voice over the din of mariachi music and people ordering burritos. "I just think it's arrogant of humans to assign bipedalism to all aliens in movies."

"They aren't all bipedal," Dan replies. "Some are quadrupedal."

"But those are always pets or beasts of burden," Luke continues. "By and large, the aliens that are intelligent look like us with different heads." He takes a swig of Modelo and runs a hand through his walnut brown hair, rumpling it in a different direction. He does this when he's excited about a discussion, so he always looks windblown when in a verbal melee.

I've heard this conversation before, and I know it ends with them examining every sci-fi movie, show, and adaptation of their favorite books, hunting for aliens that support their argument. Luke inevitably wins because 1) he is single and has way more time to dive into this stuff and 2) Dan usually gives up good-naturedly and offers to buy him another beer, which he always accepts. I'm certain this is Luke's way of getting free beer.

Twyla pats the seat beside her, so I sit down.

A few moments later, as I'm hanging my jacket on the back of the chair, I hear, "You win, Skywalker." Dan throws his hands up and chuckles.

Luke touches his hands in prayer position and bows. He loves it when people call him by his middle name. His parents were really into *Star Wars*, and apparently the first name "Luke" wasn't enough to satisfy that itch.

I lock wide eyes with Twyla and shake my head. She laughs.

"How are things with Derek going?" she asks with a little twinkle in her eye. I notice that she has rolled up the sleeves of her pink button-down blouse, so Twyla is in full celebration mode.

Derek is the guy I've been seeing for the past two months. He's adorable and clever. He runs an investment group with his best friend Richard, who is incidentally *not* a Dick. And doesn't go by a nickname either. Derek is always curious about my work, which I appreciate. I haven't often dated someone who wants to hear me talk about fish and their various parasites and gut bacteria, so I gotta enjoy that whenever it comes along.

I'm not big on listening to the investment talk, but I always do listen. Right now, he's involved with a big client in farming or something. A sustainable and eco-friendly project. He can't disclose details, but it sounds like a good idea. Who doesn't want to be more ecologically responsible?

"It's going well." I answer, flagging down Carla, the server, for a raspberry margarita, the best of their specialty drinks. "We went golfing over the weekend. He's a little more serious about it than I am, but we had a good time." Carla flashes a smile when she recognizes me from all the other times we've eaten here and takes my drink order.

"I'm happy to hear that," Twyla says. She sips her lemon water. "You know, when Sam and I got together, we loved to sit around and talk about our interests so much that we barely left the house. We had to make ourselves get out and do things." She laughs the crinkle-eyed laugh again. "I'm glad you two aren't just *twittering* each other all the time."

I seriously don't know if that's slang she picked up from her kids that I don't understand or if she used a word wrong.

"I said something funny?" Twyla said. And it clearly shows on my face.

I blink and register what she probably means. "Tweeting? You mean we don't just talk to each other on social media?"

"Yes, tweeting," she waves it off.

"Good! I was afraid it was something you and Sam do at home." Violet with the snipe. She winks as the rest of us cackle.

"You know what's funny?" Luke says. "We never did find that missing specimen of *Loma salmonae* last week."

"I swear I put it back in storage after examination," I say for the fiftieth time. "It's been driving me nuts."

"I'm not worried about it," Twyla answers. "We already had all the counts we needed."

Luke shrugs and takes another sip of his beer. "Another mystery we shall never solve."

The evening presses on with more light ribbing, talk about our results and the excitement of pitching to journals and conferences, as well as enough fish tacos to sink a very happy ship.

I'm the happy ship.

I'm also floating from my twelve-ounce margarita. "I'm going to run to the ladies' room," I tell Violet. She gives me a thumbs up and a nod as I hop out of my chair.

On the way back, I pause while walking past the bar. There is a news story on, and I swear the lab was in the background of the shot, but they cut back to the reporter in the studio and start talking about something else before I can be certain. Huh.

"Hey, Red," a guy at the bar says.

I realize I'm about two feet away from him, so definitely in his personal space. "I'm sorry. I was looking at the news." I start to walk away, but he puts a hand on my arm.

"I've seen you before. Are you a model or a basketball player?"

Because clearly I'm tall so that's all that's open for me. "Scientist," I respond.

"Can I buy you a drink?"

My retreating form should be enough answer.

"What did that guy say?" Luke asks when I get back to the table.

The server has cleared everything, so I sign the check and shake my head. "Same as usual."

All four of my lab mates roll their eyes. "Let's head out," Dan says. For good measure, he glances at his watch and lets out a deep breath, as if we've been here for hours and us crazy kids kept him out late again.

As I pull onto Exploration Drive a few minutes later, I get a sick feeling in my stomach that it really *was* the lab in the background of that news story. It's dusk, but all the parking lot lights are on, so I can see a swarm of blue vans clustered close to the entrance to our building. People in hazmat suits are shuffling about by the vans, carrying briefcase-looking boxes, making notes on clipboards ... Something is definitely not right. My chest gets tight as I wonder why.

I don't know whether to park and go in my apartment or turn around.

Chapter Two

My apartment ... that's when I finally look at the nondescript beige brick five-story where I live. People are coming out with suitcases. A woman in baggy sweats is wearing a full backpack and carrying her cat. A girl about my age has a laptop bag and a huge rolling suitcase. I can only hope they are all going on vacation and I've stumbled through some sort of rift in the space-time-continuum. Their grim faces are telling me otherwise.

I spot my neighbor, Drew, with a backpack and carry-on heading toward the parking garage, so I pull up and roll my window down. "Hey!"

He gives me a tip-lipped smile. "Lacey, it's not good. Park and I'll tell you what's up."

"Hop in, and you can tell me while I drive." Our spots are side by side, so I might as well get the low down before my stomach squeezes itself to death with nervous curiosity.

In the car, he tells me what he knows. "They aren't telling us much." Lovely. "Some guys in hazmat suits— I'm sure you saw them—are checking out the labs. Something leaked, and they are afraid that it could get in the air and groundwater."

My heart almost stops. Drew works in my building, studying infectious disease, and is the lead for their lab. He never talks about it because they have a government contract, so "it's classified," as he always jokes.

"What were you guys working on?" I whisper.

Drew blows the hair off of his eyebrows. "It's classified."

"Hardly time to joke."

"It really is."

"*Time to joke?!*"

"No. Classified. I had to talk with the guys out there about it, though, so they know what they are dealing with. As soon as they called, I ran over to the vans to let them know. Then I packed up." As I pull into the parking spot, I feel him staring at me. "They told everyone in the building to pack for two weeks away. Whatever it is, it's something bad."

"You don't think they are just being cautious?" I'm hoping.

"No. Definitely bad. I overheard someone mention involving federal agencies when I was filling them in on my group's work."

"Huh."

Drew opens the car door. "Pack up and get out of here. Be safe. I'm sure after they talk to Dan, he will call you guys with instructions."

I rummage in my glove box for a stray plastic-wrapped N95 from Covid times—I think that like it was the Dark Ages—and don it while I dig out my phone. Then I look up to see Drew waving at me while talking on his phone.

I pop out of the car. "Yeah?" A drum set is doing a show-stopping solo behind my ribs.

"I've got someone from that lab here," he says into the mouthpiece. "Should I send her over?"

My lab?

"Okay, I'll tell her." He hangs up and exhales. "They want to find out what chemicals you guys were using, so I said you could talk to them. They don't seem to have Dan's number on their emergency list. Go see Brad Nelson. He'll meet you by the van closest to the entrance."

"Am I safe to go over there? They all had on hazmat suits. All I have is this thing." I point at the flimsy paper mask on my face.

"He would have said something if it was dangerous. Like I said, they are taking this pretty seriously."

A man in a dark blue jacket stands at the end of the sidewalk with a clipboard in hand. He's just wearing a mask. I mean, he's not naked and *only* wearing a mask. Yikes! It's regular clothes, not a hazmat suit. That must be Brad. He locks eyes with me amidst the bustle when I'm a couple parking spots away.

"Dr. Sturm?" When I nod, he starts asking me about the work we did in our lab and what sort of chemicals we were using. I rattle off the list. Nothing toxic or lethal, since we were studying bacteria and trying to keep it alive. That's the only bit of reassurance I have that it wasn't us. Then my heart sinks.

"There was a delivery last week that should have gone to the geological lab in building C," I offer. "I believe that was straightened out, though. We don't know what was in the tank." I don't know if it's important, but I should disclose it, right?

Nearly an hour later, he has as much information as I could give him about compounds that had passed through our lab recently. I've given him the name and number of both Dan and the lab tech in supplies, who tracks stock and ensures that it goes to the correct rooms. He would have rerouted the lost tank. Plus, Brad has my name and number, just in case.

I barrel up the stairs past the few people left lugging their things to the garage. Once in my apartment, I pull the mask down for a moment so my phone can see my face and unlock. Then I replace the mask and text Derek, letting him know that there's an emergency and I need a place to crash.

Have you ever packed for a vacation in like ten minutes? Try it. It's super exciting.

I quickly select outfits for a couple weeks. Will I need work clothes? Casual? Athleisure? Workout? Going out? Warm weather? Cold weather? No idea. I pack it all. Five pairs of shoes. Now I understand why that one lady had a huge suitcase with her.

My phone buzzes as I zip the suitcase, but it's just a social media update for MyCircle, the app everyone's using now. I tap the text icon and see that Derek hasn't read my message yet, and a flicker of disappointment crosses through me. It's only nine p.m., so it shouldn't be a problem. I can always surprise him. Surprise! Your newish girlfriend may need a place to crash for a couple weeks.

I can find a solution tomorrow. I definitely don't want to impose.

Right as I'm about to duck out the door, I remember the most important thing. I jog back to the refrigerator for the seafood linguini. Priorities.

Chapter Three

With my ridiculously large suitcase, my seafood linguini, and a couple smaller bags loaded in my car, I head over to Derek's. It's a twenty-minute drive through a couple pretty neighborhoods, and I obsessively tip up my phone at every stoplight, thinking I heard it vibrate.

Nope.

I ease into a parking spot on the road across from his house, and for the first time since I pulled onto my own street this evening, I just breathe. I didn't realize how clenched my chest was till now. Tipping my head back, it's a relief just to focus on the starry sky above. It's a hodgepodge of mottled purples and deep blues from the swirls of wispy clouds playing peek-a-boo with the tiny pinpoints of light, shimmering forever away. It's a moonless night, so I don't see much down here on the ground aside from where some porchlights and a lamppost on the next corner illuminate the two-story homes lining the block.

Gazing back at the sky, I breathe in four, hold four, out four, hold four. And again. After a few more times, I feel like I've stretched my lungs enough that they should inflate all the way now. Shallow breathing makes you feel anxious, and I don't need to encourage that emotion right now.

A final glance at my phone confirms Derek still hasn't seen my text, so my showing up is going to be a surprise. Now that my pulse has settled, the exhaustion hits all at once, and part of me just wants to talk it out with him. I want to feel safe. To curl up against someone. To breathe in that familiar mix of his cologne and shampoo and whatever laundry detergent he uses. It's a scent I'm still getting used to—clean, warm, almost comforting—if not for that faint edge of cloves that never quite fits.

Maybe I'm a little excited at the idea of spending the night at my boyfriend's place. I haven't seen him since Sunday, and I've been itching for something more than our usual calls and scattered texts. Not that those aren't sweet—I do love when he sends me a meme or a quick *Thinking of you, babe* with a kiss emoji. It's corny, but it's cute. Still, it all feels a little... surface-level tonight, like I'm reaching for something deeper than what we usually do.

Derek lives in this adorable craftsman-style home with a beautiful big front porch in a nice neighborhood. The two shades of gray with white trim and black shutters looks really sharp. I actually love looking at the house whenever I pull up, thinking about how nice it will be this summer to hang out in his backyard. Host a barbeque together. Cuddle on the porch swing ... I'm big on cuddling. The house is lovely, even now with only the glow of his porch lights. It looks like a peaceful port after a raucous storm.

I grab my overnight bag from the back seat because—whoa—I don't want to scare the poor guy with the big honkin' luggage. I'm only staying the night, unless he says it's okay to stick around, so I just have what I need in here. I'm actually a little giddy that I might get to stay *two* nights in a row and finally spend some time together this week. Next step is a shared Amazon account. Not that I'm pushing. I throw my purse over my arm and snatch the food container from the floor. Not letting *that* spend the night in my car.

Derek's doorbell has been broken for a couple weeks, so rather than pressing the button and making us both listen to the whining noise it now produces, I dig the key from under the mat.

When I get to the entryway, I say, "Hello?" in a surprisingly normal voice. I chew my lip, nervous that he could be asleep already since he hasn't seen my text, and also, I suddenly realize he could be mad that I just came in without him giving me permission to do so. Navigating this early phase of a relationship can be quirky, delicate. He told me about the key "in case I need it," though, and being homeless definitely falls into that category.

The living room off the entryway is empty, but I hear voices coming from the sunroom at the back of the house, which he also uses as an office. Setting my bag on the storage bench, I head toward the sound of Derek's laughter.

"Uptown Funk" is playing in the background, which is probably why he didn't hear me come in. The obnoxious fluorescent light is on in the office, so I peek around the corner from the kitchen and give him a winning smile. "Hey, you." His business partner, Richard, is leaning over the desk, gesturing at something on the screen.

"Hey, babe, I didn't know you were coming over." Derek immediately steps from behind the desk and wraps me in his arms. I close my eyes and melt into his embracing, instantly feeling somewhat better after the chaos of the evening. "Richard, I'll be a sec," he says. "Go ahead and wrap up." He ends the hug a little faster than I wanted and gently nudge-walks me from the room.

I lean back into the doorway before I explain to Derek what's up. "Hi Richard, how are you doing?" I say. And then I realize that Richard is hurriedly shoving something from the desk into a bag. "Do you want some help? Or is it a secret?" I joke.

Richard's cheeks have flamed pink by this point, and I approach the desk. *I think ... it's money.* Is he shoving *money* in the bag? Quickly? Why does he have stacks of money? Is this weird? Should this be weird? This isn't a movie! Nobody has a bag full of money!

"Playing Monopoly?" I half joke, my voice quivering slightly. Derek wraps an arm around my waist, but it feels urgent rather than warm. I know I look like I've seen a ghost when I turn to Derek, and I return to square breathing, counting in my head, while I wait for a response. "What are you guys doing?" I finally say. *Drug deals? Robbing banks? A jewelry heist?* Calm it down, Lacey! He has to have an explanation. That thought at least helps me slow my breathing.

Derek runs a hand up the back of his head and sighs like it's going to be a big story. "Remember that organic farm project that we aren't allowed to talk about? We're bringing on a couple consultants to help on the scientific end of it. We're meeting with an expert in aquaculture tomorrow, and we wanted to sweeten the deal with some extra money up front. It's really nothing." He shrugs.

But my Spidey senses are tingling at this point, and I don't think that's the full truth. "Why not just cut a check?" I'm trying hard in my head to make this normal, but I feel like it's not. Not the way Richard was scooping up the cash. And why did they have it out? Were they going to throw it in the bathtub and swim through it like some crazed billionaire? My parents used to joke about doing that with our allowance money all the time when I was little. So *maybe*?

I'm thinking this is not normal, and my breath catches in my throat.

"Some people are really impressed with cash, babe," Derek says. My arms are limp when Derek takes both my hands in his.

"Oh." Of course they are. It makes total sense.

"Richard and I are pretty excited about the prospect of this project. There's no way it can fail because this is what people want. Who *doesn't* want high-quality, farm-raised food?" He squeezes my hands. "Maybe we can take a nice vacation this fall, once we start seeing a return on investment."

I perk up a little at that, though my stomach remains knotted. We've both talked about how much we want to go to Napa Valley in the fall. It feels oddly like a really grown up vacation, but I bet it's gorgeous. We've done a lot of the local touristy stuff like hiking around Mt. Ranier and Mt. St. Helen's. We both thought it was so cool that you could still see the lava flow from where it erupted in 1980. It was still chilly out when we hiked it, but it's so beautiful that you hardly mind, especially with the company.

"I'd like that." Maybe this is okay. It totally makes sense that they would be waving cash around for a big project. The knots loosen a smidge.

"We really need that aquaculture expert to come on board since her background is in the same fish they want to raise on the farm," Derek continues.

Richard coughs out a laugh. "Unless Lacey wants in."

Derek shrugs and turns back to me. "Honestly, you have a lot of the same knowledge we're looking for. Maybe we could talk about it."

"I like my job, but I appreciate it."

"You just wrapped up your project this week though, right? Maybe take tomorrow to talk it over with us, since you won't be going in." Derek kisses my forehead, and Richard nods a little too enthusiastically.

Should I at least find out what they are looking for? If it's just a couple questions I could answer for them, that might work. I glance back at the desk where the money had been, and my chest tightens up.

"The lab is almost set up, so you could even take a look at the facility." Richard shoves his hands in his pockets and leans against the front of the desk like he's trying to be casual about the conversation.

"The owners of the fish farm have a lab facility?" At first, that sounds kind of cool. I never thought about the science behind raising food, but … no. That's odd. Why would they have their own lab? "They aren't paying a lab to do the research? That's a lot of work to set up the facility."

"Ah … they want to ensure total secrecy." Derek's eyes dart back to Richard, and I don't miss the exchange. What's up with them? "They patented a technique last year and are waiting for a couple more patents to come through, so once we have this specialist on board—"

"They have a patent already, but they don't have the lab ready? How did they pull that off?" It's starting to feel… fishy. And not just because it's a fish farm. My heart starts pounding hard. *Is he actually involved in something illegal?*

"The owners are building on some current research and, uh, had another scientist working on it. The lab makes it more convenient and ... lets them keep the project more confidential." Derek nods now, like maybe I'll agree with him because I see that.

Maybe, right? My insides twist a little. I don't know how a small business would handle this. Though ... if they need to keep it all confidential, maybe once they got the ball rolling and saw that their idea had merit they would invest in a lab. *Hey, wait a sec.* "How did you know I'm not going in tomorrow?"

"The news," Derek answers way too quickly. He's staring into my eyes like he's trying to drill the idea into my brain. "We had it on earlier, and they said there was a leak at the lab from one of those trucks that's always going in and out. The tankers with frack water, I guess." He shrugs. "They said the lab would be closed tomorrow." *This. is. the. truth.* waves are being beamed directly from his brain to mine, but something is really off.

Something isn't adding up. I saw the news story at dinner, then talked to Brad-Whatshisname about the chemicals we use in the lab. When I left, they still didn't know what caused the spill—they were scrambling to track everything down. So either Derek didn't see the same report I did... or he's stretching the truth about the tankers. And I can't figure out why.

A tight pressure builds behind my eyes as irritation creeps up my throat. What a night. Then another thought hits, sharp and unwelcome: If he *did* know, why didn't he call to check on me?

He rubs his hands up and down my arms, but I barely register it. "Anyway, the owner wants to make sure their product is identical to wild-caught fish." He's talking faster now, eyes flicking toward Richard. Something is definitely off. I shouldn't be here.

"No." I pull back from his hands and take a step toward the entryway. "You couldn't even call to check on me if you knew all that was happening? Weren't you concerned?" I grab my overnight bag, my pulse thudding. "And I don't want to be part of whatever this is. This scheme. I'm leaving."

"It's not a scheme." Derek looks annoyed now. "It's a business opportunity." He throws his hands in the air. "Why are you turning this into something it's not? Richard and I have put a lot of work into this. We're trying to help the company grow, and now you're just... dismissing everything like you know better. Like you're the only one who sees the big picture."

I blink at the sharpness in his voice, my step faltering. "Whoa. Okay." It stings that he thinks that's why I'm asking questions, but mostly it just throws me. "I'm not trying to make this a fight. I just... don't want to get mixed up in something that sounds shady." My voice stays steady even though my heart is thudding hard. I hate conflict, especially with someone I care about. "You said it was nothing, and then I walk in to a pile of cash. That's confusing, Derek. Anyone would have questions."

Derek seems to cool down and grabs my arm, looking pleadingly at me. In a softer tone, he says, "Come on, Lace. Let's just sit down. We can talk more about it. I have that tea you like."

I give him a look (he knows I hate being called "Lace"), shake my arm free, and push on the storm door before I realize that I still have his house key in my hand. Shoving my bag further onto my shoulder, I drop the key on the porch and take on the awkward task of trying to shove it under the mat while balancing a food box and holding the door open. It's taking longer than I thought it would. I could put my stuff down and lift the mat up, but I'm committed to this now, ridiculous as I look. I don't even care. "I'm done."

"Lacey?" Derek mutters. He has to know I really meant I'm done. *He didn't even text to see if I knew they were evacuating.* Am I making that mean something? No, any normal person would have been concerned. So why wasn't he? Does he even care about me?

My chest clamps around my heart like it's protecting it as I stomp to the car. My face is hot, and tears are starting to slide down my cheeks, but I maintain my stony look, and I don't turn back.

Chapter Four

Back under the sky I found peaceful and soothing just a few minutes ago, I throw my bag in the back seat and climb into the driver's side. Staring at the food container, I wipe my face on a napkin from the center console and sigh before plopping my leftovers back on the passenger seat. *I don't know what to do, buddy*, I think, as if talking to the seafood linguini, my travel companion. And I can still see Derek out of the corner of my eye, silhouetted in the open front door.

"Why couldn't they just play video games together?" I say through clenched teeth. Stomping on the brake, I press the button to start the ignition and am greeted with a coughing and sputtering sound. *No.*

Just to delay the inevitable, I go through another round of square breathing—I never thought I would use that so much—and try again. Sputter and wheeze.

As much as I hate to do it, I look back at the doorway, but Derek is gone. At least he's not watching me try to coax my car to life so I can drive off angrily.

My brain swings away from the calm of my breathing and starts unraveling. *I didn't come this far to only come this far. I've made it through tough times before. This is only one day. And I know it will end. The lab will open. I'll go back to my place. The car will start. Someone out there will let me fall in love with them …*

Searching for hope, I glance at the food box on the seat beside me. At least I didn't leave the best damn seafood linguini of my life in that felon's house.

Alright, focus. I wipe a finger under my eye to catch the tear threatening to ruin my mascara and take a shaky breath.

Now what? Dad will know.

I tap his name on my phone, and after a couple rings, he answers cheerily. "Hey, sugar. Mom says *hi*."

My whole body buzzes happily at the sound of his voice. Warm. Safe. I suddenly can't hold myself together any longer and just start sobbing. "Tell her I said *hi*, to," I manage before the sobs take over.

"What's going on? Are you hurt?" Dad has swung to full parental concern now, so I need to knock it off.

"Not hurt." I wipe my nose with the napkin, calculating how much to tell my dad without causing him to worry. "I broke up with Derek." Let's just start with the one normal-sounding thing today.

I hear Dad let out a long sigh and give him a second to sign to my mom what's going on. She can read lips, but he always gives her the courtesy so she doesn't have to. A moment later, he asks, "Do you want to talk about it? Mom and I are walking on the beach. It's beautiful here this evening."

I mentally smack my head. I was hoping for an offer of a rescue drive home and an invite to just stay there tonight, but they're at Pismo Beach on vacation. "No. I just needed a friendly voice." I sniff and immediately feel guilty because I know I'm making *him* feel guilty.

"Sugar, I bet your cousin would love to hear from you. She's not too far away. Why don't you give her a call before it gets too late. See if you two could meet up. Maybe she would be up for a chat."

I blink, and suddenly I'm back in our basement the summer after eighth grade—Rona and me sprawled on the carpet, flipping through Teen and my sisters' contraband *Cosmos* while we demolished cheese fries from Sal's. *Gossip Girl* on the TV, *Kim Possible* queued up for later, both of us pretending we were so grown up even though we were still giggling about everything. That was the summer we dyed her platinum hair with cherry Kool-Aid and were convinced her mom would actually murder us. We thought we looked amazing. In reality... early-teen fashion and my braces were doing us no favors.

I haven't talked to Rona in years, but my dad always tries to get us to reconnect. Her mom, my Aunt Mindy, is his only sibling, and they've always been really close. Mindy was on the road so much for work that Rona practically grew up at my house. We used to be close, too...

My dad must have taken my silence as a chink in the fortress wall that I had built between Rona and me. "I'll send her contact info. Think about it."

"Thanks. Goodnight, Dad."

When I hop off the call, I mentally scroll through a list of all the people nearby who might be able to help. Mostly, I have acquaintances here, not the kind of people you should call for something like this.

My sister Haley lives close-ish, but she has a new baby, and I don't think she would appreciate driving to pick me up. Her husband wouldn't either. They are both so sleep-deprived. Also, *I* don't want to be a zombie tomorrow, on top of everything else. Baby Hudson has a set of lungs. Maybe I'll call tomorrow about stopping by. I haven't seen him in a few days, and I need my baby fix. That would help my mood.

It still doesn't solve my current problem, though. I sigh. I probably shouldn't have let my AAA membership lapse last year.

Think. Think.

A moment later, a contact labeled "Macaroni," my dad's nickname for Rona when we were growing up, shows up in a text from my dad. "Any port in a storm, right?" With no other viable options, I hold my breath again as I click on her number.

It goes straight to voicemail, which means that either 1) Rona already has me in her phone and still has beef with me or 2) Rona thinks I'm someone calling to talk about her car's warranty. I've never been mistaken for a spam caller before ... but regardless of the reason, I leave a quick message. Now I'm debating calling a tow truck or one of my lab mates, who would not be under any obligation to save my butt and would definitely need the full story. I would never hear the end of how I owe them because Luke would remind them *every day*.

It's probably best that Rona didn't answer. I love her, and she was my best friend for a long time, but she was always pretty irresponsible, even before she disappeared. I bailed her out in our high school classes so often that I just assumed she wouldn't take notes in class, forgot her book at a friend's house, wrote the test date on the wrong day in her planner ... Several times, I covered for her because she ran out to smoke weed at a friend's house on the weekend, and her mom would ask later if she was with me. She leaned on me a lot when she was finding herself, and then she left me to deal with—

Then my phone rings. *And it's Rona.*

"Lacey?" She sounds surprised. No doubt she should be.

"Hey, how are you?"

"I'm good. Where are you? I can come jump you."

"I'm really sorry to bother you after all this time. Dad said you live nearby ..."

"It's not a problem. What's the address?"

A few minutes later, I see a little red hatchback pass under the street light, heading my way.

Biting my lip, I watch as it creeps down the avenue toward me, feeling immensely guilty. For years of not talking. For years of not understanding why. For years of not asking. For just years of ... of missing my best friend and never doing anything about it. I turn on my headlights so she knows which car is mine and then wave her down.

When Rona Richards climbs out of the car, she looks like some sort of ethereal Rastafarian being— long blonde dreadlocks swinging with her gate, shining the same pale blonde in the light of my headlights that her hair always was, without Kool-Aid in it. She's dressed casually in a hot pink jersey knit jumpsuit and a paisley satin bomber jacket. Her presence is easy and calm, nonjudgmental, and I'm thankful for that. I feel like squirrels and birds are going to swoop down and help her jump my car the way she glides down the sidewalk to me.

"Hi." Her gentle smile reaches her eyes.

I smile back, nearly in tears again. "Hi." Our eyes search each other's for a moment as the silence settles around us, broken only by the sound of crickets.

"Let's take care of the car. Maybe talk afterward?" She grabs the cables from her trunk as I pop the hood. "Heading back to your house?"

"Actually ... I was leaving my boyfriend's house." I point my thumb in that direction. "We just broke up." I don't feel like giving details right now. I'm even more worn down just thinking about that part of the evening.

"Sorry." She throws me a sympathetic scrunch-face.

We continue for a few moments in silence before I decide I have to spill the important parts of the story. "Actually, I'm not sure where I'm going. I can't go back to the apartment because there was a leak at the lab, so they closed the Plateau and kicked us all out. I think there is a Fenton Inn on Grant Street. If I can make it there, I'll grab a room for the night and deal with the battery in the morning."

"Oh, no. I won't let you do that. You'll stay with me." She touches my arm gently and then pulls back, like she's afraid of the contact. "I know it's been awhile, but you're family." When I don't reply, she sighs. "You can't say *no*. You're coming."

"I didn't say that to make you offer." Major guilt. God, I hate it when people feel sorry for me. "The hotel is fine, really."

Rona gives me a look that reminds me of Aunt Mindy catching us sneaking in the back door after curfew. "I will disconnect these cables if you say *no* again." She crosses her arms for emphasis.

I glance back at Derek's house in time to see a curtain twitch. Ugh. But I shouldn't care what he thinks. "You win." I start the car, it roars to life, and we wait. "Guess I'll follow you."

Soon, we turn in to a neighborhood of mid-century modern homes with neat little yards spotlighted by a periodic streetlamp. We make a right at Hollenbeck Street and pull into the first driveway where I park beside Rona so I don't block her. We will have to go get a battery in the morning ... or whenever she can take me.

It just occurred to me that I don't know what hours she works. Or if she lives with anyone. Maybe I'm blocking *them* in?

I pop out of the car. "This okay?" She nods and motions for me to follow her to the front door, so I grab my overnight bag and food and start walking.

She futzes with her keys. "The lock is tricky. One sec."

I glance around, searching for anything to fill the silence, and my eyes catch on the nearby street sign. A memory hits me so hard I almost laugh. "Are you a *Holl-en-beck girl?*" I blurt in rhythm, the words coming out with way too much confidence for a joke that dumb. In my head, I'm suddenly back in my basement with Rona, jumping on the couch and screaming Gwen Stefani at the top of our lungs. God, we thought we were unstoppable.

Rona sings a line from the song, ending as she spells *bananas*, wigging her head side to side with each letter, and we both chuckle. But when the lock clicks, she stops and looks at me for a moment. Almost reading my thoughts, she says, "Want to get cheese fries?"

A quiet laugh slips out of me, surprising both of us. "More than anything. You don't have to be at work early?"

She glances at her Apple Watch. "It's fine. Sunny's is on the next street."

Chapter Five

When we're seated in a booth at Sunny's, I can hardly believe the turns my day has taken from submitting my abstract to a prestigious conference and celebratory fish tacos to becoming a refugee and eating pity cheese fries. Really good cheese fries with bacon, mind you, but the mood could stand to be on the positive end a little more. At least this place seems cheerful.

It's a little hole-in-the-wall, and for as late as it is, it's crowded. The servers are dressed in white tees with "Sunny's" arcing across the front over a bacon-and-eggs smiley face, yellow sunshine streaks bursting from over the "S." They're scrambling to grab orders from the kitchen, where a combination of '80s metal and sizzling bursts through the swinging door. The floor repeatedly kisses my feet as I move them under the table, telling tales of syrup that dribbled off of pancakes, and I kind of like it. It's very real.

Rona plucks a fry and dunks it into the cheese and bacon. "I know you've had a rough day, but there isn't much that Sunny's bacon cheese fries can't fix."

I snort. "I wish. This one has been a doozy." As we munch on our snack, I repeat the events of the day, ending with my boyfriend ... ex-boyfriend trying to cover up something fishy right before I ran out of the house to a car that wouldn't start.

As I tell my story, Rona squints in disbelief, opens her mouth wordlessly, and then squints in disbelief again. She clearly doesn't know what to say to my stranger-than-fiction tale. Finally, she crosses her arms and leans back against a worn maroon cushion. "Man, that's something else." There you go. My story is that crazy.

"Thanks for listening. I actually feel better about it now. Plus, the fries help. And the company." I swallow hard, and my eyes start to water as I think about the time that slipped by after the last time we hung out. "I missed you. A lot," I say softly.

Rona eyes me for a moment before she breathes out the weight of whatever was holding her back all these years. "I missed you too."

We eat fries in silence, no doubt both thinking about what we gave up. "What happened, Rona?" I venture.

She chokes on her fry and grabs her water. "Sorry, no one has called me that in a while. Wow."

I raise my eyebrows. "You go by your full name now?"

She coughs out a laugh. "Don't be silly. How popular do you think I'd be if I introduced myself as 'Corona'?"

Good point. Covid would have been brutal for that. "It's your choice. I'm not about to judge." I sip my soda. "So what do you go by?"

"Saoirse Ember. I had my name legally changed in mid-2020. I had thought about it before because of ... well, lots of things. But I found something I liked, so I went with it. Appropriate timing and all that."

I mouth it slowly to get a feel for the name. *SEER-sha ... EM-ber.* This is so not the Rona I knew. How do I respond to that? About ten different thoughts go through my head, and I somehow land on, "That's really pretty. Do you write vampire romances now?"

"What happened to not judging?" Saoirse gave me a sour look. "No. But I see why you would say that. I actually design websites for health and wellness practitioners. People who do yoga and reiki and have metaphysical stores and all kinds of wonderful things. Health coaches and masseuses and sound healers and even an acupuncturist a few months ago."

"That's ... wow." I don't know what half of that is. How do you heal someone with sound? And what are you healing? Like an injury? Is this like when an opera singer hits a high note and shatters glass? Probably not. Maybe I'll ask when it's a more appropriate time. "Websites, huh? I bet that's a really cool job."

I remember her being more flighty. Not the type of person who would learn about computer coding and be able to build a business. She actually showed up at track practice without her tennis shoes before. I imagined her as an adult waiting tables or selling jewelry online while living with ten of her closest friends.

"It is." Her smile is genuine, and I'm glad to see that her life makes her happy. "I meet a lot of wonderful people. I've been at it for a few years, so my clients are mostly referrals from other clients now. It took a while, but it's steady. I have a team. And I can take breaks when I want ... which is lucky for you because I'm off tomorrow. I had already scheduled it."

"I'm glad you're so fulfilled." I'm still itching to know why we stopped talking before, but the moment has passed to bring it up without force. "How did you choose your name?"

"Oh," Saoirse got a dreamy look about her, "the name chose me." I blink, not sure if she's joking. Then she clears her throat. "Actually, it was my grandmother's name."

"I thought you didn't know anything about your dad's side."

"I met her right before she passed, maybe five years ago."

"I'm sorry to hear that. I'm glad you got to meet her though." I grab another fry. "What was she like?"

"Warm. Gentle. Fragile." Saoirse's faraway look tells me she's imagining her. "Her eyes crinkled up when she smiled or laughed. It was strange because I could see myself in her then. And a few days later, she was gone."

My heart twists. "It's nice to remember her with her name, though."

"It is."

We continue eating in silence a few minutes, and I debate about bringing it up again. I have to know why she left. But is this the right time? I feel pretty battered. Maybe it's a convo for another—

"Do you remember when you used to have dreams about that boy?" Her smile is pure mischief.

Now it's my turn to almost choke. This is something I haven't thought about in a long time, mostly because it seems silly.

When we were teens, I used to dream about a boy around our age. He would hang out with me, doing whatever I did in the vision. He wasn't one of my friends or a boyfriend. Just some strange kid with sandy blonde hair inserting himself into my dreams.

"I actually forgot about that." I tap a fry into the cheese. "Remember we called him *Edward* after the guy in those vampire movies."

Saoirse launches into ripples of laughter. "I remember that! Did they actually look anything alike?"

"Vaguely? Maybe?" I frown. "No."

"What did we call them? *Transome?* Like *so handsome that you're in a trance*?" Her voice is mocking, but that's a great memory.

I can't help but snort laugh. "That was the word. What were we on?"

"High on life and our own cleverness." Saoirse wipes a tear of joy and lets out a long sigh. Calmly, she adds, "I still think that was your soulmate calling out to you."

I roll my eyes. "Well he stopped calling, so I'm guessing he either got bored or hooked up with someone else."

"Maybe you stopped wanting him to call." Saoirse shrugs. "Maybe it's none of my business."

The last time I dreamed about him was right around the time of my diagnosis. "I had other priorities," I say flatly, a sour feeling in my stomach. I don't want to talk about that.

"I get it." She swirls her straw in her water.

I decide to change the subject. Maybe we shouldn't touch on anything more from the past tonight. "So are you seeing anyone? Do you live with anyone? I didn't think to ask earlier. I hope my car isn't blocking them in."

She grins like she's thinking about someone special. "Anthony doesn't live with me, but yes, we are pretty serious."

"Tell me about this guy." It's so weird to get a peek into her world after all this time apart, but she seems willing to share. It's a good start.

"He's really great! He works as a pianist at Riff's."

"The piano bar on Brinkley Street?" I ask, and she nods. "So is that how you met him?"

She laughs. "No. I, uh, donated a kidney to his aunt."

Everything I ever thought about Rona ... Saoirse is flipped on its head. *Donated a kidney?* By the time we stopped talking, I was fairly certain she was going to be a pothead who followed bands around her whole life and cared little about herself or anyone else. "Wow, so how do you know his aunt then?"

"She's a local organizer." I must have made a face, because she elaborates. "Traci helps people declutter and organize their homes. I met her at a networking group and then worked on her website. Not long after I finished, I found out she needed a kidney. She's one of my favorite clients, so I checked to see if I was a match. Turns out I was." Suddenly, Saoirse laughed again. "You don't have to look so shocked. I have the scar to prove it, if you want to see it."

"That's just … that's really selfless of you." All this time … I had this picture of Rona in my head. She was only concerned with herself. I mean, she had to be, to just leave the way she did, letting go of a friendship so tight for no reason. I knew she packed up and ran off with her mom when she turned eighteen, right before our senior year. It was when I needed her most. I was surrounded by my sisters, my parents, my other friends … but she was my bestie, my other half. And it hurt to be abandoned. I thought she didn't care. Back in the present, I see her in a new light. "That's really brave," I whisper. And I mean it.

"We all have to do brave things. After what you did, I feel like I got a late start at twenty-six." Her eyes look glassy, but she blinks and tips her drink toward me. "Cheers."

"Cheers. You're not at all what I expected." I sip my soda and nudge the fry container toward her. She deserves the last one.

"Don't award me sainthood just yet." She snaps it up and pops it in her mouth. "So, I'm really curious about the lab thing. What do you think actually happened?"

"I must have left one of our cultures out on a table, and the janitor dumped it in the trash." I'm fully aware that this theory is delusional, but it's too funny not to share. "And somehow it reacted with a rotten ham sandwich that Dan threw out that day, which created a toxic runoff that leaked out of the trash bag and into the ground, eventually setting off one of the monitors set up outside of the lab, and that's why there was a swarm of dudes in hazmat suits there this evening."

Saoirse bites her lip to keep from laughing. "Interesting theory. What's your evidence?"

I wave my hand like *obviously*. "Dan threw out a ham sandwich because he said the ham tasted funny. The same day the culture went missing." I chuckle. "In all seriousness, though, a culture I was examining that day actually went missing, but I'm certain I put it away after I collected the data. For the last few days, Luke has been on me, jokingly, about leaving stuff out, but I swear I always clean up."

"You've always been pretty neat."

"I know, right?" I can't help the wave of guilt that washes over me though. I feel like it's something I did, even if it wasn't the culture. I'm the newest one in the lab, after all. It wouldn't be surprising. The rest of them probably blame me for it anyway, especially since Luke keeps mentioning it. Sometimes, I feel like I'm never going to measure up. Like I'm always behind. I'm just starting my career, and everyone else is lightyears ahead of me.

"That's frustrating. Doesn't sound like that Luke guy would be much fun to work with."

I frown. "Nah. He's good. Just likes to tease people. Luke has actually been really supportive. Occasionally annoying, but supportive. He's a few years older than me, and his career—and Star Wars fandom—is his life."

"Gotcha." Saoirse takes the check from the server as she passes by. "Ready to go?"

I nod and follow her to the cash register. I know deep down that it wasn't the missing culture and a ham sandwich making nuclear babies together, but at the same time, I have this weird feeling in my gut, like when you think you've left the curling iron on. It's a shame they aren't giving out any info so I can stop feeling like it was me.

In the car, *Champagne Supernova* softly plays while we drive. The song came out the year I was born, not that I remember that. My parents had an old mix CD with that song on it, and they used to play it in the car when I was little. I could fall asleep to the crashing waves at the beginning if it weren't for four older sisters chattering away around me. It's tough being little in a big family.

Now, though, it's strangely quiet, just me and Saoirse, and I catch myself humming along, almost missing the familiar chaos as I'm lost in a strange new one. Sitting beside someone I thought was the left shoe to my right one who somehow now feels like ... I got nothing.

Not a shoe at all. A boot? Are we flip flops? Maybe two different shoes. I let it go and sink into the moment. "Someday you will find me ..."

The blinker clicks in rhythm as we turn onto Hollenbeck and pull into the drive. It's nearly midnight, and a wave of exhaustion overtakes the one of guilt, building into an "I can deal with it in the morning" feeling oozing from my worn out brain.

Chapter Six

When I wake up the next morning, I am struck by three things.

It doesn't feel like a Fri-yay. More like a Fri-why--did-I-think-yesterday-would-be-normal. Even the thought of an extended weekend—because, surely, we will be back at work on Monday—isn't exciting because I have this overwhelming feeling that *I* did something wrong. I can't shake it. Despite my joking about the ham sandwich and the missing culture, I really don't *believe* it's my fault ... yet there's that little poke in my gut, like my anxiety is holding a sign that says, *Probably your fault.*

Plus, what happened with Derek curdles my stomach. How could I have been so wrong about him? I let my guard down. I let him in. And he turned out to be ... what? Sketchy? Secretive? Definitely not the guy I thought he was. And uncaring? Sounds like it.

Two, when I open my eyes, I discover that I'm not in my own room at home, with the white walls, dark wooden furniture, and the warm-colored batik bedspread that Rhiannon, my oldest sister, found at some obscure market in the LA area and bought for me. This room is all smoky blue, white, and mocha ... calm and curated, but not mine. I feel like a foreigner. I get it—I'm in a guest room, but still. At least the sunlight streaming in the windows is the same, right?

And third, as I'm coming into all these strange feelings of not belonging, betrayal, and failure, something soft and strange drifts up from my subconscious.

It's fuzzy at first, but I begin to remember a dream I was having right before I woke up. I was in a hot air balloon, floating around aimlessly. I wanted to land, but I didn't know how to control it. I was completely helpless. I was alone for a bit, but then there was a man in the balloon with me, and I felt like I knew him.

Sandy brown hair with a cowlick that refuses to be tamed and eyes that couldn't decide between ocean blue or amber. He looked impossibly familiar, like when your soul recognizes someone before your brain does.

We seemed to be friends in the dream, and I kept asking him to help me. He didn't know what to do either. Then he was just playing a guitar in the basket of the balloon. I have no explanation—it's dream logic I don't remember any sounds from the dream, but I saw him strumming. And I knew it was nice. I felt calm.

Then I stopped worrying about landing and just looked around me. We floated over lush green hills, a majestic waterfall, a billowing field of wildflowers. And then we were in my hometown, Issaquah, floating over the streets.

I woke up when we were hovering near my house, a sense of calm wrapped around me like a blanket.

I flick the covers off, my feet hitting the cool floorboards, and pad to the bathroom in my pjs. Then out to the sunlit kitchen where Rona, sorry, *Saoirse*, is brewing a pot of coffee and eating granola. She's in a knotted gray tee and pj shorts, her dreadlocks piled in a scrunchie the size of a small planet.

In the daylight, I get my first good look at her. She looks almost exactly the same as when we were fifteen, which hits me in a place I'm not ready to unpack. Same twiggy legs. Same high arched brows, now with a scar by one, likely from a piercing. Same tiny but mighty stance with her legs apart, chest thrust out, like she's taking up extra space somehow that way. But her face tells stories that only someone who used to be so close to her could see evidence of, beyond the thinner cheeks and wise eyes of today.

She covers a yawn and looks at me with droopy eyes. "'Morning," she says. "What do you usually eat?"

"Cereal's fine." I pour a bowl of granola too and join her at the table.

"Did you sleep well?"

"Yeah ... weird dreams, but yeah." I brief her on the hot air balloon ride.

"Is that Edward?" Saoirse cocks an eyebrow, looking suddenly wide awake.

"Edward?" My stomach does a weird hopeful-dreadful flip, but something isn't clicking. "I don't know his name. Could be a barista ... or maybe the UPS guy ... or someone from my apartment building." My brain is only half functioning, so I'm running out of ideas. "He looked familiar in that *déjà vu* way—like we've crossed paths in another life." I frown as a ripple of memory zigzags through my soul. "Oh! Are you saying ...?"

She nods excitedly. "The dream guy. When we were in school."

I laugh. Huh. It's certainly been awhile. "Maybe. He's all grown up now. But that sounds about right. Not so statuesque when we were kids though."

Saoirse laughs. "Clearly. It would be weird if you dreamed about men, aside from movie stars, when you were young."

"Totally." Thinking that this is over, I scoop a large bite and shove it in my mouth.

"I think your soulmate is calling out again. Just my theory."

A tiny, ridiculous spark lights in my chest. "Mmmm," I mumble through my breakfast. I somehow feel a mix of longing and disbelief because this stuff doesn't happen in real life ... but I wish it would.

"I'll get us some coffee." She gets up and heads to the kitchen. "You like milk and sugar?"

"Yes please." I follow her because I'm pretty particular about how much. My last boyfriend, the guy before Derek—maybe two years ago?—used to load up my coffee with so much cream and sugar it tasted like a milkshake. Acts of service was his love language, but that one felt like sabotage. We broke up for other reasons, but I really thought *that* would be the straw.

Saoirse hands me a cup, and I proceed to add the *correct* amount of whole milk and sugar. I feel like the silence is stifling, so I'm debating telling her about my ex trying to give me diabetes because it's kinda funny, when my phone buzzes with an email. I look at the screen for a couple beats, but I'm not close enough for it to register my face, so I have no information other than *it's an email.*

But I don't pick up the phone or lean over or tap the screen. I feel frozen in place, pulse thudding in my throat like someone pressed pause on me, but the rest of the world is still swirling by. My brain spins because I'm in this momentary bubble where I'm focused on reconnecting with my cousin and then a reminder of the outside world smacks me. I'm not sure I'm ready for the outside world this soon.

"You look freaked out." Saoirse leans over my phone, but the screen goes black. "What was that?"

"An email."

"Have you received those before?" she deadpans.

"Ha ha. I don't know if I want to look. It's work."

"Oh." She stirs her coffee and takes a sip, letting the silence stretch again. "You could just open it to see what's going on instead of assuming it's bad." She rests her mug on the white granite countertop.

"Yeah." I still don't move. If I did something wrong, they would call me. Right? Not email. That would be for general info. I take a deep breath before grabbing the phone and opening it. "Oh." I let the breath out. "Dan, our lab lead, wants to meet with us at Monroasters Coffee at one. He probably booked the private room."

"That's not so bad. Maybe he just wants to touch base. Make sure you guys know everything he knows."

"True." As far as "bosses" go, Dan is a pretty good one. He's jovial and smart, pretty quiet. He has high expectations for the group, but we tend to reach them because he's pretty positive and supportive. I have no complaints within our lab group. Overall, I have a great team.

I bet Saoirse's right. Dan probably wants to meet and talk about what's going on because he knows we're all worried and confused. Even Laid-Back Luke has to be a little curious about why Taco Thursday led to a random day off, though I'm sure he's sitting around this morning playing Battle Cry on his gaming system and hoping Dan changes his mind about the meeting. That is, if he's even up yet, now that I think about it.

I tap out a quick response to let Dan know I saw the email and will be there this afternoon. Then I type the address for Monroasters Coffee into my maps app and see that it's just a few blocks away. I can walk if we don't get the car battery taken care of in time. A quick check of the weather assures me that I won't need a heavy coat, which I forgot anyway, and I also won't need an umbrella. How's that for luck? I mean, *after everything that happened.*

Balance, maybe? Or the universe throwing me a pity bone.

The rest of the morning with Saoirse is nice. We talk about Derek a bit because I need to rationalize my decision to leave and stay strong about not dating someone who will likely soon be on the FBI wanted list. Saoirse jokingly talks me out of trying to call in a hot tip. I don't know what they were up to anyway. But being evasive is *no bueno*.

For a minute, I actually pity myself until I realize that it all brought me back to Saoirse, which is bound to be good, right? We were like PB and J for so long. Maybe we can be like that again someday. Later. When we have a chance to talk through what happened properly. And when I'm not held together with duct tape.

My stomach is in knots. It's a wonder I keep the tree bark we had for breakfast down.

I had packed a book because I thought I would be hanging out while Derek worked today, so Saoirse and I head to her living room once I think I can focus. I need to relax and get my mind off of everything. I plump up the tangerine pillows on her couch and create a safe space that I then drape myself across, feet dangling over the arm rest. I somehow manage to prop my elbows up perfectly in my little haven so I have an almost ergonomic position to read from, and it's divine,

Saoirse is flopped on her stomach on the opposite couch with a copy of *Cosmo*—ha! I look over the top of *Twitter Crush* and a gentle smile spreads across my face. It's easy being with her in our comfortable-avoidance-of-important-issues hangout, and it makes my chest ache a little. But honestly, I'm okay with it for now.

It's just enough to be back together, though as I think about it, a tiny bubble of acid pops in my belly, reminding me of how we left things all those years ago. It will have to wait.

Right now, I let myself sink into the homey feeling of being back with my best friend. It's warm and weightless, almost like drifting in that hot air balloon from my dream.

Chapter Seven

After a shower, I throw on a buttercup colored short-sleeved sweater and linen pants so I'm "professional" enough for a meeting but will be comfortable at the café. Then, I help Saoirse make a pasta salad with veggies and chunk chicken, and we eat lunch. When it's time to walk to Monroasters, I throw on my shoes and the biker jacket from last night and start down the street.

My phone buzzes right before I grab the sleek door handle at the coffee shop, so I pause to check it. Derek is calling. I send him to voicemail because he doesn't deserve my time.

When I enter, I see that Dan has commandeered the private room. I eye up the settee by the floor-to-ceiling glass windows. The furniture looks newish and firm, and I sink into the mocha micro-suede cushion, suppressing a moan. I do love a firm chair. God, I'm getting old.

Dan looks up from his tablet and smiles. "Go ahead and grab whatever you need while we're waiting on the others." He nods toward the counter. As I get up, though, he looks back at his tablet and frowns. Ugh, why? What does it say?

I order my vanilla oat milk latte and lean against the wall as the barista makes it. A glance back at Dan tells me he's either deep in thought or reading something disappointing. And I know that he's going to tell us what it is, but that doesn't stop me from future-tripping down a scary alleyway because I know I have to wait. Might as well fill the time with my nerves.

More than likely, it's about last night, but it also could be something to do with our results or submissions to journals or conferences. We just started pitching and submitting yesterday, though. I doubt he's already received a rejection.

Unless there's something glaringly wrong.

I twitch as I think back to yesterday afternoon when I hit the button to submit my abstract for the Parasitic Research Symposium and Luke interrupted me. What if that was divine intervention, and I ignored it?

I almost laugh out loud at the thought that the universe would be using Luke to stop me from doing something stupid, but I'm sure weirder things have happened.

I checked over our results and the way I described them about fifty times before submitting that paper. I also had Twyla look at it, since she offered. But what if something slipped through? What if we both missed it? Sometimes, I wonder if I only made it this far because the rest of my team is so thorough. Would I have completed research at this stage in my career with a different team? Certainly not on my own.

"Lacey," the barista calls, and I'm forced to jam my harried thoughts back into Pandora's Box and reach for the cup. Still though, *am I faking it as a scientist?* It's the first time I've really let the question surface, and I'm almost afraid of it.

When I return to my chair, the rest of the team has found seats and are taking turns placing orders and greeting each other.

"You never answered my texts last night." Twyla crushes me in a motherly hug that I wasn't expecting, almost spilling my latte. "I'm glad to see you're okay."

"I didn't get a text from you," I respond. I pull my phone out to confirm. Then, I show her our last thread, where she was offering me a lemon lavender bread recipe for my mom, who has become more interested in baking since she retired.

Twyla pulls her phone out, and sure enough, there is a series of red exclamation points alongside texts where she was asking if I was okay, since they announced on the eleven o'clock news that the Plateau apartment building had to be evacuated. She offered me a place to stay too. So sweet, if they had gone through!

I take her phone and click on settings. As I suspected, "Your Wi-Fi is off." We both laugh and sit down as my phone dings a dozen times with her worried messages from last night.

Dan clears his throat, and we all come to attention. He's perched near the front of his chair, like a serious Buddha with a mustache. "Thanks for meeting me. I'm glad to see that everyone is safe and no one reported to the lab this morning." He grins. "I guess this will be a case to make everyone have their work email on their phones." We all glance at Luke, who has been fighting it, but he's not acknowledging the poke. I'm certain that Dan had to text him about our meetup.

"Anyhoo ..." Dan continues. "I wanted to make sure everyone knew what I know because that's only fair. Last night, Colton D'Angelo, the lab's lead of safety operations, called. Normally, the sensors we have positioned around the Plateau would pick up on gas or liquid leaks pretty quickly, but remember that storm a couple months ago?"

Everyone nods.

"The sensors were damaged by an electrical surge, and no one was aware till they went back this morning to check readings. So the leak compounded before it triggered the emergency alert system."

I gasp, but Dan continues.

"The ppm for a few dangerous chemicals was so high by the time anyone realized something was going on that they had to evacuate the campus. Right now, they are investigating the source and type of chemicals in the leak. From what Colton said, the leak happened on the ridge between Guttmann and Parsons & Brewster, but they aren't sure exactly where."

"Sounds like it's not NLBS, though," Violet says.

I breathe a sigh of relief when she says this because it confirms that it's not my fault. Unless, of course, it has something to do with that package that was supposed to go to the geological group but showed up at our lab instead. But I suppose that wouldn't be my fault either. I just told them it wasn't ours and pointed them in the right direction.

Dan makes a face that makes my stomach drop. "I'd agree, but that's where the dumpsters are for the entire Plateau, along with a delivery area. None of the facilities on the Plateau are off the hook. They're checking garbage trucks that have been in and out, along with all delivery trucks for the past couple months. This ain't over."

"Dang nuclear babies ..." I mutter as I tip my cup to my lips. Luke gives me a wide-eyed side eye that certainly says, "Come again?" but I ignore it. Focus on the coffee.

"What did Kendra say?" Twyla asks. She clasps her hands and rests them against her chest, elbows propped comfortably on the chair arms.

Just hearing our lab coordinator's name gives me the twitchy feeling everyone gets when someone mentions surprise audits. She's our lab's resident storm cloud — always hovering, always judging—Dan's direct boss, only two steps below the director of the organization. I want to be on her good side, but I don't seem to be right now. Maybe I have to earn my stripes at NLBS, but she has given me a hard time since day one. Kendra once told me my phone greeting was *highly unprofessional*, which is wild because all I said was *hello*. Apparently, warmth is a crime now.

Kindness is unprofessional. Got it!

She once looked me up and down—jeans and a long-sleeve cotton shirt, totally normal lab wear—and rolled her eyes like I'd shown up in my pajamas. Once, I accidentally dropped mail on the counter when I was leaving the mailroom, and she handed it to me like it was biohazardous waste. The closest her face gets to happy is smug. I wonder if she's like that with all the newer hires.

A few weeks ago, she actually stopped Twyla in the hall, and I overheard them talking about me as I was leaving the restroom. "You guys are too easy on her. You can't baby her just because she's new." It was like I got slapped—

"Lacey?" Dan is looking at me with concern. *Was I talking to myself?*

"Sorry, what?"

Luke guffaws. "You looked like you were trying to set your coffee on fire with your mind."

"Oh." Now I feel dumb. "I'm just ... a little tightly wound today. Go on with what you were saying."

Dan nods sagely. "Kendra commented that we're actually lucky that this timed so well with the end of our testing. And she will give us information on a need-to-know basis." Of course she will. "I'm calling

her Monday morning for progress if I don't hear anything." Dan smiles. Okay, he knows how she is. He's got
us. "For now, we are looking at being away from the
office all of next week. It's just not safe. Director Burgess
is sending out a directive to all the staff via email later
today, so watch for that."

"What do you think our group should do?" Twyla
asks. "We all have remote-access keys, so maybe keep
working on submissions?"

"That's what I was thinking, too." Dan nods. "Keep up
on the submissions. Don't forget to fill out the spreadsheet so we don't duplicate efforts."

"Think there's a conference in Spain this winter?"
Luke taps his finger on his chin for a moment before
his patented Big Stupid Grin spreads across his face.
"That's my goal this week. I'm going to nail that one
down!"

The rest of us shake our heads.

"We all need goals." Dan chuckles. "I'll stay in contact
with Kendra. She's supposed to check in with the safety team every day, so when they have news for us, I'll
pass it on. Let's meet again Tuesday and Thursday next
week, same time, same place, unless we get back in the
facility faster than expected."

Oh. *Will I be able to go back that soon?* I make a mental
note to email Dan about my concerns and get in touch
with my doctor. I "should be fine" since it's been years,
but I also don't want to take any chances.

My phone buzzes, and I peek at the screen, curious
if it's that email from the director, but it's a text from

Derek, asking if we can talk. I'm tempted to text back that I don't talk to sketchy men who make questionable life choices, but I decide to take the moral high ground and ignore him.

A short time later, the meeting ends, and I start walking back to Saoirse's house, thrilled that it's warm enough now that I can carry my jacket. Sunglasses on, I breathe in fresh spring air and just try to appreciate the beautiful day. There are clouds, of course. There are always clouds, but I suppose I can deal with them.

I feel weirdly empty not being in the lab today. Not to mention, I'm worried that I may not be able to return to work with everyone else. Plus the gut-punch of knowing that I was almost willing to rationalize whatever Derek and Richard were up to because I just really wanted to feel #safeandhappy in Derek's arms. It's like my life is a snow globe and someone shook it hard, then tossed it down a flight of stairs just to make sure the snow really flew.

I don't like this not-knowing phase, this which-way-is-up day. I like a steady, straight path. I like measured steps. I like feeling like I'm making progress toward my dreams. I know, it's cliché, but honestly? A stable relationship and a career I love is the dream. I think having these dreams and staying so focused on them helps me forget my own mortality.

As a cloud drifts in front of the sun, I frown. Maybe I feel rushed for a reason I won't let myself look at too closely.

When you're sick, like really sick, you start to wonder if you'll ever get better or if your body will just keep betraying you. Your friends get to measure time by when they get their license, the moment of their first kiss, when everyone knows the lyrics to a certain song that is iconic for your generation ... while you get to measure time by a treatment schedule.

The milestone years seem so far away. Eighteen. Twenty-one. Twenty-five. Thirty. And as you get closer to thirty, you start feeling like you're on borrowed time—like every near miss in your life is stamped with an expiration date you forgot to read. So you cram meaning into every corner, just in case it all disappears tomorrow.

Do people who haven't had cancer wake up wondering if they get to do it again tomorrow? Wondering if they want to? Wondering what the point is? What it's all about?

I have to push it aside, into a box sometimes, all the wonders ... and just pretend they aren't there. I pretended like my brain was focused on prom and shopping and friends and music and jobs and falling in love and out again and all the things that teens and young adults feel are the center of the universe. And that box just stays there, getting heavier.

At twenty-eight, the box is so heavy, so dense, that it's almost like a black hole inside of me, and I've been healthy for a decade.

But in the lab, I can focus on someone else's problems. The fish, for one. The salmon are in trouble. And tons of other species, of course, but the salmon are my responsibility. Without having my career focus front and center, I'm honestly not sure how I'm going to handle the next week, especially being a nomad.

Right now, the box feels like a second heart. One that only beats when I'm afraid.

Chapter Eight

As we're enjoying our Saturday-morning, brunch of grilled veggie and goat cheese omelets, Saoirse and I decide we need a day in the wilderness. We pack a picnic and head out I-90, past Issaquah, straight to Snoqualmie Forest, where we used to spend hours hiking and exploring as teens.

We're in Saoirse's car, though I offered to drive. While I was at my meeting yesterday, she asked her neighbor if her son would bring a battery home for me and swap it out. As luck would have it, he works at Fulton's Automart and is training to become a mechanic, so he had easy access *and* the skills to do it. I couldn't believe it. Again, she's surprising me with how much she's changed, how thoughtful she is. How much she's willing to care for me totally out of the blue. It feels weird, but also, so nice. I hope she doesn't feel like she owes me, but honestly, a part of me feels like she does. And I feel guilty about feeling that way. Ugh.

We park close to a picnic shelter and climb out of the car. I'm glad I packed leggings and my aqua fleece jacket; I'll need it with the chill in the air. I'm a little sad no fellow hikers will see my t-shirt though, because it says "I told a chemistry joke and got no reaction." It's always good for a laugh.

So technically, it does get a reaction.

"It's been a while since I've been out here," Saoirse says. She reaches toward the sky and pops her heel, stretching her calf, alternating with the other one. Then she bends at the waist, curving her back till her hands are on her ankles.

I copy her routine; one we've done a million times together before hikes. We finish by pushing our hips side to side and stretching out our shoulders at the same time. I grin at Saoirse. "You ready?"

We throw on drawstring backpacks, which we packed with water, a sandwich, and an apple for our picnic and approach a path that winds down the hill. Then it meanders through the forest, past a stream, and up to an overlook. I've taken this one so many times before. In fact, I was here a couple weeks ago with Derek. As we start along the compacted dirt and gravel path, I feel a little saddened by the memory, but I shake off the feeling and focus on enjoying my time with my cousin, here. Now.

The air smells thick and woodsy, of fresh sprouts and blooms and of loam and decaying leaves. The stream is gurgling with the recent rainfall and runoff from the melting snow in the mountains, and it appears fresh and clean, begging us to dip our feet in. But we both know the streams here are also frigid this time of year, so we avoid temptation and keep walking.

We're both fairly quiet on our walk, enjoying the peace of the mid-day, middle-of-nowhere outdoors, appreciating the tranquility, the simplicity, of finding this place of wonder so close to the hustle and bustle of city life. To be on this spot on the planet, to have this luxury, is a miracle that I note in my musings. How many people get to have it all? I do. Or most of what a person would dream.

The overlook is a place that takes you by surprise. No matter how many times you've done this walk, it's always glorious. You come around the bend and then, bam, you're suddenly standing at the edge of the wood, at the edge of the world—with a huge drop off in front of you—at the top of the mountain, with the sun oozing through the clouds and enveloping you with its warmth, the love of the universe.

I feel alive here, in a way that I can't describe. It's like being a part of everything that has ever been and will ever be created, while breathing in the chill of the forest and bathing in the cozy playfulness of the sun. It's a spiritual moment for sure, a moment of awe, a moment where you wonder how and why and all the other things ... and nothing at all.

And I'm here with someone I haven't seen in years. My wonderings halt as I fully take her in, dreadlocks back in low pigtails, a berry-colored fleece that hangs to mid-thigh like it's trying to swallow her, her bird-like legs below that. And obnoxious shoes the color of tennis balls.

How and why and all the other things ...

Saoirse breaks the silence first. "Remember when Autumn wanted you to ask Pierce to come up here with us so he would finally notice her? She had a huge crush on him," Saoirse says. Her eyes are distant, staring into that place where memories lie.

"Yeah. Funny that it actually worked."

She squints. "Didn't they end up going to prom together?"

"They did. And that's when we all realized he was a gorgeous idiot."

Saoirse cackles. "I remember that now." She repeats the moment when we knew. "We all had dinner at Giovanni's, and he ordered coconut shrimp. But when the food arrived, he only ate the rice and broccoli. Autumn asked if there was something wrong with his shrimp." Then she takes on a dumb-jock inflection. "He said, 'I didn't know it would have coconut on it. I thought it was an expression.'"

I hoot out a laugh before finishing the story. "Everyone just stared at him. So then *I* said, 'I get it. Popcorn shrimp is the size of popcorn, so you thought coconut shrimp would be the size of a coconut.'"

Our ripples of laughter echo through the canyon, turning to tears of joy as we relive the moment. "That was a helluva night," Saoirse finally says.

Flashes of my dress dance across my memory. Gold like a sunflower, beads and sequins all over the top, a flowing floor-length skirt. I loved that dress. I wore a wig of red curls because my hair was gone by then. I barely had the energy to get through dinner, let alone dance. Thankfully, I had enough battery for that one-liner though.

I sober a bit as I recall that junior prom was one of the only times that spring that I got Rona to hang out with me. And she was distant the whole night, just a couple months after my life-changing diagnosis. When our group was going into the dance, she and her date—Shane? Shawn? one of the potheads—went behind a dumpster to get high, so we didn't even walk in together. She missed the first hour of the dance, and I sat inside, nervous that she was going to get caught. Talking with my date and Autumn and some of our other friends who came over to check on me. But no Rona.

A tiny part of me, deep down in my stomach, burns with the frustration of being left to deal with it by myself. To worry about her when *I* was going through so much. While she did what? I guess she wasn't sipping mai tais on a beach, though. She was working with her mom. Life on the road, especially with a band, was a hard life. Aunt Mindy talked about it a bit whenever she came back to see Rona on her breaks before senior year. The long hours. The constant travel. Packing, unpacking, packing. Teaching new crew members about the lighting instructions—they had frequent turnover. Adapting to a new venue. Telling men to knock it off, to back off. Watching the bass player slowly destroy his career. There was so much. And it was such a different world. No doubt, it was a world where a freshly minted eighteen-year-old didn't belong, especially when she was home schooling herself so she could graduate. I'm sure Mindy and Rona both had their hands full.

Rona … Saoirse missed so much that last year. The good and the bad. The hard and the very hard. Memories that I treasure, as well as those that I would rather burn.

I swallow and lock eyes with her. I wonder if she's thinking the same thing, but she breaks contact and looks out over the valley.

"Have you talked to Autumn since high school?" she asks, her voice tight. Her words are swallowed by the wind.

I guess this isn't the time to talk about where she went our senior year, why I never heard from her again. "I saw her the first couple summers I came home. After that, we drifted apart. I still have her on MyCircle. I think she's on the East Coast somewhere for grad school now. She worked for a couple years and then went back for a master's."

"Hmm." Saoirse pulls her knees to her chest, glances at me, and turns away again. She seems lost in a memory, but she's not sharing what it is. "She was always so smart. Good for her." Another pause as the tree branches rustle around us, sounding like they're playing in the breeze. Sunlight flickers across our faces, the ground, our memories. "Should we eat?"

After lunch, we continue along the trail, past the river, around the long loop that leads back to the other side of the parking lot. I usually just go back the way we came after stopping at the overlook, but the loop is such a pretty trail. Loads of red columbine along the path are about to bloom, and the red-osier dogwood is already wearing its lacey clusters of white blossoms. Plus, the trail meanders by an old house just past the edge of the protected woodland that I have always found fascinating.

A long drive winds up to the house from the main road, probably half a mile away. The stately brownstone is visible on the hill across from where we are walking. It seems to belong there in the thick of the woods with its deep brown hue, but the locals know: it's really a secret haven for someone longing to hide in style.

It used to belong to Gloria Brennan, 1940s movie star, famous Washingtonian, champion recluse. Having a house back in the woods here, you would have to be.

My sister Fallon was obsessed with Gloria when we were growing up. She's my second oldest sister, ten years older than me, and she used to tell me about the star all the time when I was in early elementary school. As a teen, she was big into classic movies, music, and other popular culture from the mid-1900s, which is probably what makes her a great eighth-grade history teacher now, but back then, she would tell me things that blew my little mind.

"Did you know that Gloria Brennan won an Academy Award for her performance in One Man's Summer *after being nominated six times?"*

"Did you know that Gloria Brennan's one of the first fifteen hundred people to get her star on the Walk of Fame?"

And probably some things a six-year-old shouldn't hear about.

"Did you know that Gloria Brennan built Cedarbrook House here because she murdered her husband and needed to spend the rest of her life somewhere where people would just forget about her?"

I remember looking wide-eyed at Fallon when she was on a roll talking about it, till Rhiannon told her to shut up because she was scaring me.

It was just a rumor anyway. I think the murder is still unsolved. But the house has that reputation.

Today, as we round the bend at the bottom of the path, Cedarbrook House comes into view, looking a bit menacing, a bit grand, and a bit sad, peeking through the patch of western red cedars that takes up much of that particular hill, dotted with oaks and maples. It has a view of the Snoqualmie River, nestled in the valley. Clouds float across the sky like computer wallpaper from the '90s, blocking the sun momentarily, and we exit the woods, staring up at the house.

"I ran into Haley the other day at the store." Saoirse thumps along the path, seeming to admire the flowers. "She mentioned that Cedarbrook House is actually occupied again. She and Tyler brought Hudson for a walk here last weekend."

I still think Haley's nuts trying to leave the house with a baby *ever*, but I know she wants him to be super portable and got one of those crazy long windy wrap things that fastens the baby to you so you can run errands and do yoga and whatever. Tyler was adamant that he's not wearing it, but when Haley bats her eyes … he caves. I guarantee Ty was the one loping along this path with baby on. And Haley was trudging ahead, determined that she's going to lose all the baby weight in a month by staying active while teaching Hudson good habits like exercise and appreciating the outdoors at the ripe old age of like fifteen days.

"How did she know?"

"Moving vans. They were unloading."

"Huh." I crane my neck like that's going to make any sort of difference seeing what's going on in the house. No one is outside. The lights aren't on because it's daylight. "Doesn't look any different than before. I'm glad someone is living there though. It's beautiful. I wonder if the house was passed down through her family or if they sold it."

"Not sure. I know Gloria Brennan had a son. I think he was a doctor in the area, so maybe he's still around. She died like sixty years ago though. If he held onto it all this time and never lived there, it has to be in rough shape."

"Maybe they fixed it up." When we hiked here as kids, my older sisters, Saoirse, and I always snooped around the house a bit. Someone told Rhiannon that it was haunted, so she dragged all her younger siblings up here to check it out because none of her friends would go. Rhiannon was in college, home for the summer. Our group varied widely in age: seven and seven, ten, thirteen, seventeen, and nineteen. Rona and I were the sevens. Rhiannon tried to talk Morgan, the thirteen, into staying home with the little ones while she and Fallon explored, but the thing is, you don't talk Morgan into anything. She's the adventurous one. The one who wants attention. The one who got a tattoo of a phoenix the moment she turned eighteen, not because it held any special meaning to her but because it was her birthright to get a tattoo as soon as she was of age.

I was equal parts scared and curious—Rona too—so we managed to peer through a few windows. It was full of covered furniture, though. Nothing interesting or even mildly spooky. And the only ghosts were the ones that Fallon and Morgan—my chaos-gremlin middle sister—created to freak us out. Didn't work though. I was so used to her shrieking from behind the garage, short sheeting my bed, and putting Dad's shaving cream in my shoes that I knew it was her. How she roped Fallon—our resident mother hen—into it was beyond me.

Saoirse gets that mischievous glint in her eye. "Want to go see?" She shrugs innocently.

I don't know why, but despite the butterflies in my stomach, I'm game. "Just not too close. We can look around for a minute." It's less the thought of ghosts and more the thought of getting caught trespassing that almost deters me. I am, unfortunately, a rule-following gremlin.

We pick our way through the denser brush off the path, crunching over leaves till we are a few yards from the house. If someone's there, surely they'll tell us to go away, right? I admire the building in a way I never could as a kid—its stately dignity, its loneliness. "I don't see any signs of life though." The front stoop is empty. No little flags in the garden or yard. The mailbox is rusted. And the shrubs are overgrown, though they appear to have been trimmed maybe a year or two ago.

I stride around the house, giving it a wide berth, and Saoirse follows. The back porch is empty, like it's waiting for lounge chairs and a fire pit, maybe even a tricycle or a sandbox. But there's nothing. I glance at the windows. No blinds, curtains open. I don't feel comfortable going right up to the house, in case someone is inside, but from the looks of it, no one will be. I look at Saoirse and shrug.

"You're right. Doesn't look like anyone lives here," she says.

We return to the trail and finish the loop back to the car, both of us quiet, thoughts rustling like the leaves under our feet.

On the return trip to Saoirse's house, I can't help but think about Cedarbrook House and how it's been empty for so long. It didn't look like anyone had broken in. It looked untouched, like time had been politely avoiding it. I wonder if the inside is like a time capsule for the 1950s, full of memories from Gloria Brennan's life.

I wonder what it would be like to walk through a place that's been frozen in time, holding its breath. I wonder who might have bought it and if they will update it.

"You thinking about Cedarbrook House?" Saoirse says.

Her soft voice startles me. I love that she still knows me that well. "Yeah, funny how it's still there, unchanged, after all this time."

"I agree. I sort of wish that I had peeked in the windows. When you're an adult, though, you can't claim you *didn't know better* and get away with it." She chuckles and turns onto the highway back toward her house. "Did you want to do something tonight? We could go to Riff's. You could meet Anthony."

"Anthony?" The name rings a faint bell, but I can't place it.

"My boyfriend. He wouldn't be hanging out with us, since he's working, but I'd love it if you could see him play."

"I'd actually love that." I can't help but grin. She sounds like she really likes this guy. And I love seeing her happy. "I'll call Haley tomorrow and see about staying with her for a few days. I don't want to overstay my welcome. I know I kind of dropped into your life like a tornado."

"I really don't mind you staying with me. It's been nice having the company. I haven't had a roommate in a few years, not since I bought the house." Saoirse's voice dips. The way it softens makes me wonder what she's not saying. Did something happen? "Besides," she seems to perk up, "I don't have a screaming baby waking you up several times a night. That's a bonus, right?"

"An *adorable* screaming baby," I add.

"True. But a good night's sleep is better. By a little bit."

I laugh. "If you're sure." Then I decide to ask, "Why haven't you had a roommate?"

Saoirse bites her lip. "I had a few roommates during college, but we weren't close. I lived by myself for a few years. Then, when I bought this place, I didn't know anyone who really needed anywhere to stay. It just never worked out for me to have a roommate." Straightforward enough, but I feel like that's not the whole story.

"Oh." I want to ask more, but the moment feels fragile, so I let it drop.

Chapter Nine

That evening, I change into my favorite jeans, a brick red peasant blouse, and a pair of low-heeled ankle boots to go to Riff's. I went a few months ago for Haley's birthday, and we had a great time. I was pretty impressed by the musicians: a trio of piano players who appeared to know every popular song from the 1950s on without needing to read music. I have zero musical talent aside from a chaotic but heartfelt karaoke rendition of *I will Survive*, so I was in awe.

Riff's is swanky, and I love the atmosphere. It's all shades of smoky gray with a huge red theater-style curtain flanking the stage. Tables and chairs encircle the stage, tapering off to high tops where people are standing and walking around near the back of the room. Servers dressed all in black weave through the crowd, taking orders, bringing fancy plates of appetizer samplers and cocktails. As a server rushes past us, the air thickens with the scent of maple syrup and bacon.

We find a table near the wall and order wings with honey barbeque sauce. A rum and soda for me and a ginger beer for Saoirse.

A few minutes later, the crowd erupts into applause as two men and a woman enter the stage. They smile at the audience as they approach the instruments, waving and nodding when someone whistles or catcalls. I'm sure it's such a rush being in their positions.

"Anthony's on the left, closest to us." Saoirse nods at the man. He's cute—objectively cute—with dark wavy hair, just long enough for a ponytail. She waves while he scours the audience, and finally, recognition spreads across his face as he pumps a fist in the air and winks at her. She lights up like the Beacons of Gondor. Adorable. My nerd heart approves.

When the two men are seated at the pianos and the woman at a small drum set between them on a riser, the lights dim. I don't recognize the opening chords, but the audience immediately starts grooving and cheering. It's clearly a club favorite. Once Anthony starts the lyrics though, I know it—"I Saw her Standing There," by the Beatles. Good pick for an intro!

I find myself singing along the best that I can, even on the high "Oooooh!" as the whole place cracks discordantly while all the patrons strain for the pitch. The trio not only nails the instrumental part of the song, but they completely kick ass on the singing, with some really nice harmonies. Anthony's tenor voice is rich and strong, and I see that Saoirse is completely mesmerized by his talent. No doubt everyone in the room is too.

After a couple more songs, the food arrives, and we munch on the wings while we enjoy the tunes. It's a great distraction from the craziness of the past week, and I feel so light and joyful that I hardly want to think about the lab or Derek or even the fact that Saoirse and I still haven't talked about The Great Big Thing.

The woman switches spots with Anthony for a couple songs, including Whitney Houston's "I Want to Dance with Somebody," showing off her range and skills with some complicated piano licks. Then, the other man switches with Anthony and pulls out an acoustic guitar for Justin Timberlake's "Like I Love You," where all three performers take turns singing.

Then the lights dim further, and the guitarist is spotlighted. He begins playing solo, improvising the introduction to a song with a series of complicated runs and strumming. It goes on way longer than a normal intro, and I know he's hamming it up as he's shaking his head, biting his tongue, and really getting into what he's doing. It's so beautiful and not something I would expect to hear in a piano bar. This man is seriously talented, not that the others aren't. But it's clear that his guitar skills are a gift, and he's eating up the attention he's getting for this part of the show.

I feel suddenly like he no longer realizes the rest of us are there, like we're all watching something very private and loving as he plucks away at the strings, eyes closed, brain clearly a million miles away focused on the sound.

It's sensual and haunting, and I feel my heart beating faster as he takes us on this melodic journey.

And that was just the opening of the song.

When he starts in on the chords and sings the first line Bryan Adams' "Have You Ever Really Loved a Woman?" the depth of his baritone voice is like honey, warm and golden, pouring from his lips. There are audible gasps from the crowd, and I glance around, fully expecting the other ladies in the room to slingshot their undies onto the stage.

What am I witnessing? Oh my God!

They don't. But I swear the air gets heavier around us.

I have never heard that song performed like this.

During the first chorus, the man exits the stage and moves through the crowd like he owns the room, greeted by cheers, pausing by tables to really play it up. His mischievous grin reveals a dimple on his left cheek I absolutely should not be noticing as he leans toward a woman here and there, like he's singing it just for them.

And yes, there is swooning. Not from me. Probably.

I glance at the stage and see the other two performers acting like it's another day at the office, chugging water, flexing their hands, and generally chilling and chatting while their colleague sweeps through the room, enchanting everyone.

His playing is so intense and sensual it feels almost intrusive to watch. I can't help but wonder if music is the only profession you can be in and experience your work that way. What scientist looks at a petri dish like that? A beaker? A spreadsheet?

Certainly not me.

Do I feel like that about my work? Should I? Can I? Is that weird? Probably weird to be thinking about this right now.

I notice that I'm humming along as he weaves his spell, but my brain is spinning. *Why is my brain doing this when I'm being entertained?* He plays like no one else is in the room. And maybe I feel like that when I'm deep into my research. Okay. That's a good thing. But there's always been this little piece of me that feels like my work isn't important. Like I'm doing something frivolous. Am I?

And what about this? In the grand scheme of things, what does one guitar player do to impact the universe? Is he making the world a safer place? Curing cancer? No. But does *joy* count? Because, oh my, he has brought joy to this room! Like capital-J joy.

I remember wondering if I was supposed to do something big with my life. I felt like I should, you know, do something big. I'm here. I survived. But ... that's a tall order. And I couldn't talk it through with my sisters. Or my parents. I wanted to talk to Rona.

But she wasn't around much. I tried to reconnect when I felt better, when we were in college. Aunt Mindy said she went to a trade school but didn't mention what she did there, and I went to Stonegate University, south of Seattle, to study fish. They have a great program. I thought it was the right thing. But I felt so much pressure, you know? I *have the brain for it.*

I knew when I was growing up that I wanted to go into research—"save the people," as everyone thinks when they are little. I had a rare form of bone cancer when I was in high school, and you would think that would seal the deal. But ...

As the guitar player approaches the aisle by our table, Saoirse lets out a playful "ow-ow!" that pulls me back from my reverie. He tips his chin at her, probably recognizing her as Anthony's girlfriend and sashays up to us.

First, he sidles up to Saoirse, leans down, and gives her a playful mini-serenade. Then he swings around to me. And when I grin and lock eyes with him, something strange happens—a jolt, a hitch, a tiny ripple in the space-time continuum. I can't explain it.

The flecks of gold in his eyes catch the light, his smile wavers, he hits a wrong chord, and the moment is gone.

My breath stutters. I don't know if anyone even noticed but me. And him. And the planets.

I shiver and look at Saoirse as the guitarist leaps back on stage to finish the last strong chords of the song to thunderous applause. The crowd hoots and hollers, as my heartbeat slows to a normal rhythm, and my clapping shakes my brain from its trance.

Still catching his breath, he looks back at me once. Twice. A third time. Like maybe he felt it too.

Or I'm weird and should probably lay off the drinks for the rest of the night.

Chapter Ten

I t's been four days since the lab closed down, and I am absolutely *not* going stir-crazy.

Four. Loooooong. Days.

Actually, it's not *that* bad. I keep telling myself it's like a long weekend. There's work I *could* be doing—submitting for more journals and conferences ... I miss my space though. My home space and my lab space. I miss my colleagues. And I miss just, you know, normalcy.

Is this what it's like for people with desk jobs? Do they just compulsively check their email every five minutes? How does anyone sit still that long?

Okay, new mindset. This is just a plot twist, not a crisis. I'm going to be great at this. I know I am. I am in control of my day. And ... it reminds me of the pandemic, honestly, which went *really well*. People weren't going crazy locked up with their roommates. No one murdered anyone because they were practicing the same song on the clarinet fifty times a day while we were all figuring out if we were going to survive the apocalypse.

That's a really specific example for a reason. RIP Christy. Kidding—she's thriving with the Boston Symphony, and I'm super proud of her.

So why am I watching my email? Because Dan said that he's calling Kendra today, and I'm *not* waiting till our meeting tomorrow to find out what she said. There has to be an update. Right?

Please?

With no new emails, my mind drifts back to Derek. He called again this morning, but I can't make myself take his phone calls or listen to his messages. I click on the text icon, finally, to see what he's sent, but it's basically messages asking me to call him. Except the last one, which he sent three hours ago.

> Lacey, can we talk? I think you got the wrong impression the other night. Richard and I aren't doing anything wrong. I really want to explain the whole project to you. We meet with the expert later this week, and I want your support. I wanted to share it all with you before, but there are certain aspects of the project that are confidential. You understand. Just let me explain. xoxo

I'm leaving him on read. I don't even know what to say. Even several days later, the shock hasn't worn off. A bag of money is sketchy enough, but knowing he somehow had inside info about the evacuation? That's a whole new level. They wouldn't have announced that on the news. I just know he was bribing someone, or something. But why? And what does it have to do with NLBS?

A ding from my laptop jolts me from my thoughts. An email! This one is from the *Journal of Ichthyologic and Herpetological Studies*. That's a mouthful. I read it aloud.

"Your article has been received and is being considered for the winter publication of our journal. We will inform you of our decision by July 1st."

My stomach does a nervous little flip. I published as a grad student, but this could be my first publication as a professional. Why does it feel so different?

My mind drifts back to Kendra and how she thinks I'm being coddled as a noob. Am I? Does my name really deserve to be on this article? I'm last, since I'm the newest, but I suddenly don't feel right about even being on there. I didn't come up with the research or determine the structure of the experiment. I just did what I was told—a cog in the machine. I ...

"Argh." How am I going to handle presenting our work if this is how I react to the possibility, not even the guarantee, of being published for it?

I wonder if Kendra thinks I'm a cog.

I fire off a quick "thank you!" to the sender, log confirmation in the group's spreadsheet, and stand up from the dining room table. It's three p.m. I've lasted almost a whole day.

I wish I could just have my own lab. I wonder what my life would be like. Do people really do what Derek was talking about the other night? That farm place they are working with is going to build their own. Could a person, not a business, do that? What would that take? What would I do with my own lab?

I'd definitely be an evil scientist for five minutes.

But then ... I'd probably be the weirdo at the shore gathering salmon in a bucket and then taking them back to study cells and microorganisms. In my lab. All by myself.

It's day one, and I'm already losing it.

"Are you doing okay?" Saoirse is standing in the middle of the kitchen, staring at me. She's been in her office most of the day. She said she had some meetings and then was off the rest of the week because she likes to take a week of vacation every quarter, between website builds, which sounds fantastic. After the day I've had, though, I don't know how I would handle that.

"I'm, uh, good. Just thinking about what it would be like to have my own lab."

"So that groan was joy, not pain?"

She caught me.

"Well ..." Do I want to explain that entire roller coaster of thought? "I'm impatient because Dan hasn't told us what Kendra said yet. He was supposed to call her today to see what's up. She's always tight-lipped and never tells the rest of us anything we *don't need to know*.

It's like we work in some hush-hush government facility, and we'll never be good enough for her top-secret clearance."

"Huh." She makes a plate of vegetables, olives, and hummus and brings it to the table. I realize I'm hungry as I spy the red peppers—the two of us used to devour those as kids—so I snag one and dip it. "I thought you could use a break," she says.

Closing my laptop, I sigh. "I have a lot on my mind and not enough actual work to do."

"Poor thing." Saoirse chuckles and pops an olive in her mouth. "You know, you could just do nothing. Take a bath. Take a walk. Think about something pleasant."

I smile. "You have all the answers."

"Of course I do. When you've lived as long as we have, you know everything." She winks at me and leans on the table. "So what if you don't know anything new about the lab? What else interests you?"

I frown. Saoirse's right. I can't just think about the lab all day, but if I stop thinking about the lab, I think about Derek. And when I think about Derek, I want to cry or yell. I miss the idea of him, his touch, maybe his smell. I miss being with someone in that way.

And now I want to smack myself. Were there any red flags? I don't know of anything. I never saw a map marking hidden treasure. No crowbar in the corner. No black ski masks.

I guess they wouldn't be very good criminals if they left that stuff lying around though.

This would be easier if I'd caught him kissing someone else. Then I would be mad at him and never want to speak to him again.

Saoirse cocks her head to the side, and her mouth forms a half smile. "How about Cedarbrook House?"

I raise an eyebrow at her. "What about it?"

"I know you found that interesting." She picks up her phone. "Maybe we could look up some info about it. See if there is anything new about the murdered husband. Or who bought the place. Bare minimum, we could snoop on the real estate sites for the value of the house."

I laugh at that. "okay, I'm curious now." I pick up my phone and open the browser. A few seconds later, I learn the magic number: $2.5 million. It comes with some acreage, plus being in the area it is in, I suppose that would bump the price up. Still, that's a number I never fathomed.

"Oh! A few years ago, they found the guy who murdered Gloria Brennan's husband!" Saoirse is staring wide-eyed at her phone. "So, it wasn't her. The police were investigating a strange smell in an apartment and found a man dead in an armchair. Then they found boxes of driver's licenses in his house from everyone he had robbed over the years. A box was open beside the chair, so that's why they started looking. Apparently, he kept them as a souvenir of the crimes. They found Everett Vernon's stuck in the front of a photo frame, like the guy knew it was special. He had to know that was Gloria Brennan's husband. Upon further investigation, they discovered that the dude had stabbed him during a mugging gone wrong."

"That's ... deeply disturbing." I glance back down at the single picture of the outside of the house on my phone screen. The poor woman, retreating there to heal after she lost her love. I wonder what her life was like after that, especially with the rumors surrounding his death. They were supposedly walking home from the theater and were seen arguing. Then he was found in an alley the next morning. That's what Fallon had said all those years ago. No conclusive evidence. Imagine having a fight with someone you love and then never getting to speak to them again. My heart aches as my mind drifts back to what brought Saoirse and me together again.

When I glance at her, she looks amused. Clearly her train of thought is parked somewhere completely different. "What did you look up?" she asks.

With a wry laugh, I turn my phone to show her. "The value of the house. I was actually hoping to see pictures of the inside too."

"Ahh, good call. It's a shame there aren't any."

"That probably means it was never listed. It was either purchased privately or passed down through the family."

"Huh."

"You know, Fallon told me once that Gloria never remarried. I wonder if it's because she missed him that much, or because she didn't feel like she could love again, or because she never found anyone else. I'm sure it was so hard on her, living there with just her son after she lost someone she loved so deeply."

A shadow flickers across Saoirse's face, her smile fading.

"Saoirse?"

She blinks and returns to me. "Yeah, I'm sure it was really hard for her. You have to wonder what it would be like for her living in the woods practically alone after that."

Should I say something? That was weird. She said before that she lived alone a lot and seemed sad about it. Maybe this is part of Saoirse's blank history after she left. Did she lose someone?

"Hey, Saoirse, I don't want to pry, but—"

"Oh, I almost forgot to ask you. Do you mind if Anthony comes over this evening? Riff's is closed on Mondays, so that's always one of his days off. We spend the evening together."

She definitely cut me off on purpose. Huh. I guess we're talking about Anthony now. "Of course I don't mind. Do you ... do you want me to leave?"

"No! No, no! Please stay. We usually hang out, talk, watch TV. It's a chill evening. I'd like to introduce you anyway."

I have to smile when I hear this. Something a little odd about our family is that no one ever brings up Rona around me. In fact, I didn't even know that she and Haley were talking. I want to ask but digging up a timeline of reconnection between her and my sisters would be a little bizarre. I'm a guest in her house right now, so I don't want to be nosy. Still though, I wonder if anyone else knows about Anthony. Have they met him? Does she hang out with my family still? How do I broach this … "I'd like that. Has he met your mom yet?"

"Yeah." She smiles at the memory, but there is a tightness around her eyes that tells me her mind is still on a past hurt. "I introduced him at Christmas. She likes him. They talked a lot about music, since they have that in common. It was really good."

"I'm happy to hear that. Looking forward to talking with him this evening."

A short time later, Anthony arrives. He's casual but cool in jeans and a faded Foo Fighters t-shirt. His energy is easy, caring—he helps Saoirse in the kitchen when she offers to fix a snack platter. I like him already. I catch him looking at her lovingly a couple times as we are all sitting at the dining room table, munching on the grapes he brought, along with cheese and crackers that Saoirse already had in the house. Often, he touches her arm, the small of her back. I'm happy for them.

At the same time, though, it reinforces the fact that I'm alone. I feel a little bruised about it right now. Not like I can't be completely whole without a man. I feel good about leaving Derek—most of the last few days—and confident in being by myself. But at the same time, there is this disappointment. *Single again.* Like I fell off a horse. Like I can't figure it out. I guess I've always got Edward, the dream guy.

I don't want to be desperate, but there's that little tingle of anxiety again. That whisper of "what if you never find him" deep in my chest. What if Saoirse is right, and my soulmate really was calling to me, but then he got hit by a bus or something? Do all women feel anxious when they want to find the right man, settle down, have a baby eventually? It's such a strange feeling. Like being in the calmest race ever where no one can acknowledge that it's a race, but for reals, it's a race. And it's a little nerve-wracking.

Being a human is so bizarre.

I push down my feelings of inadequacy and sadness and meh and just smile and focus on the fact that they are clearly in love. I place a silent wish to the universe for some of that for me, please! As I do, my mind drifts back to that cosmic flutter at Riff's, when the guitar player kept looking back at me. That was something, right? Maybe? The tingles in my chest seem to agree.

I look back at my cousin and her honey on the couch and smile. You can't help but be happy in their presence if you shove the crap feelings aside.

Their adoration for each other actually makes *me* feel loved.

Chapter Eleven

It's nice getting to know Anthony a bit this evening. After we talk about his background and how he got started in music, along with an abbreviated version of the craziness of my life, we decide to flip on a show and relax for a bit before making dinner.

I stretch my legs out on one couch while the two lovebirds snuggle into the other. Then Saoirse leans forward and gives me a conspiratorial look.

"Welcome to the portion of the evening where Anthony spends thirty to forty minutes flipping through show apps trying to find something that he will enjoy watching that won't annoy his girlfriend."

I nearly spit out my water. "Seriously? Who does that?" I gesture to Anthony for a response.

Anthony turns his head slowly and looks at her like she is the assiest smartass on the planet. "There are a lot of choices out there, and I want to pick something good. You gotta find what fits our mood." He shakes his head and grabs the remote, clearly used to the ribbing. "That takes time."

"And the patience of a saint," Saoirse mutters through a smile, giving him a playful shove in the arm. She turns back to me and flips her hands open. "So, we will watch a lot of previews, and he will *almost* settle on something several times, but ultimately, he will select something that we've both seen at least five times, and no one will be happy."

I'm dying now.

Anthony wraps an arm around her shoulders and gives her an affectionate squeeze. "Game on." He makes a show of staring at previews for a couple minutes, whistling while he flips through titles. "Actually, I think you might like this. My brother recommended it." He goes to the search bar and types a title in. "He watches it with his wife, and she hasn't been *annoyed* by it yet." He throws casual shade at Saoirse with a sidelong glance.

I snort laugh.

We start watching a series called *Warminster*, which is sort of like *Lord of the Rings* but scarier. It seems that Anthony did not piss Saoirse off with this choice, but I would have been happier with a rom-com. Still not bad, though. I make a mental note to let Dan and Luke know about it because this is totally up their alley.

I probably would have been more into it if my phone didn't start going off just a few minutes into the show. I see a text from Twyla and open it, ready to applaud her for keeping the Wi-Fi on this time.

> Dan, did you talk to
> Kendra today?

I smile. I'm about to tell her she texted the wrong person when I realize that she has set up a group text with all our lab members on it. Bravo, Twyla!

I see dots pop up and sit up a little straighter. Come on, Dan! Dots ... dots ... dots. No dots. Ugh.

Oh! Dots again! But it's from Twyla.

> Brody helped me set up
> this twitter.

I giggle. Ah, so she didn't figure it out herself. Her son helped her.

More dots ... okay, Dan, you can just get on and respond now. Another from Twyla.

> Sorry, Brody said it's
> called a "text thread." I'll
> get used to this.

Then a poop emoji pops up.

> He told me I should send
> you guys this Hershey's
> Kiss. It's kinda cute!

Brody is every teenage boy on the planet. I'm dying now, and Saoirse and Anthony keep glancing over at me. "Sorry," I mouth as my thumbs move furiously across the phone screen.

Thanks, Twyla! That's
sweet! Dan, what's the
news?

I just couldn't tell her that was poop! Hopefully all the activity in the thread will get Dan's attention with his phone lighting up. Texts from Violet and Luke come in, also encouraging Dan to speak up. While we are waiting, I vaguely follow their discussion of what everyone is up to today, to see that we all pretty much stalked our email waiting for more info on the lab. Glad I'm not the only one going crazy!

Finally, about half an hour later, Dan jumps on.

Looks like I missed
something! I did speak to
Kendra today. She didn't
have much to say.

Now the dots ... they will surely kill me! I can't believe how dry my throat feels as I watch for the "and?"

The good news is that
they've started cleanup
on the chemicals that
remained in the
immediate area of the
leak. Some of the
compounds that the
sensors picked up on
were absorbed by the
dirt and remained
stationary, so they
brought in a crew to do
cleanup on the
contaminated dirt.

And? I mean, that's great that they are figuring it out, but what was it? How did it happen? And whose fault is it? Aren't they going to tell us? Of course, it's Kendra, so she will probably wait till we have an all-hands meeting with sub-par pizza a month from now and drip it out slowly over two hours. She loves being in control.

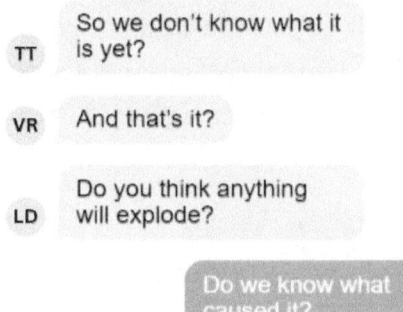

All our responses rolled in at once, but Dan isn't saying anything yet. I know we're all staring at the thread, watching for the three dots. Come on three dots! And nothing.

"Who are you talking to?" Saoirse says. "You look like you're ready to jump through your phone and strangle them." She sits up and looks at me sternly. "That's not Derek, is it?"

"No. Definitely not Derek. It's a thread with my lab group. Just a general check in. Everyone is good. No news about the lab. Just a cleanup update."

"Man, that's rough," Anthony says. "I'm sorry you guys are going through this. It has to be frustrating."

You don't know the half of it.

> **DR** No news on anything else. The good news is that everyone evacuated and is safe. Let's not worry about it. Keep plugging away on submissions for now.

More dots pop up as my soul collapses. We still don't know whose fault it is. I would think they could have run testing on all the samples of ground water and dirt this weekend since it was an emergency, but they clearly don't have all the info yet. Ugh.

> **TT** Well, I'm convinced that the tank that was delivered to our lab that was supposed to go to geological studies is the culprit. It probably got dinged going across the Plateau because it had to be loaded on a dolly instead of being delivered directly to the building by truck.

> **DR** You might be right. I was thinking that something wasn't disposed of properly and leaked from a garbage truck.

I gasp loud enough that Saoirse glances over from where they are snuggling on the couch, caught up in the show again. She raises her eyebrows, and I interpret the question, giving her a thumbs up. I am absolutely *not* bringing up the nuclear-babies theory and pointing a finger at myself. Not doing it.

> **LD** Well, whatever happened, I'm just glad it happened right after we finished. Happy coincidence! It would have sucked to be a couple days away from wrap-up and then have to wait.

> **VR** Good point.

Weird that our wrap-up coincided with the leak, but I agree with Luke. It's definitely good that we got to finish.

I notice Anthony shifting to dig his phone out of his pocket. He taps the screen. "It's Libs," he says. Saoirse smiles and nods as Anthony opens the text. Then he shows it to her. "What do you think?"

"Aw, that would be nice." She nods and then raises her eyebrows at me. "Lacey, do you want to go to Libby's house for pizza? She's one of the pianists at Riff's. She just invited the whole crew over."

"If she's cool with me tagging along, then sure." They seem like a nice group from what Saoirse has said. Then my heart stops and my brain slingshots me straight me back to Saturday night again. I remember the way the guitar player pranced around the room and how it felt like time stood still when our eyes met. So weird. Oh, I wonder if he will be there. "So who is 'the whole crew'?"

"The four of us pianists from Riff's: me, Libby, Wes, and Colin," Anthony explains. "Colin is part-time, but you know, he's still part of the family. Libby's boyfriend will probably be there. Maybe Wes's wife." He counts on his fingers. "Maybe eight total. Do you have a preference for pizza?"

"I can do plain cheese or mushroom and ham, if anyone else likes that."

"We usually do all anchovies, but I'll see what I can do." Anthony gives me a cheeky smile. Saoirse and I cackle as Anthony texts our response.

As I think about going to Libby's and meeting everyone, my stomach does a nervous little flutter. Was it the booze, or did something weird happen on Saturday?

Probably the booze, Lacey. Definitely the booze.

Chapter Twelve

I gaze out the window from the backseat of Anthony's SUV as he winds through the streets to Libby's place. This is another lovely neighborhood with a variety of houses, depending on the block, from four-square to mid-century modern to bungalows and craftsman style homes. At a stop light, I fall a little in love with the cutest bungalow. It looks like the perfect place for a young couple. It has a sweet little front porch and shutters. It's all gray with white trim and exposed beams on the porch. The bleeding hearts flanking the porch add drama with their splash of red blooms. Wouldn't it be great to live in a place like that?

Well that's rude.

A huge tanker has pulled up between me and the little house, totally blocking my view and ruining my fantasy. Clemons's Liquid Transport is printed across the side of the tanker. I think that's the same as the tankers I've seen on the Plateau at Pearson & Brewster. I mentally try to shoo the truck away, but no such luck. The light turns, and we continue on to Libby's. Bye bye charming little house.

Libby's place is adorable! She's in the top floor of a four-square house, known here as a "Seattle box," that's been divided up for apartments. The entryway has that fun huge floral print wallpaper and pops of pink that I always see on MyCircle videos and get jealous of. I'd make it look like chaos instead of whimsy if I tried to decorate like that, which is why my apartment is mostly neutrals. When we walk in, she greets all of us with huge hugs—yes, even me.

"Hey, I'm so happy to finally meet you! I'm Libby Yun." She grabs me and squeezes, her silky black hair swinging around her.

I'm not sure why she says "finally." There's no way I've come up in conversation before Friday, right? "So nice to meet you too! You guys were great on Saturday. I love your dress!" It's a red cotton midi with short sleeves. The kind that I definitely wouldn't buy because it looks like it needs ironed. But it's adorable on her. Everyone looks adorable when you're taller than most women. I suddenly feel underdressed in my dark jeans and pink watercolor V-neck. Eh. It's pizza night, right?

She introduces me to her boyfriend, Ray, and the piano player who was off on Saturday, Wes. Wes's wife is at home with their daughter, so I don't get to meet her.

The guitar player isn't here, which leaves me feeling both oddly relieved and... a little disappointed. I do not need to complicate my life right after a breakup with a potential gang member—maybe that would explain the money—and an unnatural disaster, but I also have this horrible curiosity about whatever *that* was—the look we shared at the piano bar.

"Sit wherever you like," Libby says. She gestures to her tidy little living room full of poufs and folding chairs, which she must have brought in because we can't all fit on her plump white couch. I pick a folding chair—I know myself, and that white sofa would not survive me plus pizza. "We heard your lab shut down for a bit," she says. "I saw a story on my news app. Any idea what happened?"

I let out a long sigh and give them the little I actually know, which isn't much, while everyone is grabbing drinks. Saoirse hands me a ginger beer and taps the neck of mine with her own. "Cheers," I whisper, and she winks at me.

When the pizza arrives, we descend on it like a pack of raptors.

"Looks like you're in luck, Lacey—no anchovies." Anthony laughs.

I wrinkle my nose at him and grab a slice.

The conversation shifts to plans for the summer and how busy the piano bar will probably be. I mostly listen, trying to get a feel for everyone's personalities. As they talk, I nod politely and take a bite of pizza. It's really good. I need to find out where they got it and make it my regular place. Maybe I'll suggest it for our next all-hands meeting—at least the pizza would be worth showing up for.

I'm mid-thought on making meetings bearable when everyone erupts into "heys!" Libby leaps from her spot on the sofa—huh, no sauce anywhere!—and rushes past me to the entryway. A man is kicking his shoes off and hanging his jacket, and Libby throws her arms around him for a quick squeeze.

Good thing I just swallowed the bite of pizza already. It's the missing musician, and a quiver runs through me like a plucked guitar string.

After fist-bumping Anthony and Wes, the man snags a Sam Adams from the kitchen and then sits on a folding chair.

"Lacey, I don't think you've met Colin," Libby says. "He plays piano and, oh! You would have seen him Saturday, playing guitar. Most people remember *Have You Ever Really Loved a Woman?* when Colin performs it."

"Oh yeah?" I say, pretending I don't remember every second of that performance. "That was great! Nice to meet you!" We both half-stand and shake hands across the coffee table. The touch is—honestly—electric, and I'm sure my face is as pink as my shirt. We lock eyes, and my breath catches. I see his smile quirk.

When he sits, he flashes that crooked smile across the room at me. "Libby gives me too much credit. I'm happy that I get to join the group a couple nights a week and make some magic with our music."

"It's definitely ... something magical." God, I sound dumb. "When did you start playing guitar?"

"High school. I wanted to ditch my nerdy reputation and get a prom date. Some of my friends had a band: Every Girl's Dream. Spoiler: it was not. We all ended up going to prom stag."

The whole group laughs.

"You took piano lessons as a kid, though, right?" Wes asks. "I think we all did."

"Yeah. That's part of the nerdy reputation thing. Until now, of course. We all get to be hometown rock stars." Colin does a silly groove move and tips his chin. "We're big with the thirty-five and older crowd."

"Gotta love when the local mom group does their night out and they get a little wild because they're so used to being home with their kids," Libby adds. "One of them actually yelled, 'Take your shirt off,' when Colin was doing his song a few weeks ago."

Everyone is almost in tears at this point. And honestly, I can't judge—I don't get out much either.

A while later, the pizza is long gone, and I head to the kitchen for a glass of water. I lean against the counter for a moment. They're a great group, but I'm starting to fade. Maybe I should see if Saoirse is ready to go. I'm about to go back to the living room when Colin walks in, and that familiar tremor ripples through me.

"Hey." He grins and pulls the refrigerator open. "Having fun?" He pops the cap off another beer and leans on the counter by the fridge, across from me.

I chuckle. "Just needed a minute to myself. I'm getting a little tired. The last few days have been ... a lot."

"Sorry to hear that." He gives me a sympathetic smile. "Saoirse seems really happy to have you back in her life. Anthony mentioned that on Saturday."

I frown. So they *have* been talking about me. "I'm glad we're talking again. Weird that she ended up saving my butt the other night, but I'm glad it gave us this chance." He gives me a questioning look, so I tell him the short version of how I ended up staying with her.

"Geez. Really sorry you had to go through that. Maybe it's good, though, since it landed you back in her world. It's funny how things work out sometimes ..."

I take in the look on his face, and it calls me to a hidden tale. His eyes are cast downward, distant and intense. "I feel like there's a story there," I say.

"Ah." He waves a hand, brushing the thought away like a gnat. "Just thinking about how I got into my work. My gran."

"Was she a musician too?"

"No, nothing like that." Colin crosses the kitchen and leans against the counter beside me, like he's about to share a secret. I notice he's actually taller than me. He runs a hand through his hair, brushing it out of his face, and the cowlick at his temple pops the shorter hairs there right back up. The dim lighting catches the gold flecks in his blue eyes.

"Gran had a heart problem when I was little," he continues. "Needed a transplant. She was on the list for a while but couldn't find a match. It was strange to think someone would have to die for my grandmother to live. I couldn't shake that for years. I wished it didn't have to be like that, but sadly, that's what the truth was. Eventually, she passed, and we were all crushed. Granddad moved in with us, so we got to be really close, and I really treasure the time we had together when I was growing up, but what about Gran? All those could-have-been moments with her were just... gone. And my brother and sister were younger, so they don't even remember her as well as I do."

Tears prick at my eyes as I listen to his story. How heart-breaking! "That's so hard. I'm sorry to hear that." I touch his arm gently, and our eyes lock again.

Through a sad smile, he continues. "I don't usually tell that story." He clears his throat. "But good came out of it. This is why I do what I do."

"She's why you got into music? I thought that was to get a prom date."

He chuckles softly. "That's why I started playing guitar. And I only fill in a couple nights a week at Riff's. That's not my full-time gig." Swigging his beer, he continues. "I didn't want others to go through what our family did. It was hard to lose Gran to something that felt so ... avoidable. I went into biology so I could help design artificial hearts, as an option for those who are waiting for a human heart. To give them time."

Wow. I'm sure my eyes are bugging out of my head right now. I have to say something to lighten the mood. It's getting incredibly serious in here. "You design artificial hearts? That's incredible. You know, I bet *that* story would work on the ladies." I give his arm a playful nudge.

His laugh echoes in the kitchen, and I get caught up in his mirth, laughing too. "Surprisingly, it works better than being in a high school rock band. Though I haven't tried it on the bridge club that comes to Riff's on Thursdays …" He shakes his finger at me. "You gave me an idea!"

"You could probably find yourself a sugar mama there."

"Cheers to that." As Colin leans in to clink his beer against my glass, our eyes lock again, but this time, a wisp of memory drifts through my mind and clicks into place. I've seen those eyes before—flecks of gold on blue. So unusual. And I think I know where.

Chapter Thirteen

I t's Thursday again—a whole week after the lab disaster—and I wake up with one thing on my mind:
those eyes.

It's been two days since Libby's, but they still haunt
me. It's all I see when I close my own eyes, those flecks
of gold floating in a blue ocean.

Everyone's eye color is unique. And eyes with central
heterochromia—having a different eye color close to
the iris—that are blue as the Pacific on the outside and
honey-amber near the center are rare.

We talked about this trait in a biology class years
ago, and I found it fascinating. Eye color is fascinating
to think about anyway, since there are about a million
variations due to not only pigment color but also the
lack or presence of pigments.

But that's not why I keep thinking about him, I mean,
his eyes.

That dream I had when I first came to Saoirse's house, the one where I was floating uncontrolled in a hot air balloon ... I think the man in the dream is Colin. In the dream, the man's eyes were blue and then amber, back and forth. I know it sounds completely crazy, but anytime the idea crosses my mind, it feels like a universal truth. Like capital-T truth. Like my gut is telling me it's right. It doesn't *feel* far-fetched at all.

But it *sounds* absolutely unhinged.

So, I've been dreaming about Colin for years but never met him until now? Does that happen?

My logical brain doesn't want that to be right, but when I look at things like the fact that everything is energy and everything is connected and you just *know* when a person you're meeting for the first time will end up being a close friend ... maybe it isn't as far-fetched as it seems. Was he calling out to me in my dreams when we were in high school, though? Is he soul family? A soul mate? Are friendships and relationships predestined? Wild.

So, I'm not saying a word to anyone about it, since I don't know that I would believe myself if I told me that. I keep the whole internal battle to myself—it feels like I've discovered something huge, but I'm not ready to say it out loud. When Anthony picks us up to go hiking, we return to the loop that Saoirse and I hiked on Saturday at Snoqualmie.

Rounding the bend near Cedarbrook, a tingle of anticipation curls in my stomach. Knowing a little more about the house's history makes it feel almost alive.

Anthony pulls his hand from the pocket of his fleece and gestures at the silent stone giant. "I saw a couple moving trucks here last month."

"I heard that someone was moving in." I stop and tuck a lock that had escaped my ponytail behind my ear.

"We snooped online for interior pictures, but nothing came up." Saoirse stops walking and tugs at her sock. "We guessed that the house was never listed. Probably passed down through the family."

"Gloria Brennan's son used to work for a med tech company in the area," Anthony adds. "He actually went to school with my dad. As an adult, he didn't live there, though. The commute to downtown would be hell. I think he had a loft in the city at one point. Dad kept in touch with him for a while."

"So Cedarbrook just sat empty all this time?" I say.

"Yep. Probably one of his kids or grandkids moving in now. Unless they decided to rent it out."

"Huh." A breeze shivers through the pines, filling the air with a peaceful shhh-shhh that suddenly feels ominous. I glance at the drive that winds to the back of the building and see a black sedan parked there. Maybe someone is home.

"You know what would be nice?" Saoirse says as we continue around the bend. "I'd love to see the new tenant do a before-and-after piece online so people can see what it looked like and what they are doing with it. I'd especially love to see how it looked when Gloria Brennan lived there."

"I think most people would," I say. "I wonder if her son has ever shared any pictures of it. Any idea what his name is?"

"Chuck Vernon," Anthony says. "Probably goes by 'Charles' professionally, but my dad always calls him 'good ole Chuck.'"

The wind carries voices to us, but I can't make out what they are saying. I glance back toward the house and see two people standing near the car behind Cedarbrook, deep in discussion. One has their arms crossed. The other throws their arms up, shaking them in what looks like frustration.

Anthony cuts through my thoughts. "You know who might know something?" I glance at him and shrug. "Colin."

"Does he know Chuck Vernon too?" I ask.

"Chuck was head of research at the first place Colin worked. Maybe Chuck showed him pictures. I'm not sure how close they were."

We walk on for a few minutes in silence, except for the crunch crunch of gravel on the path. Then Anthony interrupts my thoughts again. "Colin took that job so he could stay close to his family. His brother and sister both still live in the area. And his granddad is still living with his mom. He got a good offer from Cleveland Clinic but didn't want to go so far away. Said this is where he's meant to be."

"I feel the same way," I say softly. "My work is important, but everyone is within a couple hours' drive except my sisters Morgan in Pittsburgh and Rhiannon in LA." I realize Anthony probably doesn't know them, so I elaborate. "Morgan handles finances at a boutique architecture firm, Baker & Willow, and Rhiannon is an exec at Gardener Records." My companions nod. "I lucked out finding a job where I can study fish and stay close to home."

"Yeah," Saoirse whispers. "I knew I had to come back, too. This is where I belong."

Anthony puts his arm around her and pulls her against his hip. She smiles like the sun and shines her light on him.

That little tingle returns to my stomach. I wonder how long she was traveling with her mom, with the band, and what she was doing the whole time. I wonder why she sounded a little sad when she said she belonged here—like she wanted to, and also didn't. And I wonder if every little thing along the way was supposed to bring us here, to this strange place, to this moment in my life.

Chapter Fourteen

In the afternoon, I walk to Monroasters again to meet with my lab team. It's breezier today, and the wind lifts the ruffle collar of my blouse. I end up pulling on my leather jacket, as much as I try to tell myself that I'm not cold and it's spring, darn it.

With my latte warming my chilly hands, I sink into the same chair in Monroasters' meeting room that I had last time, still enjoying the firm-but-soft cushions, and nod to Violet, who is already there. Twyla and Dan enter together a moment later, chatting amicably, and Luke follows close behind them. Once the group is assembled, Dan stands and gives us a stiff smile.

"Let's start with an update on where we are pitching and what we've heard from journals and conferences." Dan nods to Twyla. "Do you want to go first?"

We do a round robin that is mostly, "I pitched, got confirmation of receipt," so there's nothing really exciting. Summer and fall publications are already mostly planned; winter ones will likely do selections in the early summer if they are still open. For late fall conferences, we're hoping to hear back by summer, and the others, of course, further out. It'll probably be quiet for the next couple of weeks.

Dan looks pleased. The funny thing is that this extra quiet time has allowed us to all search for different journals and conferences aside from the big ones, so we are spreading out our chances of getting our research in front of people. I guess that's a win, even though it's due to a weird situation.

"Good news all around then," Dan concludes. He takes a sip of his coffee. "We got an odd update this week on the investigation at the lab."

I sit up straighter, my heart skipping a beat. My chest clenches as I realize that someone could be getting in trouble for not disposing of something properly or not closing a container before storing. Or maybe someone left a valve open on a gas tank. Or maybe ...

Stop it, Lacey.

"You all probably remember the frozen pipe that delayed our research this spring." Everyone nods. Luke rolls his eyes. It really pissed him off.

The pipe in question brings water to our building, and since we didn't have running water—in other words, no sanitary restrooms—we were locked out of the building for two whole days during a major cold snap while the pipe was being thawed and repaired. It happened right in the middle of a week when we needed hourly measurements. We were taking shifts around the clock that week to make it work. Getting three days into a test like that and then needing to start over the following week was no fun, especially for those who drew the short straws and had to do measurements overnight. Luke and Twyla got those two slots. Luke opted to stay up till three a.m. to get his, and Twyla came in at four a.m. to start the day. I was the shift before Luke, so I only stayed up a little late, nothing too awful. But two weeks in a row for that was not what we had planned.

"It turns out that the frozen pipe wasn't repaired properly." Dan pauses as we all react. I know I'm grimacing as my brain traces over the different ways this ended badly. "Some of the chemicals from the spill leaked into the water pipes and got inside NLBS. Because they will have to flush out the water system and see what damage it caused, we will be out at least another week."

Wow! So, we have this really intricate water system at the lab, which is one of the reasons I love working there. I know—*nerd*. Our building has a living roof, which means there are plants up there. On purpose. The architect was someone from my sister Morgan's firm, which was a cool coincidence. Long story! Anyway, they incorporated this neat way for our building to help maintain its temperature because the layer of dirt on top of the building acts as insulation. The bulk of the plants on the roof are vegetables, so they're harvested and sold at a low cost to the area school system, helping the kids get local veggies. We actually have someone on staff who teaches area kids to grow vegetables, using the rooftop garden.

Now here's the other cool part: gray water—anything from the cafeteria sink or dishwasher—is filtered inside the building and returned to the roof to water the plants whenever there isn't much rain. I know, it's Seattle, but still, but there are always periods between storms when the veggies could use a shower. Water that isn't used on the plants goes back into a tank to be used to flush toilets. There are other environmentally friendly aspects to the building, too, which I'm really into ... but they aren't relevant here.

Now I'm concerned about the plants and the school kids and ... what else? I don't know the system intimately, but I definitely know enough to wonder what the impact is. It's good that they are taking time to ensure safety all around!

"Well, you can't be too careful," Twyla says. "I'm glad they are being thorough."

"Agreed." Dan lets out a big breath. "Last piece of news. There is a local company that makes plastic beads for body scrubs, Plastique, Inc."

I remember hearing about them. They were in the news because they were involved in a lawsuit recently. Something about an ecological group finding microplastics in the ocean and that a certain local bird was endangered because of the amount of microplastics they were ingesting. It was traced back to Plastique, the leading producer of the little plastic beads.

Funny thing, the reason I remember this story is because it gave Haley a panic, so we both immediately switched from drug store brand scrubs to natural salt or sugar scrubs. Haley and I spent the weekend online finding recipes and making our own. They kinda worked. I actually found someone nearby who makes them now, so—

"Was that the company that got in trouble for nearly killing off the Nisqually fire tit?" Twyla asks.

Luke chuckles, and honestly, I'm laughing in my head.

"Tits are small birds, Dr. Davis." Twyla shoots him the mom-look-of-disapproval. "I have boys. I know what you're thinking." I shudder. She crosses her legs and turns to the rest of us. "The Nisqually fire tit is indigenous to Nisqually Reach. They eat insects in the shallows there, and I guess they were mistaking the little plastic beads for bugs. For a while, the news was reporting a lot of fire tits found dead in the area, and after a few months, they attributed the high death rate to the beads."

"That's awful," Violet says. "I remember when the story broke."

"As much as I love talking about tits," Luke glances at Twyla, who acknowledges the joke with a wry smile, "why are we discussing microplastics?"

"Right ... anyhoo, Plastique reached out to Kendra about our research because they wanted to know if we discovered microplastics in the digestive systems of the salmon that we've studied."

"They just casually requested our results?" I ask. Can a company ask for information from a lab? Shouldn't they have to pay for info or wait till the reports come out?

"I was surprised to hear this too," Dan agrees. "I asked Kendra if there was a reason she was complying. It just sounded strange to me. She said that Dr. Burgess"—he's our director at NLBS—"referred them to her, since she's the media contact for the lab."

"Her official statement should be that they need to wait until the research comes out," Twyla says. She's speaking in a clipped tone that I haven't heard before, her face turning pink. She must be annoyed. "You don't call a lab and ask for private information like that. I wonder what Kendra was thinking!"

"Well, I told her that we are working with multiple journals to release results from the testing," Dan says, "and they will have to wait till the research is officially published. It needs to be peer reviewed first anyway. She pressed a little, but ultimately, she said she would let them know that."

This keeps getting weirder and weirder. Maybe Plastique is trying to get ahead of a PR nightmare by finding out about our research before it's released. We didn't find any microplastics in the digestive tracts of the salmon we checked, but that doesn't mean it can be ruled out completely. We only looked at sockeye salmon, not all the species that thrive in the local waters, nor all the species of fish or animals that live near the water. It's certainly not an all-encompassing study!

Clearly, they're concerned about being nailed for harming other species with their scrub nubs.

A memory flashes through my mind of Rhiannon, Fallon, and Morgan, my three oldest sisters, dancing in our basement to "No Scrubs" by TLC. They would dress Haley, Rona, and I up, do our hair and makeup, and let us have dance parties with them. They draped flashing Christmas lights across the pictures on the wall and turned off the big overhead lights. The older girls pretended they were in a club while the little ones thought it was just plain magical. I remember skipping around, throwing my arms in the air while I watched my older sisters swaying their hips and making duck faces at each other. Good times!

Man, what a weird way to remember why we don't want scrubs of any kind.

When the meeting wraps up, I start walking back to Saoirse's. On the way, I call my neighbor Drew to see how he's doing. He picks up on the first ring.

"Lacey Casey, how are you, girl?" Drew insists that my middle name is "Casey," and I have never come up with a good nickname for him. I feel weirdly inadequate.

"Hanging in there," I reply. "I'm staying at my cousin's for a few days. She was nice enough to take me in. Where did you end up?"

"My mom and dad aren't too far away, just over in Bonney Lake. They said I can stick around, but they're going to charge me rent if I'm here more than two weeks." We both laugh. "I'm starting to get nervous. Not sure if you heard the news ..."

"I'm hoping it's the same thing Dan just told us, well one of the two things." I brief Drew on both the broken pipe and the microplastics bit.

"Now hold on. Kendra knows that we can't just share information like that. If it's not published, she's not supposed to say anything. Why the heck would she even ask?"

"No idea. She operates by her own rules." Saying it out loud, I realize it's true. She does whatever she wants. I like her even less now.

"Well, it wasn't fair to put Dan in that position." Drew sighs. "Is it just me, or is it really weird to be off for so many days?"

"You're right. I think I'm starting to lose it. I can only check my email so many times. The rest of the time, I'm worried about what's going on at the lab, kinda wondering when we get our homes back, too."

"Tell me about it ... oh, hey, I gotta go. I promised my mom I'd help her pick up some flowers and start planting around the house. That's the other thing. I suddenly have a honey-do list from my parents. I'm single for a reason, man!"

I chuckle at that. "Good luck with the flowers! Talk to you soon!"

I tuck my phone into my purse and keep walking, but my mind drifts—not to the lab, not to Plastique, not even to home.

To a pair of blue and gold eyes I can't seem to forget.

Chapter Fifteen

By the time I walk through Saoirse's front door, I have some mixed up feelings. I don't know what to even think of the dreams about Colin or if that's really what was going on. I might just be overthinking it. Stuff at the lab isn't resolved, and I've let Derek's text just hang out there for days.

Then there's the Rona/Saoirse story that's been hanging around like a dog under the dining room table, hoping someone will drop a crumb. But she's not dropping any! And it's still bothering me. Clearly, Saoirse has proven herself to be an awesome friend, taking me in, letting me hang out with her and her friends. She even had the neighbor fix my car. For the love of pizza, you would think I could just let go. She seems to have.

But there is still this little edge of hurt. I'm always going to wonder why Saoirse just up and left, never spoke to me again until I reached out and desperately needed someone. It hurts to know that. It hurts to think that our friendship meant so little to her that she would turn and run, never looking back, when it meant the world to me.

On the long list of things on my mind, maybe I can knock one out right now.

I find Saoirse wrapping a present at the dining room table. *Carousel,* a creepy looking book with a merry-go-round and a scary man on the cover is lying on the table beside a t-shirt and a gift card. She's opening a gift bag.

"*Carousel*?" I say, gesturing at the book.

"It's young adult horror about an abandoned amusement park. Anthony's niece is turning fourteen, and she loves books like that. It's her birthday this weekend."

"Nice," is what I say. But what I'm thinking, despite my best effort, is "How do you abandon me and just pick up this new life, fall in love, continue on ... after our life-long friendship was ripped apart?" I shouldn't be jealous of Anthony and the attention she's giving him and his family, but I honestly am.

"How was the meeting?"

"Eh, good-ish." I brief her on what I found out. The broken pipe and the company that makes scrub beads.

"That's crazy!" She tucks some tissue paper into the top of the bag and hangs a gift tag from the handle. Stepping back, she surveys her handiwork and smiles.

"Rona, can we talk?" My tone is ... weird. But doesn't that phrase always sound weird? Nothing good comes after. It's never, *Can we talk? There's a new restaurant I'd like to try.* Probably a crappy choice of words.

Her smile appears frozen, and she looks at me for a moment, eyes darting back and forth reading mine, before she answers. "Sure. Let's sit down. What's up?" As we walk to the couch, she says, "Are you okay?"

I sigh. I want to ask, but I don't want to ask. "Rona … *Saoirse*, you've been so nice to me the past week. I love that we got to reconnect. If you had told me before that we would be hanging out together every day now, I would have thought you were nuts." I take a deep breath. "Dad tried to get me to reach out to you for a couple years, but I didn't want to." I bite my lip, but I know I have to go on.

She nods, encouraging me.

Then the words just start tumbling out. "When you left, back in high school, I felt betrayed. You left me alone when I was going through cancer treatments, and I was *so. scared.*" I sniff hard, but the tears are definitely coming. "You were more than my best friend, more than family. You were my soul sister. We were together all the time. From when we were little. It felt like … like losing a part of myself. I was lost. I wanted to share all my secrets and my fears and have my best friend tell me she was going to be by my side, but you were gone. Just *gone!* You didn't even answer my calls or my emails. Nothing."

I'm a little wound up now, and tears start to fall. I look at Saoirse, and her delicate face is creased with anguish. A tear escapes down her cheek. She plays with her hands in her lap. Then she throws her arms around me and sobs.

We're a mess, clinging to each other like we're seventeen again. It feels like the months we were together junior year, till we weren't. In my mind, we are right back on that couch in the basement, as I'm crying about all my fears, right after my diagnosis, and she cries along with me.

"God, Lacey, I was so scared too." She finally manages to squeeze the words out. She lets me go and grabs a wad of tissues from the box by the couch, sharing them with me. We both wipe and blow and generally clean up the feelings. "You remember how I was in high school. I was high most of the time." I definitely remember that. "I was totally irresponsible." And that. "I didn't want to grow up because of your diagnosis. I didn't want that shock. I wanted to coast a bit longer. Keep being young and free." She blows her nose hard, and I give her space to continue.

"It sobers you up real quick when your best friend—hell, what did you say? *soul sister*—gets that sick," she says. "I couldn't stand to see you weak and helpless. Plus, it made me reassess my life. You can't keep pretending that you're gonna live forever and just be when you're watching someone who was so bright and beautiful shrivel before your eyes. You can't just drift through life picking whatever you want anymore. You *have to* grow up. And I couldn't. I couldn't be that person. For you. Or for me. Or anyone at that point." She spreads her arms. Her eyes are wide and raw. It's so different from the calm and caring Saoirse that I've known the past few days, like I've peeled back the layers of the onion to where she's real. Where she feels.

For a second, I see the girl she used to be—scared and overwhelmed—and I lose it again.

As the tap turns back on, I wipe tears from my face with my tissue. "So it scared you to think about what I was going through? And you ran because you couldn't take it?" I put my hand on her arm. "I didn't realize this."

Saoirse half-smiles through her tears. "This was just the start. Cancer doesn't just hit the person who's sick. It hits everyone around them. Not to downplay what you were going through at all! I kept thinking about how horrible it would be if I lost you, and I couldn't bear it. At the time, it made sense for me to put distance between us because I was terrified of how badly it would hurt to lose you. I thought that if we grew apart, it wouldn't hurt as badly if you were gone. I know that sounds stupid now. Believe me, I've thought about it a million times."

"At that age, I'm sure it made sense." I give her a wan smile. "Especially with you being high all the time."

Saoirse coughs out a laugh. "I get it. I deserved that." She grabs my hand and stares at our intertwined knuckles. "Once I decided that I needed to go, I called my mom and talked her into letting me come on the road with her. She picked up the materials for home-schooling over the summer, and I did my senior year on the band Parallax's tour buses. I thought I would be escaping from reality, just letting my mom take care of me for a few months before I needed to figure out my life, but I was really wrong."

"What happened?" A dozen awful possibilities flash through my mind, and I really hope they are all misdirections.

Saoirse shifts on the couch and sniffs. "I made friends with some of the younger members of the stage crew, and I got to help out with the lighting for the shows. My mom liked that part a lot. The band paid me under the table, so things started out pretty well. I kept up on the schoolwork, so Mom was pleased about that, too."

I nod, encouraging her to go on.

"Because I was making money, though, I started getting in trouble. A couple of the kids were into angel dust. I was still trying to escape a lot of my fears about you, so I decided to partake too, to block them out. We were up late one night, close to the end of senior year, high, and Toby started hallucinating." She stops here, and I know she's watching the scene unfold in her head. I don't say a word as I wait for her to continue.

"He was telling us all these crazy things he saw, and then he was slurring his words and drooling. We thought it was funny till he started vomiting and shaking on the ground. Even in the state we were in, we knew it was bad. None of us knew what to do, and we were freaked out about getting arrested. Melanie just kept saying, 'Oh shit. Oh shit,' and pacing around the room. After a couple minutes, I finally called 911. Then the shaking stopped, and his lips started turning blue. Then he was gone. Before the ambulance even got there."

I put my hands over my mouth and stare at Saoirse. I can't believe she went through that. She meets my eyes and starts sobbing again, and I wrap my arms around her.

"It was so awful. Just what I was trying to escape had happened. It was like freaking Oedipus, you know."

"That's a really strange thing to compare that to," I whisper through tears.

"You know what I mean." She shakes her hands like the story will fall out of the air for her. "Oedipus was trying to escape a prophecy, but his actions made it come true anyway." She leans forward and places her hands on my arms. "I didn't want to see someone close to me die, but leaving made it happen anyway, just to someone else. I was so torn up by Toby's death. But that led to a couple things for me, good and bad. First, it scared me straight. I haven't touched drugs or alcohol since. Heck, I rarely use medications or ingest anything processed. I got really serious about what I was putting in my body and how I wanted to feel."

"That's a good thing, honey."

"It is. But the other end of it is that I was so scared of getting close to anyone else that I just avoided it. I became a loner. The only person I knew well was my mom, and I was so terrified of losing her the whole rest of the tour that I often made myself sick with worry. When we came back to town, Mom talked to Uncle Russ, and he said you were doing great. You came back stronger than ever ..." Then her voice dropped to a whisper. "And it just felt like ... you wouldn't need me anymore. Plus, I was still scared. What if the cancer came back? I couldn't lose you like I lost him. So I stayed away. We were so far apart by that point anyway."

"Oh." That's so much for an eighteen-year-old to carry.

"I knew I had to make a living, so I did community college courses online and learned computer programming while I worked a couple different jobs. I lived alone most of the time, only getting a roommate when I needed help with the rent. I never really got to be friends with them though. I just couldn't get close to anyone."

"I'm so sorry you went through all of that." It seems so hollow, but I don't know how else to comfort her. "You're clearly doing better now though. What happened next?"

Saoirse laughs. "Therapy. Lots of therapy. Once I got a job, I looked into it. I was so messed up." We both give a wry laugh at this. I mean, who isn't?

"But you still stayed away. Why?"

"I'm sorry. I was scared of what you would say. You still meant so much to me, and I hurt you badly. I was a coward, and I didn't know how to mend what I had destroyed."

Chapter Sixteen

*D*ear diary, it's been eleven days since we last saw the lab. Morale is low. We've started eating our horses.

I cannot possibly sit at Saoirse's dining room table all day today staring at my email. I feel like I have to be at my "desk" because that's what I'm supposed to do, but my brain hums like a beehive every time I sit down. Just another Monday for the cube-rats, I suppose, but this is doing me in.

I'm about to consider trying yoga when Saoirse bursts into the living area, arms wide and a huge smile on her face. "For once, someone recognized that a meeting could actually be an email!" She clasps her hands together and breathes in like the air is mountain fresh. "I'm open the rest of the day. Want to go somewhere?"

I pop out of the chair like it's spring-loaded. "Absolutely. What are you thinking?"

"Mount St. Helens? Pike Place Market? Space Needle? Whale watching?" She purses her lips and taps her finger against her cheek as we both consider the list.

"I haven't been to Pike Place in a while. What do you think?"

A short time later, I pull Lizzie into the lot and park. Stuffing a couple recyclable shopping bags into my canvas tote, I sling it over my shoulder, hop out of the car, and prepare to shop with my cousin for the first time in over a decade. I imagine our tastes have changed a lot!

"I wanted to stop in a little shop downstairs first, if you don't mind," Saoirse says.

"Sure."

We cross the skybridge and make our way to the main floor of the marketplace. For a moment, we enjoy the brilliant blue sky of early spring and the sound of cars and people bustling around us. I sigh happily. This is home just as much as Snoqualmie is.

As we stroll down the street to the shop, the strains of a guitar playing Jack Johnson's "Better Together" greet us, and I smile at Saoirse, like the universe queued it up just for us. She elbows me playfully and drops a fiver in the busker's open guitar case as he serenades us and she mouths the words at me. We both end up sashaying to the open door of Jekyll & Hides.

Jekyll & Hides has the delicious smell of fresh leather oozing from every corner. It's almost suffocating, but we can still hear the guitar player and peruse the merchandise with joy.

As I'm humming along, I can't help but think about Colin. The way he played at the piano bar was breathtaking and mesmerizing. And the little spark I felt when we talked in the kitchen at Libby's ... makes me wonder. I wish I could have stuck around longer, but after our short conversation, Saoirse said she was tired and wanted to head out. I was only tired *before* we started talking.

We exit the store to the strains of "I'm Yours" by Jason Mraz from the street musician, walk down the road, and enter the marketplace.

"Have you had any more *interesting* dreams?" Saoirse asks.

"Reading my mind," I mutter. "I did a couple nights ago."

"And you didn't tell me?"

"It wasn't that clear of a dream. I didn't even remember till you said something just now." We walk on in silence for a moment before Saoirse pokes me.

"And?"

"We were in a little boat. It was rocking really hard. I was pointing at the whales on the horizon, thinking they would come closer, so we should head back to shore. I'm not sure what I was afraid of, but I seemed scared. Colin said it was fine, and we should just be patient. They would come closer so we could see them. They wouldn't hurt us."

"You dreamed about Colin?" Saoirse sounds strangely excited.

"Yeah. Weird, right?" I forgot she didn't know I think Colin is the dream guy.

A slow smile spreads across Saoirse's face, and she does a little wiggle. "That's so cute! Anthony and I both think Colin is great, by the way. And he's single."

I glance at her thoughtfully before I continue. I know I will never hear the end of this, but I brave it. "I think he's the guy from the old dreams too. And the one about the hot air balloon."

"Lacey! That is so exciting!" Saoirse grabs my hand, and I stop walking. "Do you know what this means?"

"I can guess what you think this means." I give her a look.

She exhales slowly like a balloon deflating. "What do you think he was trying to tell you?"

"Not to go whale watching with you today," I deadpan.

"It sounds like he's telling you to stop worrying about the lab and just let things play out however."

"Why would Colin tell me that? What does he know about the lab?"

Suddenly, she's bursting again. "His soul was nudging you because you feel safe with him."

I choose to ignore the sudden perkiness. "Why would he be worried? I don't think I came across as freaked out when I told him what happened."

"Because you're soulmates, goofball!" Saoirse sang. "He knows what's in your heart."

I nearly sprain an eyeball rolling them.

She picks up a jar of plum preserves at a nearby stall and examines it. "I think we already agreed that there's something weird going on with you two, even if you have no idea what, so let me have my fun." She frowned at the label on the jar. "Is this what your mom used to get when we were little?"

My annoyance dissolves as I lean in for a better look. "Oh, it is! Barrow Farms. I haven't had that in years." Mom always brought home plum, apple, and pear jams from a little shop near her office when we were little. Plum was our favorite, and I'm sure we ate double our weight in plum preserves on toast growing up. "I need like three jars." I gather them, pay for them, and slide them into one of my shopping bags.

Saoirse ends up getting a plum, a spiced plum, and a jalapeño salsa. "We're having this tonight," she says, pointing at the salsa.

"I don't know about that," I murmur. I'm not a big spice girl.

We wander past a cheese stall, then a knitted hat stall before I decide to ask, "How are you doing since our talk?" I've checked in with her like this every day since our discussion of how she left. She opened up a huge wound that night, sharing about what happened to her friend. I don't want to gloss over it. "I care. But you don't have to share anything else."

"I know." She toys with a jewelry tray at another stall. It's marbled with blues and greens and has gold leaf on the bottom and outer edge. It reminds me of those geode coasters that were popular for a while. "I never told anyone about Toby except my therapist. I was always a little afraid to do so. I don't want people's perception of me to change."

I frown. "We are more than what happened to us in the past. And that was so long ago. Everyone changes. Why would people think anything of you for that?"

"The drugs, seeing Toby die … I don't want them to pity me. Or think I'm trash." She sets the tray down but doesn't move away. Her eyes are fixed on a spot on the wall, distant. "I'm not broken. I was. But I've worked through it. Mostly."

"I think it depends on how you tell people what happened. And why."

"I clearly still have issues from it. I totally broke down the other night."

"That was a little different. You were telling me why you left. I'm sure that cracked open a new place altogether."

"Sometimes I feel like a plastic lid that doesn't fit my bottom."

"Sorry what?" I let go of the necklace I was half examining and turn my full attention to her. "How does that work?"

"You know how you press down on one part and then another, but a different part always pops up. Then you press on that part and another pops up. You only have so many hands to press edges down. The lid won't stay flat anymore, maybe because it's the wrong lid, maybe because it warped in the microwave. It's not a perfect fit to keep the chaos inside."

"I think we're all a little warped." I recall that time we were making necklaces for my sisters for Christmas, wrapping them nicely in tissue paper, placing them in plastic Chinese food containers like they were fancy jewelry boxes. Smashing the lids down the best we could, but nothing fit right. We finally agreed to let Dad help us, and he started switching lids around to see what fit on what bottom. It took some trying, but we eventually did it. "I kinda get what you're saying."

"Mmm." Saoirse picks up the same jewelry tray and weighs it with her hand, tips it to look at the gold coating. "We're not always what we look like on the outside."

I nod and pick up a mug from the ceramics table, half looking at it, half thinking about what she said. "Have you ever talked to Anthony about it?"

"I haven't."

"It would probably be worth it for both of you. It was part of what made you who you are today, and that's not so bad." I wrap an arm around her in a half hug.

She returns the hug. "Thanks, girl." She glances back at the jewelry tray. "I'm getting this. It's really special." With a determined look, she adds, "Besides, I deserve it."

As she's being rung up, my phone vibrates, and I check to see who texted. Derek did earlier, while I was driving. Don't care. But the recent text is from Luke to the lab group.

Spill update: My friend Jenna in the infectious disease lab said they are all being called in to discuss their work and biohazard protocols because the hazmat people found a sample of polio in the biohazard disposal that wasn't properly wrapped. Yikes!

"That's pretty weird." I show Saoirse the text.

She grimaces. "That can't be good. I hope it didn't get in the water supply."

"Yeah. It's wild how many little mistakes are stacking up. This could get messy." I react to the text with exclamation points and quickly text Drew to see what he knows. And then I realize that I could get Luke's friend in trouble for talking about it. But I should check, right? Eh, you can't unring a bell. I slip my phone back in my purse and pretend I didn't just do something stupid.

"You're right." Saoirse picks up her bag, and we continue browsing stalls. "It's a lot of mistakes. It's starting to feel ... off. You know?"

"It's weird, but I'm not sure what you're hinting at."

"If this were a movie, it might mean something."

"It means that humans screw up, and unfortunately, when you start digging for a problem, you find one. Haven't you seen those home improvement shows where they decide to add a toilet in the basement of a hundred-year-old home and end up needing to lift the whole house to redo the foundation because termites and raccoons and rats and antelopes or whatever have caused it to shift so badly that the biggest shock is that the house is still standing?"

"You're probably right." Saoirse pauses to examine a print of a painting of the Seattle coastline. "Is the infectious disease lab in your building?"

"Yeah. My neighbor Drew works in that lab." I point to my phone. "I'll see what he knows."

"Has your boss said anything?"

"Dan is on the text, but Kendra—who's over him—isn't." I frown. "She hasn't said anything to us."

"Maybe she'll email you guys with the full story."

"I'm not counting on it." I brief her on a couple of our interactions that I hadn't talked about before. Then I add, "Once, I actually overheard her talking about me. She said I'll have it too easy and not get anywhere in my career because Dan and Luke are 'cupcakes.' She was complaining to Twyla about it and actually called them that."

"What a weird thing to say. Does she think they should be mean to you?" Saoirse glances at her phone, appears to tap out a text, and then tucks it back in her purse.

"I guess. It sounded like she had to prove herself in her career and thinks everyone else should have it hard too."

"That's ridiculous. I can't stand it when women don't support each other. Or really anyone for that matter.

When we have it hard, we should want it to be easier for others and help them out."

"It's hard enough to break into any industry." Even after all my work, my education, I still feel like an imposter. I doubt I'll ever have enough experience to feel worthy of the accomplishment I just made. There will always be someone ahead of me and a Kendra at the top thinking that she should be tough on the newbies.

Saoirse picks up an apple at the next stall. "Imagine if no one shared about how to tend to an orchard and just made people guess and made it hard for them. How many apples would we have?"

"It's nuts, right?" I pick up a couple apples and pears and pay the shopkeeper. "It's just like that in some industries. I think that especially certain women who were hurt in the past think that putting the pressure on will justify what they went through. It always feels like Kendra is picking on me, though. Like it's personal."

Saoirse shakes her head. "That's ridiculous."

As we weave through the stalls, a little chill runs down my spine. Too many mistakes. Too many coincidences.

Something about all of this feels... off.

Chapter Seventeen

B ack at Saoirse's house later, Anthony stops by with Colin. They had picked up Chinese on their way, which was deliciously convenient, since Saoirse and I hadn't made dinner yet. Libby and Ray drop in as well, and I have a feeling I'm being set, but honestly? *Singapore noodles*, so I don't mind.

As we're sitting around the table, Libby suddenly seems to have a tiny bubble burst in her head. "Oh my goodness! I don't know if you guys have heard of that old mansion out at Snoqualmie where Gloria Brennan used to live?" It's not a question, but it sounds like a question when she says it.

"We were hiking near there the other day and saw it." I shovel more Singapore noodles into my mouth and brace myself for whatever's coming.

"I was listening to a podcast this morning, Thirteen, and they were talking about it."

"The name of the podcast is Thirteen?" Anthony asks.

"Mmm hmm, it's about creepy stuff in America, fears, urban legends," Libby continues. "They were talking about how her husband was murdered. And they said that their granddaughter is moving into the mansion."

"Were they talking about it because they think it's haunted?" Colin asks. Our gazes catch for a second, and I tell myself the little flutter in my stomach is nothing. Absolutely nothing.

"Yes!" Libby says. "The upstairs window on the far right is the room where her husband died. I guess people hiking the trail near the house sometimes see a figure in the window, like he's trying to get someone's attention to come help him." Libby pauses dramatically. "The thing is, they never found the body. The podcast host was talking about how nuts it is for the granddaughter to move in there without having the house cleansed. Like to eradicate any wandering souls."

"Whaaaat?" Now I'm skeptical of the story. We know how Everett Vernon died.

Libby flips her hands dramatically. "The host was interviewing the granddaughter ... I can't remember her name. She said she didn't believe that the ghost of her grandfather would hurt her, and she wasn't afraid."

"The ghost can't hurt her anyway because she's a human," Saoirse chimes in. "All she has to do is tell him to leave her house now and head toward the light. She's in control."

I'm getting a little weirded out now, and I give my cousin a sideways glance. No idea what she's talking about or why she would have this knowledge. Ghosts are creepy, and I'm not talking to them. In fact, I want to stay as far away from Snoqualmie and Cedarbrook as I can now. But I also can't shut up when I know the right answer, so I jump into the conversation.

"Actually, we just read the other day that Everett Vernon's murder was solved a few years ago." I bite my lip but keep going. "We were hiking near there and decided to snoop around online afterward." I brief them on the story we found about the mugger and the driver's licenses he had in the apartment. "They managed to dig up evidence after that. There was an official report on a news site. *A legit news site*." Then it hits me. "I wonder why the granddaughter made up that story."

Libby looks deflated, and guilt washes over me. I knew it was coming, but that doesn't make it easier.

"I'm so sorry! I didn't mean to burst your bubble. It's just odd, you know."

Ray pats her arm. "It doesn't mean that the ghost can't still be in the house, though."

With that suggestion, Libby perks up. "Right! The granddaughter was really open about answering all his questions. Maybe she just didn't want people snooping around and bothering her. I imagine she would be a curiosity."

"It's enough to keep *me* away from the house," I laugh.

Everyone else chuckles at that. None of us are looking to hang out at a maybe-haunted house.

"It's a cool story anyway." Colin shrugs.

My phone vibrates, and I look down. Derek. Go away.

I decided today that I officially hate him, which makes ignoring him easier. Five stages of grief or seven or whatever—I'm definitely past the denial part. And the missing him part. Or missing the idea of him.

The preview doesn't show the message, just his name, but I already know it's probably the same as the last several texts.

So why do I care?

I glance back at Colin, and my stomach does that little fizzle again—the one it absolutely did *not* do earlier.

And honestly, I don't want to risk talking to Derek and getting sucked into whatever story he's spinning. It's all too fishy. But I'm still curious, and part of me is half-wondering about my job. Maybe I need a backup plan? Except... do I really want to work with Derek? And what if it's not even legit? Plus, I hate him.

It's too many questions at once, and my brain starts spinning. I need some fresh air.

I pick up my phone, excuse myself, and walk out to the back patio. I need the world to stop spinning for a minute.

Chapter Eighteen

When I sink onto the loveseat on the patio, my back to the house, I can't look at my phone. I set it on the table, face up, and stare off into the night. At the stars. The same ones that seemed so beautiful and promising just a few nights ago when I parked by Derek's house. Now, they feel cold and far away. Wise and silent. I wonder if they ever get tired of watching us humans flail around.

I glance back at the phone and shiver.

A moment later, I hear the patio door open behind me. An afghan is pressed around my shoulders, almost like I had asked for it.

"It's chilly out." Colin walks around the loveseat. "Mind if I join you?"

I nod toward the chair to my left, and he sits, not really looking at anything, but purposefully not looking at me, like he's waiting for an invitation to join my convoluted thoughts. A shiver runs through me, and the cold has nothing to do with it.

We remain just like that, in silence for a couple minutes, me focusing on not looking at him. Wondering if he's going to say something. Wondering what brought him out here besides bringing me a blanket. Half expecting someone inside to notice he followed me out here. Wondering if they're all concerned because I got up abruptly and walked outside.

Or if they're talking about me because this was what they were hoping would happen with the two single friends in the group.

That string of thoughts is completely normal. I'm totally fine.

"They were really getting into the discussion about Cedarbrook," Colin begins. "Everyone pulled their phones out after you left the room, searching for info about the house and the murder. Libby is pretty disappointed that the podcast was wrong." He chuckles.

"Oh?" I say. Is that why he came out here? "Thanks for letting me know." I think I sound perky, but it's definitely forced. I meet Colin's eyes, those ocean blue eyes with the ring of fire in them, and I feel the intensity of his gaze like a warm spotlight I'm not ready for. I finally chicken out and look away, but I can still feel the weight of his gaze pressing against my cheek.

Minutes drag, and I hear him sigh. It sounds like contentment though, and it oddly makes me feel more at ease too. He leans back in the chair and it creaks.

"You okay?" he finally asks. "I don't want to pry, but when you left, it looked like something was wrong. I used the blanket as an excuse to check on you. I hope that's okay."

I rub my hands on my thighs and breathe in. Then I pull the blanket tighter around my shoulders. "Yeah. I'm good. In theory." A sarcastic laugh escapes my throat before I can stop it.

He nods, giving me a wan smile.

Somehow, I feel like I want to talk, though, maybe let him in on a couple of the weird thoughts in my head. "Do you ever feel like your life took a weird detour you didn't sign up for, and you're stuck wondering when things are going to even out again? Like things are going to go back to normal, and you can just walk back in your apartment, say 'that was weird,' and return to what you were doing before?"

"You know that's not how life works, right?" When I glance at him, his gaze is soft, still fixed on my face. "Truth is always stranger than fiction."

I grimace and nod. "I know." My own gaze wanders to the phone, which is dark, waiting for me to discover what Derek had to say. It feels like the moments between rolling down your car window and the officer appearing there, asking for your license and registration, about to "let you off with a warning." I just don't want to engage.

Colin clears his throat. "Did you get bad news? I'll listen if you need someone to talk to."

I smile gratefully at him. "It's okay. My ex texted." Quickly I mutter, "We aren't talking or anything. I hate him. I know that sounds dramatic, but I do." Had to get that in there. "I was just wondering what he said. The home screen didn't show it, and I don't really want to open the text to read it. I'm just ... tired. Of all of it. And it reminded me of how I ended up here at Saoirse's, my job, everything crazy in my life right now." I laugh again. "You're right. Truth is stranger than fiction."

He nods sympathetically. "I see."

I don't know what it is about the way he's looking at me, but a dam bursts, and I suddenly want to spill *all* the weird stuff in my head, the fears, and hopes, and loony stuff, and just empty out for a moment to an understanding ear. "I had a little panic when I saw that he texted because, the last time we talked, he had mentioned something about a job that he's working on. I thought that maybe I shouldn't burn that bridge just in case the lab where I work closes." Then I rush to explain. "Not that I want to work with him, but I really need to keep health insurance. I—" A little too much, Lacey. Reign in the crazy. "I just thought that since he mentioned a job, if I need one, I could always ask. So maybe I *should* read his text and actually reply." I frown and then laugh, a little self-conscious. "That sounds nuts."

Colin leans forward and gives me a thoughtful look. "So your ex, who you hate, offered you a job, so you thought you should talk to him because you don't know if the lab will close and you'll need one?" He pauses, and I nod. "That's not the craziest reason I've heard for people talking to their exes." He shrugs. "So, what's the job? Does it sound promising?"

I cringe because now I'm on the hook for talking about it. "My ex is an investor, and he was working with some natural fish farm. They were looking for an ichthyologist. I have a similar skillset, and he was trying to convince me to help them out right before I broke up with him." My gaze shifts to my lap because this sounds so utterly stupid that I can't imagine why I thought this was a backup. I am healthy. I don't need to panic about health insurance. But still, that undercurrent of *what if* ... "I was tempted then, but now I'm wondering whether the job is actually all kosher."

Colin gives me a playful look. "So your ex texted to offer you a mafia job at a fish farm as a scientist?"

I laugh because that's such an absurd way of putting it, and soon, Colin is laughing with me too. "Yeah, call me Lacey the Butcher," I say in a terrible New York accent. "When you put it that way, I don't even want to open the text." My panic about actually needing a job has dropped to almost zero now. Besides, there is no way I could take that job, even if I were desperate. I could figure out something else for health insurance. I would be fine. "Okay, I'll read the text."

Letting out a dramatic breathe, I open my phone and click the text icon. Then I glance at Colin, who looks cool and relaxed, leaning back in the chair again, gazing at the stars. I bite my lip and open Derek's text.

Surprisingly, it's not a line begging me to call him. It's a thirty-second video clip. I tap it and turn the volume up just loud enough to hear it. It looks like he's in the woods, near sunset.

"Hey, Lace." Cringe. "I wanted to show you how beautiful it is near the fish lab. I saw on the news that your lab is still closed, so I thought you may want to consider what I said about the research we needed." He falls silent, and the camera pans across part of a brown stone patio with an outdoor dining set and a patch of western red cedars dotted with oaks and maples. Down the hill is a river, nestled in the valley. "It's a great view. Perfect for a quiet lunch every day. Wouldn't be a bad spot to work. Give it some thought! Let me know." Then the video stops.

I place the phone face down on the table and look at Colin. He raises his eyebrows. I frown. "That was weird. He's trying to entice me to take that job."

"Maybe he figures you aren't going to talk to him without an incentive."

"Yeah … he sent a video of the area where the lab is. Not of the lab itself, but the woods outside. It's somewhere rural."

"Did that push you over the hump?" Colin smirks.

"Nooooo. I definitely don't want to talk to him. The lab looks like it's somewhere nice, but I'm just going to hope my lab opens again. That's a safer bet. All legal work."

Colin chuckles. "Always a good thing."

We fall silent again, and I shove all thoughts of Derek from my mind. "That reminds me ... Anthony said you used to work with Gloria Brennan's son. Did you talk to him much?"

Colin leans forward, the chair creaking in the silence, and we lock eyes. My pulse jumps. "When I worked there, I did. He was a really good mentor, and we got to be friends. I don't have the 'inside scoop' on Cedarbrook, though." I laugh lightly. "He had a picture on his desk of his mom and him when he was probably ten. They were outside, sitting on deck chairs. He had a book in his hand, and she had a coffee mug. Looked like a candid shot. They were smiling, but I remember the weird, haunted smile his mom had. Like she was trying to be happy and make everyone think she was. It was the kind of smile people wear when they're trying too hard."

"That's awful."

"Yeah, it kinda reminded me of how my mom was for a few years after the divorce. Chuck and I bonded over that." He shakes his head, looking amused. "I brought it up during my interview, which I *never* intended to do, but when I saw that picture, I felt like that would be a good connection."

"Really? I would be so nervous to bring up something that could be painful like that. You wouldn't know how a person would react."

"I trusted my gut." He shrugs. "I thought, 'If this popped into my head, then it's probably a good thing to say.' I just mentioned the picture, asked if that was him with his mother. I didn't say anything about who she was. Then I said that my mom always smiled the same way after my dad left. We talked for another half hour about our experiences growing up, and when we wrapped up, he offered me the job."

I imagine myself talking with Kendra on my first day of work, trying to find common ground, as she showed me around the building. The silence between us felt like a wall. I always wondered what it was like for the previous generation when they were starting out. Is that wall from her contact with other employees? From her early days as a researcher? Is it protective? I know about the harassment women went through, and sometimes still do, but what about the subtle ways that women were shut out from connection? I imagine some of the men were overly conscious of how they interacted with them as rules were put in place. Was she keeping people out because they were tentative anyway?

I've never felt weird among any of my male coworkers. And we've had some good conversations about family and friendships and experiences, but I wonder if that would have been different thirty years ago. What made Kendra *Kendra*?

"Lacey?" He's searching my eyes for something. Did I just zone out?

"Sorry, I was just thinking about your conversation with Chuck. That's really bold."

He raises his eyebrows and nods. "I always trust my gut. If it feels wrong, don't do it. If it feels right, proceed." He gestures wide with his hands. "It's never steered me wrong." Somehow, he looks amused, like he's surprised that things work this way.

I nod, still looking into his eyes. "Do you stay in touch with him?"

He hums in response. "A little. I have him on My-Circle, so I see updates sometimes. I don't have those day-to-day interactions with him that I used to. I kind of miss it." He casts his eyes down. "I didn't get to be around my dad much after he left. He was busy, traveled a lot, and I think we became an afterthought." He shrugs.

I make a disapproving face.

"I was lucky to have my granddad around a lot when I was growing up, though, since he lived with us after Gran passed. We went camping and fishing all the time, and I loved that."

"My dad used to take us camping and fishing, too." I smile at the memory. "Well, my sister Morgan, Saoirse, and me. My other sisters weren't big on it, but we all hiked."

"Granddad and I hiked a lot too. We loved going up to Snoqualmie and just wandering the trails."

I nod, appreciating that we have this in common. A little voice in my head that sounds a lot like Saoirse whispers *soulmates*, but that's just silly.

"I had a couple really great professors in college who took me under their wing," Colin continues. "No fishing but tons of talk about research and my goals. Chuck, though, was something different. Like he got me because we had a similar situation."

"That makes sense."

"I ought to reach out sometime, see how's he's doing."

"Sounds like it would be nice. I always appreciate those connections that just feel like—" I search for the word, "home ... you know?"

Colin's voice gets low and soft, "I know what you mean ..."

A shiver runs through me when his eyes meet mine, and I pull the blanket closer, but I can't look away. The firelight catches in his eyes, dim but steady, leaving a bare bit of ocean to drag me under.

A half smile plays across both our faces. Crickets chirp around us, the night settling close. He parts his lips like he's about to say something, takes a breath. Stops. I raise my eyebrows, encouraging him to go ahead.

"Ow!" A mosquito chooses that moment to bite my arm, and I react by smashing it. It was already engorged with blood, so now there's a dead bug and a bloody smear on my arm. I gag and abruptly stand. I'm so smooth.

"Get bit?" Colin asks. He stands too, and we both head toward the patio door, but we're stopped by Libby and Ray as they step onto the porch.

"We need to head out," she's saying. "Thanks for letting us hang out!" She quickly hugs us, and Ray throws up a wave as they head toward the driveway.

Colin follows Libby a couple steps, asking something about arrangements for the next night, so Ray and I both stand in silence as they chat. Buuuut, it turns into a funny story from Saturday night, when a bachelorette party was at the bar and got a little too excited when the musicians played "Lady Marmalade" for them. The I Do Crew almost got kicked out because of their vulgar dancing.

We all have a laugh, and Libby and Ray head to their car.

Finally, I beeline inside for the sink to wash my arm. As I'm there, I note that Saoirse and Anthony appear to be having a very serious conversation in the living room. Colin hovers awkwardly near me in the kitchen for a moment before packing up the Chinese food. I join him once I'm clean and start putting it in the refrigerator.

When I glance toward the living room, I see Saoirse wipe a tear. Then they both stand up. Anthony hugs her, and she squeezes him hard. He strokes her hair for a moment before letting go.

Colin and I share a look.

"You about ready to go, Col?" Anthony asks.

"Yep," Colin responds. "We just put the kitchen back together, so we're good."

"Sounds good." Anthony turns to Saoirse. "Call me tomorrow?"

"Of course," she says weakly. He gives her a quick peck on the lips, and relief washes through me. At least I know they didn't break up. No idea why she's upset though.

Anthony and Colin head outside, while Saoirse and I wave from the doorway. As they pull away, I turn to her. "What happened?"

"Just ... talking," Saoirse says. "Don't worry about it. Nothing's wrong." Her tone says that's the end of the conversation.

I nod. "I got bit while we were outside." I show her the welt, which I had smeared up with bite cream a few minutes before. "Colin and I were talking about Cedarbrook House. A little about work stuff." I didn't need to repeat the whole conversation. It wasn't that important, and she doesn't seem to be fully focused on our conversation anyway. She only responds with a shrug.

My chest tightens, and I start doing that thing where I nervously babble to fill space. "You know, I keep thinking about what musicians are like when they play. I was thinking about Colin playing that song the other night, and it's just ... he becomes part of the music. He is so present with what he does."

She hums in response.

"You know, it's like he is living a life of purpose with his work, too. Did he tell you why he does research?"

"No, I don't know the story," she replies dully.

"Ah. He did say he doesn't tell many people about it."

"Maybe you shouldn't tell me then." She sounds a little annoyed, so I heed her warning.

"Right. It's just ... he has purpose. A clear reason for what he does ..." Somehow, I can't shut up now. "And I feel so *purposeless* because I am studying salmon instead of cancer." I know I'm rambling, but I feel like something has been split wide open inside of me.

"Lacey, you chose that."

"Right. And you keep talking about my soulmate calling out to me, which makes me think that maybe there are other things that are meant to be. That we don't get to really choose. Maybe I choose wrong things. Like my career."

"Could be."

"What if what I'm doing isn't important? If it's not big enough?"

"What you're doing is helpful. You're looking at processes in the natural world that are impacted by climate change." She sighs, sounding emotionally drained. "You have evidence in your research that the change over time in that species of salmon is more than what it would be without human interference. That's plenty important."

I frown. She sounds moody, but I somehow can't stop myself when the realization hits me. "Ohmigod. What if someone doesn't *want* this research getting out?" I start pacing, nervous energy coursing through me. "I know it sounds ridiculous, but everything feels off lately." I stop with a sudden realization. "Or, what if it's the place that makes the plastic beads for body wash? Maybe they caused a leak at the lab? I know they wanted to know about the research, but I didn't think that—"

"Look." Saoirse's tone has gone straight to stern here. "Lacey, you're jumping to the worst-case scenario again. Not everything is a sign or a mission." I stare at her with my jaw open, but she's not done. "You just assume that you're supposed to have some big purpose because you survived bone cancer, so you went into biology, just like everyone else does. Maybe it's not a sign that you were 'saved' because you *have to save the world*." Her voice gets a little higher than normal. "When you talk about purpose like that... it makes me think about Toby. And it hurts. A lot. He died right in front of me, and I like to think that it wasn't because he was a throw-away."

"I—I don't know what to say."

But she barrels through like she didn't even hear me. "What, he didn't have a purpose, so it was okay for him to die? Sometimes it feels like you put so much pressure on yourself that you forget the rest of us are just... trying to get through the day." Her face is streaked with pink and crumpled in frustration.

I gasp, and the tears I've been holding back since she changed her tone finally spill over.

"All you really have to do with your life is live what's in your heart." She jabs a finger at her chest, sobs loudly, and jogs down the hall. "I can't do this right now."

Chapter Nineteen

A short time later, I slump into bed and, unsurprisingly, can't fall asleep. I had waited in the living room for a while, but Saoirse stayed in her room the rest of the evening, so we haven't spoken. I did hear her talking to someone on the phone when I walked down the hall to go to bed, and it sounded like she was crying. I'm guessing she called Anthony.

I feel awful for a couple reasons. One, I hate that Saoirse and I argued. Two, I'm pretty sure I pushed her to snap when she was already upset about something, though I'm not sure what. I just had to purge all the thoughts in my head, and I wanted to have a conversation about the lab and the stress that it's causing. I didn't even get to tell her about the video that Derek sent. Ugh.

I guess I'm out of practice at living with someone — and knowing when to shut up.

Oh, and three, I feel awful that Saoirse thought that about me. It sounded like she was calling me selfish, like I think I'm more important than others. That's not me at all.

As I'm lying in bed, it's so quiet that I can hear the murmur of conversation on the other side of the wall for a while. Even when silence envelops the house, though, I still don't fall asleep. Guilt and frustration and nerves and so many other things pile up enough to knock me out, and I pass out sometime around one a.m.

I'm not sure if I'm glad I fell asleep, though, because that's when the weird dreams start.

First, I'm in the lab, white coat on, brushing test tubes and samples and papers and whatever else off the counter and into the trash can. The fluorescent lights pulse brighter and brighter, like they're about to pop. My stomach is in knots, but I don't stop myself. Petri dishes and bags of specimens and notes go in the trash … My gut tells me that this is wrong, but I feel almost panicked, like I have to throw it all away, even if it feels icky. Desperate.

Other people are in the lab, but I don't know them. Faceless dream-people drift around like background characters—like video game NPCs. None of them seem to care that I'm dumping everything from the counters, though they are all dressed in lab coats, too, posing as researchers.

I make my way around the lab tables and reach a fume hood with the exhaust on, roaring loudly in my ears. Under the hood, a fish is lying on the table, rotting.

Its tail flips like the poor guy still has a breath of life left in it, and the lighting reflects dully off of its dead eyes. I shudder, and my heart starts pounding. It's not supposed to be alive. I realize that it has an incision and that thick blood is oozing from it, almost like ketchup. I look at my hand and realize I'm holding a scalpel.

I can't drop it, though. I'm somehow concerned that the NPC lab people might get it. I feel rooted in place, watching the thick, ketchup-like blood ooze out, holding the scalpel like maybe it's my fault.

I feel a hand on my shoulder, and I nod at no one, turning from the table finally, like that was my signal, that's what freed me for the next quest. I think they want me to leave the room, so I do. I follow a presence—not a person, exactly, but close enough. No one is there, but I feel like I know what they want me to do. I feel safer.

Leaving the room, I find myself in the forest, and it's pretty dark. I wander through the trees, over the mossy earth, somehow unafraid. After a few minutes of walking, though, a suffocating sense of being watched presses in on me. Shapes crowd around me—until I realize it's just the trees. They whisper to me, soft rustling shhh sounds. They have a secret.

I'm not sure if I'm scared or if I should be, but I continue through the woods, drawn by a strange light ahead. Suddenly, I'm walking on a path, leaves and brittle pine needles crunching under my feet, the sound of a river nearby, and I know exactly where I am.

The beautiful brownstone mansion of Cedarbrook House rises from the hill ahead of me, but it seems huge: that disproportionate dream wonkiness in full effect. It doesn't bother me though. I continue through the woods till it seems that the trees fall silent. Waiting on me. Apprehensive. Curious.

And then he's here. A man is standing beside me, and he touches my hand with his own. His face is in shadow. I press my fingers into his palm, and together, we approach the house. I feel safe, somehow, with him by my side, like a missing piece was slotted into place.

The house doesn't feel welcoming, but rather standoffish. It feels hollow, like a façade propped up for a movie set.

The man motions for me to follow him, and we walk quietly around the side of the building. When we get to the back, there's a party. Lights have been strung between the house and poles around the patio, and there are chairs and loveseats everywhere with bold crimson cushions. More NPCs are milling around, but there's a festive atmosphere.

My lab coat is gone. Now I'm in a beaded turquoise cocktail dress, long ivory gloves, and a fur wrap. Not my thing, but I'll play along.

I let go of my companion's hand and approach the food table. On one end are several bottles of liquor and mixers, along with antique Waterford crystal goblets. Following that are the plates and silverware and several dishes—a casserole with vegetables and rice, dinner rolls, something gross that resembles a pastry, a tray of meat cutlets, and a fruit salad. Finally, I get to the good stuff at the other end of the table: pineapple upside down cake, lemon chiffon cake, shoofly pie, and a huge stack of whoopie pies. I snag a whoopie pie, but when I try to eat it, nothing happens. Bummer.

NPCs wander close and try to strike up a conversation with me, but I don't know what they are saying or how I respond. Then my whoopie pie is missing, and my companion has grabbed my hand again, bringing me to a circle of exquisitely dressed people surrounding one fabulous-looking woman.

The lady radiates confidence and something ... special. I feel like it's *je ne sais quoi*, like you always hear people say, but that's not a phrase I would ever use. I feel important just being in her glow.

The woman wears her hair pinned half up in big victory rolls, and her soft green knee-length dress is made of a flowy fabric with a sheen. The fairy lights make it look like a quick fish flitting through the shallows as she moves. At her neck, she wears a huge peridot set in gold on a short pearl necklace. And she is stunning with her ruby lips and huge brown doe eyes.

I feel like I should know who she is, like she's someone important, and then I realize she must be Gloria Brennan. She's talking, and everyone floats on her words like kites on the wind. Her laugh tinkles like glass in a breeze, and the crowd answers with laughter. Then we all clap, and the NPCs wander off to mingle. But I'm stuck in place again, wondering if she will notice and make it awkward.

Swing music suddenly swells in the background, but I'm not sure of the song. My sister Rhiannon or Aunt Mindy would know. I can't find a purse or pocket in my gown, so I don't know where my phone is to text them a clip and get the answer.

Then, Ms. Brennan approaches and conveys a thought—like telepathically?—to me. She's asking if I would like some fish. She gestures to the buffet.

"There isn't any fish," I say.

My companion takes my hand, and the three of us wander across the patio. It's a gorgeous night out. I hear my heels clicking on the stone with each step, oddly not muffled by the noise of the party.

Ms. Brennan shakes her head and conveys, "Why did you bring the fish inside?" It seems like she's asking me.

"I didn't see any fish here," I say. "Can I have some cake?" Because priorities, even in a dream party with a dead movie star. I point at the pineapple upside down cake, and my companion hands me a plate.

"Yes. But don't bring any more fish inside. I don't want them here." Now she seems angry, and her face is contorting.

"I'm sorry." I feel personally responsible for whatever happened. "No fish inside the house." I shake my head to show I understand.

"None. Never. Don't do it." Her voice is full of venom, but I don't know why.

My companion pulls me away from her, and I realize that I have cake on my plate. I need a fork. Now there aren't any forks. And the NPCs are crowding me. Claustrophobia clamps down on me again when I see tiny cheese crackers that look like cartoon fish, the kind little kids like, scattered on the ground. I'm afraid I'll step on them after what Ms. Brennan said.

Click click click as my heels hit the stones, and my companion and I walk to the edge of the patio. We sit on the wall, and I pull off my gloves. Then I break off pieces of cake, feeding myself clumsily with my hands.

"No fish!" I see our host pointing at the crackers, which I must have smashed, and a man in a dark suit is sweeping them up. A little boy, probably around age five, runs through the crowd, and now, I'm afraid he will smash the crackers while the man is cleaning them up. I try to stop him, but my mouth is all gummy and won't make any sound. I strain to force a sound out, like pushing against a locked door. Come on!

I glance at my companion, and his eyes are fire and ice. *I know those eyes.*

A strangled sound finally tears loose, which wakes me up.

And now, I'm lying in bed, a little sweaty, hoping that I didn't just wake up my cousin because I yelled in my sleep. She already mad at me, and a surprise wake up call wouldn't help the situation.

What the hell was that dream about?

Chapter Twenty

Saoirse stays in her office all morning, while I work from my bed with one of those little cushion tray things on my lap. It's not terrible if I bunch the pillows against the headboard and move around every fifteen minutes. Not *totally* terrible. It's not like I'm accomplishing anything anyway between being tired, being haunted by that bizarre dream, and researching new places to pitch.

I still feel a little warm after my weird night of crazy dreams and interrupted sleep, but there's a chill in the air when I leave my bedroom for the bathroom, so I throw an oversized navy cardigan on over my tank.

Still no sign of Saoirse, and I'm worried that we'll bump into each other in the kitchen before she's ready to talk to me, so I decide to walk to Sal's Diner for a bite. I could use the fresh air to perk me up.

On the marker board by the fridge, I write a quick note for Saoirse, in case she checks it. I put on a little makeup, brush my hair, and grab my purse and a new book, *The Memory of Cotton*. Fallon's daughter Annabel wanted me to read it so we could talk about it, so I may as well get started. The reviews make it sound good!

After a delicious lunch of a Reuben and half a salad, I walk back through the streets and am unfortunately lost in my thoughts. The sandwich was great, but that's not where my mind wanders. I hope Saoirse is ready to talk when I get back.

The GPS tells me to turn a couple blocks earlier than I expect, so I switch my focus back to the phone again as I walk. I really don't want to get lost and need help getting back. I really don't want to bother Saoirse till she feels like talking.

The street I turn onto is lined with pretty, modern homes, and I wonder what happened. Most of the homes in this part of town are much older. Was there a fire? Did a developer buy up the block and knock down the older homes, rebuilding afterward? As I approach a set of five townhouses that can't be more than ten years old, I hear someone strumming a guitar, and the song is familiar. I can't place it though. It feels like a long ago memory.

I see a man sitting on the stoop of the unit farthest from me, strumming away. He appears to have the guitar in an embrace as he's playing, and the two almost meld together. The air around us is filled with a passionate melody. I see him shake his head as he plays a complicated riff, like the song is rippling through his soul, and I'm struck with realization.

It's Colin.

Was my phone conspiring against me? Or doing me a favor?

It would be rude to ignore him, even though he's so deep in the music, so when I get near, I pause on the sidewalk. It doesn't take long for him to note my presence and look up. His mouth forms an "o," and then a smile. He jerks his head toward the steps, so I take it as an invite to join him. A warm shiver passes through me like a breeze as I sit against the railing opposite him and drink in the song like lemonade on a summer day.

Now that he has an audience, he turns on Show Colin. Swaying to the music, he grins at me a few times and leans into a difficult riff at the end. Flicking the last note, his hand flies away from the guitar and then returns for another quick ripple of notes that he clearly added to be fancy.

I smile and applaud, now feeling completely awkward as the one-woman audience. We look at each other, and my brain presses a "now what?" against my temples. Finally, I go with, "That was great! I didn't mean to interrupt your practice."

"You're not interrupting!" he assures me. "I was just playing around. Besides, when I have someone to play for, I usually try harder, which is good, since I have that bridge club coming to Riff's later this week." He smiles smugly. "Don't want to miss my shot."

We both laugh, and then it grows silent again.

"What song was that? It sounded familiar, but I can't place it."

"Oh, you've heard it?" he says. "Usually no one knows that one. It's 'Daphne' from *Swing Kids*."

I frown. That sounds like something I should know. "Is that the movie about teenagers in Germany during World War II?"

"It is."

"I remember watching it in high school when we studied that unit in history class." Rona sat behind me. I had to tutor her that whole year because she would get high in the parking lot during lunch and go to history class right after. "The music was great. I don't remember much else about the movie though."

"I mostly fell in love with the music, too. We played a piece from the movie in jazz band, but I can't remember which one now. I was always partial to 'Daphne' though. The character who plays guitar plays this song after he gets beat up. They broke his hand, which is a pretty damning injury for a musician. It threatens his livelihood."

"Okay, I remember that part now." I scrunch my face as I recall part of it. When I come back to the present, I can almost feel the intensity of Colin's stare. His pupils are shrunken in the bright light of midday, and the flecks of gold are dancing in the sun. I feel my breath catch. *That's the last thing I saw before I yelled and woke myself up in the middle of the night.* Probably shouldn't tell him that. Then he clears his throat and the moment is gone.

"Anyway, I think it's pretty inspiring how the musician comes back from that injury and keeps doing what he loves. That's something that I hope people take from the song when I play it ... even though I don't often get to play it for an audience." He lets out a laugh suddenly. "I'd be pretty surprised if someone actually requested 'Daphne' at Riff's."

I smile. "You mean 'Put a Ring on It' is more popular? How strange!"

"Yeah, it's not exactly booty shaking music." He shrugs.

"Are you off today?" I ask.

"Not quite, dentist appointment a bit ago. Got my all clear, so I figured I'd come out and enjoy the weather since I took half a day for it."

"I see." It is a nice day. Too bad it's a little overshadowed by Saoirse not talking to me.

"So what are you up to today? Just out for a walk ... with a book?" He points at the novel in my hand.

"Not exactly. I walked to Sal's for lunch. I'm walking back now."

"Is Saoirse working through lunch today?" he teases. "She couldn't take a break to hang out with you?"

"I'm not sure she would want to ... we had a fight after you guys left last night." His concerned look tells me he's curious but isn't sure if we're at that point in our friendship where he should pry. "You saw that she looked upset when we came in from outside, right?" Colin nods. "I don't know what she and Anthony were talking about, but she was clearly pretty irritated. And I made it worse. I started rambling about all these things I was wondering about the leak at the lab, and then she got frustrated with me and went to bed." I bite my lip and then decide to continue. "She said that I always think that I survived cancer because I have some special mission on earth. But that's not true." I cross my arms and hunch over them. "I don't *think* it's true."

Colin is still watching me, a sympathetic look on his face. He raises his eyebrows and nods encouragingly, so I keep going.

"She was talking about this difficult time she went through back when we weren't talking," I have to be careful about sharing this, "and I think that had something to do with her reaction, since she brought it up. It must have been on her mind, so I can see why she got upset the way she did. It still bothers me though. I don't want to upset her. Or anyone." I let my forehead rest in my hands and lean my elbows on my knees. I stare at the concrete steps for a moment, breathe deeply, and then look at the sky. "I'm sure we'll talk later, but this is just hard when we're finally back to talking and hanging out. I don't want to push her away, like before."

Colin frowns and nods.

"I mean, she left," I add quickly, "but I don't want to be the reason ..." I sigh.

A couple cars pass us, and we watch them pause at the stop sign and continue.

Then I keep going. "I know you have zero context for this, and I probably shouldn't have dumped this all on you. You were just sitting out here trying to enjoy the day and practice and be normal." A short laugh escapes my lips, and I suck the air back in to help keep the tears from falling.

"Is there something I can do to help?" Colin asks. He shifts a little closer, just enough to make the moment feel more private. "Do you want a hug? My sister says they solve every problem. You look like you could use one, but I don't know if we've known each other long enough for that?" He sets his guitar against the railing and shrugs, eyebrows scrunched together in a "maybe?"

I laugh again, and a tear almost escapes. "Yeah, actually, I wouldn't mind one." He slides across the steps and wraps his arms around me. He smells like pine needles and sandalwood and fresh air. And there's something deeper that isn't quite a smell or a feel but more like a tiny piece of me deep in my belly that I never noticed had been clenched tight, like a little seed, all my life, that is suddenly relaxed and open and free. Like I've awakened something dormant.

Maybe Saoirse is right after all.

My shoulders relax, and a tear finally drips down my cheek. I discretely wipe it with a finger.

He gives me a quick squeeze and moves back a bit. "You okay?"

I sniff. "Thanks. I will be." I dig in my purse for a tissue. "I'll see if Saoirse is ready to talk when I get back to the house."

Colin nods. "Why are you so worried about the lab? This seems like something you just have to wait on, to let it play out."

"I guess that's why I'm so worried. I'm used to jumping in and trying to solve puzzles, take care of everything. Isn't that what us scientists do?" I bump his knee with mine, teasing a bit, but also trying to satisfy this strange need to touch him again.

"Of course." He gives me a soft smile that makes my stomach buzz. "But if we're always worried about every little thing, that takes a lot of the fun out of life, right?"

"I suppose it does."

"Look, you're not the lab lead, and I bet they aren't even that worried. You know they'll figure out what's going on, clean it all up, and let you guys back in as soon as it's done."

"But what if it's my fault?"

He gives me a skeptical look. "*How* would it be your fault?"

"Don't you have any weird fears about screwing up something major? Maybe you've been a professional longer than I have. I got my job a year ago."

"I've been at it for three years. First with Beekman Labs—that's where I worked with Chuck Vernon—and now with my current job at exCorde." Colin stretches his legs out and leans back on the stairs. "I learned the first time that I dumped chemicals down the lab sink in my freshman chemistry class that you can't sit around worrying about making a mistake. If the mistake comes, someone will definitely let you know. Especially when they see a big plume of multicolor smoke puff out of the drain. And then you can apologize and correct it. You do better when you know better. Then you dump the chemicals into the neutralizing solution under the fume hood like all the other good boys and girls."

I can't help but laugh. "Oh my God, you didn't?" He nods, looking amused by his own story. "Yeesh. I always feel like I should know everything, and I should already be doing everything perfectly. Everyone in my lab has so much more experience than me. And then our lab coordinator thinks that everyone should have it hard because she did, so she likes to make things difficult whenever she can."

"I know we don't know each other that well, but if I can share something ..." He pauses, and I gesture to continue. "You know, the moment I truly started living my life was when I finally decided to say 'F it' to all the *shoulds*. If you're always caught up in thinking that you should have cured this or solved that or achieved a certain status by a certain time, then you'll always be behind." He leans over and pokes me in the knee. "And you're the one putting that pressure on yourself because you're trying to control more than you actually can."

I flare my nostrils at him and give him a look, which makes him laugh. "I suppose you're right." I debate about sharing with him and then cave. He calls all my deepest thoughts and secrets from me like a siren. "I had cancer when I was in high school, halfway through my junior year, and it made me feel like life was so scary and unpredictable. I felt like I had no control over anything, not even my own body." I jab my fingers at my chest and then clench my fists. "I know we all go through things, but that … that was what gave me so many of my strange ideas about the world. That I wasn't safe, no matter what I did. That I lacked control. That I was a ticking time bomb and had to live so much in a short amount of time …"

Colin puts his hand on my forearm and squeezes it. "I'm not going to pretend that I understand that completely because I've never been through what you have, but I'm sure that was so difficult. I bet it makes it hard to let go and just be."

"Sorry, I don't usually spill my guts like this." I have to acknowledge the weirdness.

Colin glances down at his guitar. "I don't mind. I'm just enjoying this beautiful day, when I don't have to be anywhere," he looks back at me, "and getting to know an interesting woman."

If I could bottle this moment—the way he's looking at me—I would. And I would take a sip every day and get drunk on the way that tiny seed in my belly is starting to spread its warm tendrils throughout my abdomen, into my chest cavity, and around my heart.

Certain that my face has turned a bright salmon pink, I grin like an idiot and drop my gaze. "Thank you. I'm appreciating the time with you, too." We lock eyes for a beat, and I turn away.

"By the way, you have the most beautiful whiskey-colored eyes …"

"Thanks," I whisper, trying to keep from smiling. I know I'm failing. And I can still feel him staring at me.

Just then, a school bus pulls up in front of the building and several elementary-age kids clatter down the steps, running down the sidewalk to their respective homes amid the yelling and laughing emanating from the bus. The door of the townhouse beside Colin's swings open, and a woman in joggers and a t-shirt steps out to greet a little girl with braided pigtails and a puppy-print book bag as big as she is.

I smile as I watch, and Colin waves. The little girl waves back, and Colin signs, "hi" and the letter "s" over his heart. I glance between Colin and the girl, following the exchange.

"You know ASL?" I ask.

"Only a few signs. Sabrina has a moderate hearing loss, so she signs. However—" He scoops up his guitar. "She can hear some sound and loves music." He calls out to her mom, "okay if I play her a song?"

"Of course," she responds. Sabrina and her mom sit on the steps in front of their townhouse and watch as Colin starts strumming.

I recognize the song immediately. It's "Never Grow Up" by Taylor Swift.

"It's one of her favorites," Colin says during the introductory chords.

I watch for a moment, touched by the fact that he's playing a song for this little girl, and then I get an idea. I know the words, thanks to being a Swiftie back in high school. I remember signing them to my mom so she knew what I was singing, so I start signing for Sabrina.

When Colin realizes what I'm doing, he gives me a huge grin, and I'm completely melting. I might cry again, but I don't even mind. I watch Sabrina as she dumps her backpack, runs down to the sidewalk, and starts dancing. She watches me for a moment and then gets caught in the music again. This might be the sweetest thing I've seen in ages.

After the final chords, Sabrina and her mom clap for us ... well probably for Colin, and then they head inside.

Colin and I look at each other for a second with completely satisfied smiles.

I hate to interrupt this beautiful moment, but I also can't possibly keep my mouth shut when something funny is in my brain. "You must be really secure in your masculinity to sing Taylor Swift with such gusto."

Luckily, it lands, and Colin is laughing again. "That I am. I also happen to be a sucker for making her smile. She's a sweet kid."

"Mmm." I nod. Then I realize that I've been sitting here for a long time, and maybe I should head home and see if Saoirse is ready to talk. "I should probably get going. Thanks for hanging out with me—and letting me join in." I wink. *Why the hell did I wink?* I gather my purse and book and stand up.

"You're welcome to any time," Colin says. He stands too and looks like he wants to say something else.

When he doesn't continue, I lean in and give him a quick half-hug. I take a deep breath, partially because he smells so good, and then I let go and step back. "I'll see you later."

"Hang on. Can I give you my number?" he says. "In case you want to talk?"

"Sure." I hold out my phone for him to type it in. "I'll let you know how things go later."

"Please do. I'm sure you'll be fine though." He touches my arm and then turns to get his guitar.

I'm impressed that I somehow I made it through the whole conversation without blurting out my bizarre dream about him. I still haven't puzzled out what that all was supposed to mean.

As I walk down the street, I hear "Here Comes the Sun" floating on the spring air from the direction of his porch.

"It's alright ..."

Chapter Twenty-One

When I get back to the house, I'm surprised to see Saoirse sitting in the living room. She's not doing anything. No books or magazines. Just sitting. She's perched on the edge of the couch looking very much like a barn swallow with her tiny features and slim limbs. In her blue jersey knit jumper, she reminds me of little Rona, so tiny and fragile and alone.

My heart sort of breaks because I don't want to have a conversation about last night, but that's clearly why she's there, waiting on me.

"Hey," she says. There's no edge, no excitement. It's sort of a tentative greeting. Dipping her toe in the water.

"Hey." I respond with warmth I hope she can feel.

"I'm sorry I yelled at you. Can we talk?" Saoirse bites her lip, her eyes crinkled with worry. She looks haunted suddenly, but now some of her ghosts are familiar, and I welcome them.

"Sure," I set my stuff on the table and join her in the living room. "I didn't mean to run over you last night. Sometimes, I have trouble shutting up. Are you doing okay?"

Her gaze drops to the edge of her long-sleeve shirt where she picks at a loose thread. "You told me I should talk to Anthony about what had happened with Toby all those years ago." When she pauses, my heart drops. *Did I give her bad advice?*

But she continues. "It's okay. Don't be worried. I just thought that last night was a good night to talk because he said something about me living with a roommate and how he was impressed that I could share my space for over a week. He was joking, but I thought I could open up about Toby and why I always lived alone. We talked about living together recently, and I sort of dodged around the question then. I love him, and I want him to move in, but it's a weird step for me. But then with you here, it sort of made me look like an ass if I didn't tell him why being this close with someone is tough."

"What did he say?"

"Mostly, he listened, but then I started crying because, clearly, I haven't healed from all of this yet ... And then you and Colin came back inside."

"Yeah, that was bad timing on our part, but we didn't know." I shrug.

"I know," she whispers. "I felt really frazzled and embarrassed. I shouldn't have tried to have that conversation when I didn't know if it would be private. Then when you were telling me all that stuff, I just sort of snapped. I know I shouldn't have. It's been a lot to take, digging all of that up again. I guess last night it was too much"

"I know."

"I'm *really* sorry for what I said. I didn't mean to make you feel bad. That was all my crap, and I dumped it on you." Saoirse takes my hands. "I feel like I have to keep asking forgiveness for all the terrible things I've done, for the way I've treated you in the past. I thought I was making up for it by being supportive now, and then I screwed it up again." She bites her lip and wipes the single tear that trails down her face.

We've done a lot of crying on this couch over the past few days. "I'm not saying that what you did was right or okay, but I know why you did it. I forgive you." I grab her in a huge hug. "And I'm sorry I trampled over you without shutting my mouth. I just felt like I suddenly had so many things I wanted to share with you, you know?" I feel her nod against my shoulder. "Hey ... why don't we play hooky the rest of the day?"

"I'd like that." Saoirse gives me a weak smile. "Anthony and I talked a lot about what I said last night and about Toby. He has tonight off, so we were going to hang out anyway, but he suggested we go out to dinner. He's so sweet. He wanted to cheer me up."

"Okay, I'll have you home in time to get ready for your date." I squeeze her hand, glad that things are working out again.

We head to Newcastle Beach Park for a walk and to chill on the beach. Literally chill: it's not quite beach weather. There's a food truck parked nearby, so we get coffee and nachos to warm up. It's a nice afternoon, and honestly, I'm a little sad to go back to the house and spend the evening alone.

When Anthony picks Saoirse up, I notice that he's wearing a sports jacket and dress shirt. Turns out he's taking her to see the musical *Rainy Day Fund* and then eat at Nines. It's so sweet of him to take her out for a nice dinner when she's having a rough time. I'm happy to see how supportive he is of her needs.

I hope I can find something like that someday. And for the first time in a long while, it doesn't feel impossible.

Chapter Twenty-Two

Once they're gone, I feel a little aimless, like I've been set adrift. I have no idea what to do. I don't want to read or watch TV. I decide to mop all Saoirse's hard floors just to show that I appreciation her giving me a home, but that doesn't take very long. Finally, I give in and sit down at the computer in the dining room.

Luckily, my phone rings. It's Fallon, sister number two.

"Hi!" I answer.

"Hey, how are you? How's Saoirse?" I texted Fallon the other day about Rona's new name when she was telling me about the book Annabel wanted me to read with her.

I answer truthfully, and I'm happy that I can. "I'm good. She's good. Anthony is taking her out to a musical and dinner tonight."

"Is it *Rainy Day Fund*? A bunch of the faculty wanted to go together, take advantage of the special teacher discount, but everything is sold out for months."

"That's the one."

Fallon sighs. "Lucky. Anyway, I was wondering what you're up to on Tuesday … like the whole day."

Wallowing in self-pity? Reconsidering all my life choices? Running off with the circus? "Oh, Tuesday, let's see … I'm pretty busy what with all this keeping my laptop from floating away business. What did you have in mind?"

"That's a bummer that you can't get into the lab." Fallon legit sounds disappointed for me. That's what I love about her. She's always been the "mom" of our sibling group, the sensitive one who always gets our feelings. "I actually thought this would cheer you up. The school has a 'career petting zoo' planned for Tuesday with a bunch of local professionals, and another researcher was supposed to come but can't now. I told them I'd ask you if you would mind stepping in."

"When you say 'petting zoo,' you're not counting on me to bring in dead fish, are you?"

Fallon scoffs. "Ew. No. Can you stop being weird for one minute?"

"Nope." I chuckle, pleased with myself.

Fallon lets out a huge sigh, so I know it's time to stop giving her crap. "What do you need me to do? I'll be there."

"I knew I could count on you," she says. "You'll be giving five, half-hour presentations about what you do on a normal day—" Fallon pauses because I snort-laugh.

"Um, *normal* isn't exactly what we're doing right now."

"Like *normal* when the lab is open," she continues. "That's point one. Point two: what you enjoy about the work. And point three: your education and what inspired you to go into your work."

"Oh good. I really, really like telling people that I'm a doctor. Not joking." I mean, a girl's gotta brag, right?

"As someone with a *measly master's degree*—I think that's what you said—I know." Fallon loved the whole month when I made everyone in our family call me "Dr. Sturm" or I wouldn't answer them. As the baby of the family, I feel that I was owed that power trip.

When I hang up, of course, my stomach ties itself into a knot that a boy scout would be proud of. I have to create a presentation and talk to middle schoolers. *Middle schoolers!* Raging hormones and boredom painted all over their faces, regardless of the topic. I'm hoping I get all the groups that just stare and pretend to be interested instead of the ones that heckle and ask insane questions.

If anyone but Fallon had asked …

I pull myself out of that tailspin and try to regroup. There are bound to be at least a handful of kids there who love science. Or who love nature. Or who love pyrotechnics … probably a fair few of those. Maybe I can come up with something fun for the presentation.

Maybe creating this presentation will help me finally have total confidence in myself and my work. *Said no one ever.* But I can at least try.

For now, though, I need to get back to my work. I pull up a blank document and start jotting down ideas of where else I can pitch our results. After five minutes, I still have a blank document, which is unfortunate because it means I'm going to start soul searching.

"Okay, Lacey. What actually matters to you?" I start typing whatever pops into my head. "I'm a Pisces. I live in Seattle and study salmon." *How do I feel about that?* "I love the work I do because it's helping people, and it's fun doing research, like putting together a puzzle."

So why am I so unfulfilled?

Hmmm. I don't have anything to type there. And I didn't realize that the feeling was "unfulfilled" till it just popped into my subconscious. I wonder if this is why I'm obsessing over what's going on at the lab and when I can get back. I need control. Did I feel like this about my work before the lab shut down? Hmmm.

So what matters to me? Maybe that's more the direction I should go. Maybe that will inform my search for new places to pitch the work.

Again, I type. "Who do I want to share it with?" New line. "People who care about the environment. People who want to understand what scientists do and why it's important." Ohhhhh. That's not journals or conferences, is it? Or is it?

What else matters? To me?

When I don't come up with anything else, I decide to clean again. I do the tub and both toilets. I dust the living room. As I'm moving the books in Saoirse's bookcase—because no one is more thorough in their cleaning than someone avoiding something—I see that one has been pushed back and lost behind the others. I pull it out and note that it's *To Those Who Wait*, a novel by author Tallulah Carney, who wrote in the early nineteenth century.

It's been a long time since I read this one, probably ninth grade, but I still remember the story. A young woman is betrothed to a baron who then dies of "consumption," what we call "tuberculosis." Because it's only a week before their wedding, she is then sent off to live with an aunt in the country till her father can figure out what to do with her. While there, of course, she falls in love with another nobleman who conveniently lives down the road. There's a lot of awkward old-timey courting, "turns about the room" and other such things. He has to go away for some reason I can't remember, but then when her father has finally found a "suitable" marriage agreement for her with an icky old man, the other nobleman arrives and declares to her father that he loves the woman, saving her from the arranged marriage.

Of course, they live happily ever after in his giant mansion full of servants where she writes poetry and plays the pianoforte while popping out numerous male heirs.

But something I loved about Carney's work was that the women had real opinions and desire for the direction their lives took, despite being trapped in a world where they had no control.

I put the book aside on the dining room table, intending to reread it after I finish *The Memory of Cotton,* when I notice a paper stuck between the pages. I open the book and see a junk mail postcard, but the page that it's marking has nothing but a quote on it with beautiful framing around the edges.

Even when the odds are against us, we must still pursue what's in our hearts and sets our souls on fire.

Ohhhhhhhhh. I feel like I was meant to find that.

Who says procrastinating isn't an effective way of getting your work done?

What actually lights me up? I pause in my cleaning with the hope that this is what will get me going on more places to pitch our work. Maybe I should start with everything that's brought me joy over the past few days.

I begin typing. "I love seeing pretty houses and beautiful decorations in other people's homes, like Libby's. I love meeting new people and seeing what brings them joy. I love seeing the world through their eyes. I love listening to live music. I am overjoyed that I got to reconnect with my cousin and finally resolve the mystery surrounding her disappearance all those years ago. I love being around my lab mates. I love the work that we do because I get lost in the puzzle solving."

That last one ... that still rings true. Okay, so I'm not looking at an overhaul, just a little change in direction or an addition. Maybe *this and.*

My mind floats back to right after lunch when I was able to sign for that little girl. American Sign Language isn't something a lot of people know, but I know that it makes a difference to those who need it. My mom always appreciated when someone knew a few signs anytime we were out with her. Of course, my sisters and I could always help with communication, but it was easier when we ran into people who already knew it. Now that I think about it, the lady who owned the store where my mom got the plum jam could sign ...

Maybe I love bridging the gap. Helping those who want to connect with something. What if ...

I google "deaf scientists organizations" and land on a winner. The Association of Deaf and Hard of Hearing Scientists has a yearly symposium in the fall, and they are looking for submissions for speakers and breakout sessions. *And what else* ... I dig around some more and find that they have a magazine. There is also a group that works with high school- and college-age budding scientists who have hearing loss.

I think I've stumbled onto something that actually excites me.

I add all three options to my list (the former blank document) and begin researching other places to reach scientists with disabilities or students with disabilities who are interested in science. There are actually a lot of options. Jackpot! I add these groups and publications to my list too. Now we're getting somewhere.

Because I actually have a special connection to the deaf community and the skills to be able to sign while I'm presenting, I pitch that one first. I start with the conference talk and young scientists group, then the publication, since that isn't something you would need those skills for. It does say that if you are chosen as a speaker, you will also be published in their magazine, but I want to cover all my bases.

I need to call Dad and let him know so he can tell Mom! It's been a few days since we've talked anyway. I pull out my phone and am about to tap his name when another call comes through. It's a number I don't recognize, so I almost send it to voicemail, but I figure I'll just check, in case it's legit.

It could be important.

Chapter Twenty-Three

"Dr. Sturm, this is Kendra Glass from NLBS."

My stomach drops as I think about all the reasons she could be calling. Did I do something?

She continues. "I need a copy of the report on gut bacteria in *Oncorhynchus nerka* forwarded to me. The one you plan to send to the Ichthyology Association of America should be fine."

"A copy of the report?" This seems strange since we don't open our findings up completely to anyone, even within the lab. "You have the summary, correct? That's what we're presenting as our official statements on the work until it's published in a journal."

"The media needs to know about it, and they reached out to me since I'm the press contact for the lab. Nothing has been published yet, so there was no other way for them to access it."

"Why do they need to access the report?"

Kendra sighs like I'm a moron. "It has to do with the leak. They wanted to present something to the public that shows the lab isn't a danger to the area. The news stations are getting a lot of calls from concerned citizens."

I almost scoff aloud at this. It's ridiculous that people would worry about us.

"They think the lab is poisoning the water supply," she says. "The reporter I'm working with agrees that information about the work at the lab will be good press at this point."

I'm getting a funny feeling in my stomach about this. *I don't think I should give her the information.* "What did Dan say?"

"I couldn't get ahold of Dan today, and Twyla's cell has been going straight to voicemail. You know how she is with technology." Kendra sounds dismissive, but there is an edge to her voice that I don't like.

"What about Luke or Violet? They've both been at the lab longer than me, so they're higher rank."

"The list I have is alphabetized, and you happened to be next. Can you send me the paper? Please." The please was a little forceful. I still don't like this.

"That's weird. I would think 'Sturm' would fall after *Davis* and *Rodriguez*." I'm not trying to be a smartass, but seriously? This just sounds so strange to me.

"It was by first name." Her voice sounds strained. "Dr. Sturm, could you please forward the paper to my email address? I don't want to report you to Dr. Burgess for being disagreeable. I have a job to do, and you're holding me up."

I'm taken aback by her brusqueness, but I still feel like this is wrong. What are my options?

I could fake being sick, but then I should have reported a sick day to Dan. I could tell her I'm not near my computer, but since I'm supposed to be working, I could get in trouble for that. I could say I'm having a late lunch … a quick glance at the clock tells me it's too close to dinner time to pull that off. Mercury retrograde? Freak power outage? What about the internet being down?

"I'm sorry about that. I was just curious." I'm stalling, but it can't go on forever. "The internet has been down here for the past couple hours. Could I try to send it to you later, whenever it comes back on?"

"You're joking. The internet is down?" Kendra sounds angry now. After a brief silence, she finally says, "Get it to me as soon as it comes back on. We've wasted enough time on this. The lab looks bad, and I need to fix that." Then she hangs up.

My stomach twists, and I flop down onto the couch. What was that all about? Why would she call *me* about the results? She just called Dan recently about them and got shut down. Did she think I would cave? What's going on? Kendra knows that we don't release anything till we've been published. I know Dan just told her the same thing recently.

Things are getting super weird.

Obviously, I immediately call Dan. I need to see what he says about this.

He answers his phone with his standard, cheery, "Yellow."

"Hey, it's Lacey. I just got a really strange phone call, and I wanted to talk to you about it." I brief him on what Kendra said.

"Hmm." Dan is always super steady, so I'm not surprised that he's taking his time responding to this. He always weighs his words. "I don't have any calls from Kendra. And my phone has been on all day. You told her your internet is down?"

"Yeah. I hated lying, but giving her the paper felt wrong." Then I have a weird thought. "Why does she keep asking us instead of just turning on the computer in the lab and getting it herself?" She would have passcodes to all the lab's private portals. It would be easy for her to do.

"The electricity is off at the lab because of the leak and the water issue," Dan says. "Won't be back on till they're almost ready to welcome everyone back. She can't access it at home because she's not able to log on to our portal through her personal laptop. She would only have access through her work computer with the master code. As long as we aren't in the lab, she can't get to anything except her own files."

"Oh." Now I get it. Well, part of it. "What do you think we should do?"

"I think it's time to report this. Once is a mistake, but she flat out lied to you about calling me. Something is up. I'm calling Cliff—" Cliff is the director, Dr. Burgess's first name. "—as soon as I get off the phone with you. If Kendra calls again, don't answer. I'm sure she will be getting a call from Cliff shortly."

When I hang up, I exhale and sink into the couch. At least I won't lose my job because I pissed Kendra off. Now I'm curious what Dr. Burgess will say to Kendra. And why would she want our paper?

Super weird.

I return to dusting the living room and put everything back on the shelves. Because I already accomplished what I wanted to with the research and submissions today, I decide to shut down the laptop and pull out my book to read for a while. Soon, my stomach is growling, though, so I take a break to make dinner: grilled chicken with red potatoes and a salad. When I'm done eating, I roam around the house for a bit, searching for something to do.

It's funny being alone when you're not accustomed to being alone. I used to fill my time easily with puzzles, TV, books, a couple hobbies I've attempted. I had a window container garden of spices for a few weeks: rosemary, basil, cilantro, oregano, and sage. Then we had a few hot days that coincided with me forgetting to water them ... and then I had dried herbs. Or dead herbs. Anyway, not a great hobby for someone who forgets to water things.

... TV it is!

Sometime around nine thirty p.m., the door opens, and Saoirse and Anthony literally float inside. Well, not *literally*, but you know. I'm reading on the couch again and look up to greet them.

"Lacey!" Saoirse exclaims.

She's all bubbly and weird. I don't know why she yelled my name when she came in.

"Yeah?" I say. She's grinning, and I get this feeling I actually *do* know before she says it.

She races to the couch and holds her hand up. "We're engaged!" She flutters her hands in excitement and then grabs me.

Of course, I wrap my arms around her and squeeze. When I let go, I grab her hand and do the girl thing. "Let me see!" Like that's the most important part. It's gorgeous though: a large tanzanite center stone with a row of diamonds flanking it, graduated from large to small around the band. It really is breathtaking. "Beautiful! I'm so happy for you."

Anthony is beaming in the entry, hands in his pockets, watching Saoirse as she's talking to me. I throw a *congratulations* his way and he nods. "Thank you."

"Do you mind if I stay at Anthony's tonight? Will that bother you? Would you be okay here?" Saoirse is still grinning like she just won the lottery—she kinda did—and I want to laugh. She just asked me like my opinion should matter.

"Go! Don't worry about me." As she heads down the hall to pack an overnight bag, I walk over to Anthony.

"I'm really happy for you guys." I give him a big hug too. He's family now, and I'm thrilled about that. He seems really good for Saoirse.

"Thanks," he says. He leans back against the wall. "I actually thought that last night was going to derail things. I've had this planned for weeks. But we had a long talk about her past, and I think it was the best thing for us. Then today, I said I was trying to make her feel better so she didn't suspect anything was up when I took her to a musical and a fancy restaurant."

"Good point." I guess it did work out. "How was *Rainy Day Fund*? And *how* did you get tickets? I thought they were sold out months ago." Rhiannon had begged me to sell my soul for tickets the next time she visited, and though I hunted for a place that would accept a soul, a kidney, or a ridiculous amount of cash, I couldn't make it happen.

"One of my college buddies is in the pit." Of course, orchestra connections. I nod. "The show was great. Good acting, loved the songs. They do a lot more tap dancing than I was expecting, but I know Saoirse enjoyed that. Overall, I'd recommend it."

Just then, Saoirse appears in the kitchen with her bag and a huge grin. "I'm ready."

There's something weighty in the way she says it—like she's ready for more than just the evening with Anthony, but *ready ready*. Like for the rest of her life.

I can't stop smiling. I'm really happy for them.

Chapter Twenty-Four

When they go, it's okay. Really. But again, I feel unexpectedly alone. I'm not used to it anymore, and it's strange. I return to the couch and read a few more pages, but nothing is sinking in. I can't explain what's going on in my heart, but it's part happiness that Saoirse has found *the one* and part feeling like I'm behind. Again. Like everyone else my age is moving forward and I'm still waiting at the starting line. I didn't need to beat *her per se*. I just … want to feel like I'm in the game. Like I have someone too.

Clearly, a night like this deserves cheesecake. I remember seeing some in the case at Sal's at lunch, so I check their hours on my phone and jump in the car. It's five minutes from idea to *table for one*, which is honestly one of the best things about living in the modern world. *Cheesecake? How about now?*

The turtle cheesecake looks divine, and I actually debate if I want to take a piece home with me. Because there's only one piece left. It's the last slice. Somehow that feels symbolic. What if it feels abandoned?

Clearly I'm losing it. Dreaming about strange men and empathizing with cheesecake. How's that for a dating profile?

The server brings me a water—to balance out the calories—and a slice of the turtle cheesecake, and I was right. It's divine. Hand-crafted by angels, probably. I bet the pope blessed it.

As I pop the second bite into my mouth, I have to wonder if it actually makes me feel better. Eh. Not sure whether that's the point though. I think I just needed an excuse for cheesecake.

As I take a third bite in slow motion, savoring the creamy, sweet tang of the caramel dripping onto the plate and the rich sugary smell, I glance up and do a double-take when I spot Colin strolling toward me, a novel tucked under his arm, following the hostess. When he catches my stare, he stops near my table and asks her to wait a moment.

"Hey, are you doing okay?" He glances from me to the cheesecake, and I realize he probably thinks Saoirse isn't talking to me yet because *I forgot to text him*. Of course.

I finally swallow and grimace at him. "Yeah. Good. Fine. I'm sorry I forgot to let you know how things went." He's still standing there, so I guess I should offer him a seat. "Are you here alone? Want to join me?"

He lets the hostess know the plan and slides into the booth across from me. "What happened with Saoirse? Is that homeless cheesecake?"

I have to laugh. "Not quite. We actually talked when I got back from my walk, and it was nice. She's good. We're good. She apologized. I did too. I caught her at a bad time with my," I wave my hands in the air like I'm swatting gnats, "avalanche of questions."

"I guess that can be overwhelming," Colin agrees.

"Oh, and they got engaged this evening." I smile at the memory of her face when she walked in and told me.

"Yeah, Anthony told us the plan. Show, dinner, proposal. I'm really happy for them." He gives a satisfied smile, picks up the menu, and says, "Ah, I should pick something," at the same time that I say, "I recommend the turtle cheesecake." We both laugh.

"Turtle cheesecake it is then." He exaggerates looking around to make sure no one is watching and then whispers across the table, "I was actually going to get cheese fries, but since you twisted my arm, I shall succumb to your wicked ways."

Be still my heart.

"You could do both, but that's a lot of dairy." Grownups say the dumbest things. I'm grownups.

Colin raises his eyebrows at me. "I bet you also have a favorite burner on the stove, don't you?" He chuckles.

I sip my water, smirking. When the waitress arrives, she nods at Colin's order and makes a beeline for the desert case up front.

"How was the rest of your afternoon?" I feel like it would be rude to keep eating my cheesecake till Colin's arrives, but our server better be quick.

"Not bad. I was thinking about Cedarbrook a bit, since you brought it up the other day. Then I noticed that Chuck Vernon posted about it on MyCircle today. I still have him on there from when we worked together. He said that his daughter was moving into the house, and it was bringing back old memories."

"That's really nice." I play with my straw a bit, creating a vacuum with my finger on the top, pulling the straw out of the water a little, and then letting go so the water dribbles back into the glass. "The river by Cedarbrook would be a great spot to fish. It must be nice living there. Just going down to the water and sitting for hours whenever you like."

Colin nods in approval. "You're right on that count. I wonder if Chuck or his daughter like to fish. He's never talked about it." I hum in response.

When the server sets Colin's cheesecake in front of him, I grab my fork.

"Cheers," he says, lifting his own fork in the air in a salute. I salute with mine too, and we both dig in.

After a moment, Colin looks like his mind is far away, and I initially assume he's in la la cheesecake land. Then he says, "Chuck's post said that when he was little, it was really hard after his dad passed, so they got a dog. Then they got a cat. And another dog. He brought home an injured bunny. Then they had a bunch of painted lady cocoons that didn't hatch before the school year ended, so he brought them home."

"I'm sure it was hard after they lost his father. Maybe caring for all those animals helped some."

"Yeah, he said his mom was fine with all the animals, even the lizard he got as a teen, but she absolutely didn't want fish. Couldn't stand the idea of having an aquarium in the house. She was certain that it would crack and get water everywhere."

"Huh, I can see that being a fear." Unease at the thought coils inside of me.

"He said that every time he would walk in with *that look*, like he found another rescue, she would pretend to get angry and say, "Fine, just no fish inside the house.""

I freeze. *Isn't that what she said in my dream?*

"Something wrong with the cheesecake?" Colin looks concerned.

"Noooo. Nothing wrong with this cheesecake." I swallow again and sip my water, unsure how to answer. "It's just ... that sounds like something she would say."

"Gloria Brennan?"

"Yeah."

"Do you watch a lot of her movies?" Colin takes another bite.

I frown. Now I have to explain. Why did I say that? "It was a weird dream I had the other night. I swear I was at Cedarbrook talking to Gloria Brennan, and she was telling me that she didn't want any fish in the house."

"Ah," he nods. "Makes perfect sense." A smile plays about his lips. We continue in silence for a couple minutes before he gives me look I can't quite read. "Do you always remember your dreams?"

A wave of panic hits—the kind that makes me over-share—and I sip my water to stall. It's a shame that I can't claim that the internet is down again and not respond to his question. "Some of them." My voice sounds oddly high ... "That one was really bizarre, very vivid. I think that's why I remember it." I set my glass down and gaze off for a moment, remembering the bold colors, the loud music, the pineapple upside down cake that I ate like a Neanderthal ... I give him the short version. "It was such a strange dream. Probably brought on by my fight with Saoirse."

Colin is oddly quiet, and his face is completely expressionless. But I don't think I said anything creepy or weird.

"What's up?" I finally ask.

He shakes his head like he was deep in thought and needs to dust off the cobwebs. "Ah, just, sounds ... kinda like the dream I had last night. Gloria Brennan was at her house, and there was a party. She seemed upset at one point." He brushes the remnants of the dream away. "I imagine she's on everyone's mind now, especially after Libby was talking about her house the other day."

A small thread of doubt pulls tight in my stomach, but I choose not to say anything. "Huh. Weird."

When our server drops off our checks, Colin swipes them both up and grins. "My treat."

I smile back. "Thanks."

We walk back to our cars, the only ones left in the lot aside from the staffs'. Colin chuckles. "I was just thinking about how Chuck met his wife."

"And how is that?"

"It's a cute story. He was telling us about it once at work." When we stop by my little blue Lizzie, Colin brushes a stray hair from my cheek with his knuckle, leaving a trail of warmth on my face. "He played guitar in a band in high school." He barely gets the sentence out before he laughs.

I blink a couple times, trying to decide if he's kidding. Then I laugh too. "You almost got me there, but I *know* that's not how one gets girls."

He raises his eyebrows and nods. "Actually, he met her at a bookstore. He was having coffee and reading a book at one of the chess tables. He put a little sign on the table that said, 'Chess anyone?' She actually stopped by and played. Kicked his ass, from what Chuck said."

"*That* is adorable!" I can't help but flash a big, cheesy grin. "And now the house he grew up in is being passed to his daughter, all because of a game of chess."

"It's funny how things work out, right?"

"Yeah." I skip over a joke about her having "all the right moves" as my brain flashes to my life a couple weeks ago and how one little thing rippled into so many things happening at once. The weird path I traveled to get here, in the parking lot of a diner, in the evening, with the man with the amber and azure eyes. Definitely funny. Now.

In the sodium lighting of the parking lot, the rings of fire in Colin's eyes blaze, and I'm snared again, staring into their depths. Wondering about the fact that we both just dreamed about Gloria Brennan. Wondering what other dreams we shared. And what dreams we might. And how people find each other if they are ... what Saoirse thinks we are.

My gaze falls to his lips and flickers back to his eyes. I debate about hugging him and gingerly lay my hand on his arm. And then his hands are on my face, and my arms are around his neck, and he touches his lips to mine so gently that it starts like a breeze ... and hits like a hurricane.

Chapter Twenty-Five

S aturday morning, I'm sitting in the living room, half reading a book and half patting myself on the back again for suggesting that Colin order that turtle cheesecake. Saoirse interrupts my fantasy, though, approaching me at eight a.m. with a pair of scissors, a trash bag, and a conspiratorial grin. "It is time."

I cringe and follow her onto her back porch. It's such a pretty place for ... whatever is about to happen here. Agatha Christie would approve. Saoirse's patio has a charming, peaked roof with natural timber supports shading it from the sun. A border of golden catalpa, beautiful pink dianthus, and some other flowers just opening their blooms encircles the concrete slab we're standing on, surrounded by a broad grassed-in lawn. And we are about to do a task that was definitely not on my bingo card for this year: removing her dreadlocks.

I should not be trusted with scissors, especially near someone's hair. Anyone who's seen my Barbie's accidental Mohawk when I was five agrees. Yet, here we are.

She talked me into it. Over three days. She assured me that I couldn't screw it up and that she was ready to move on to a new chapter of her life and that included her natural hair in all its glory.

Did I mention that her natural hair is baby fine and poker straight? If the cut is crooked, she can always wear a hat. Or two.

Let's not talk about the time we gave each other bangs ...

So we're outside, I have scissors, and Saoirse is sitting on a dining room chair with a plastic painter's drop cloth on the concrete slab. She's wearing a garbage bag over her clothes with a hole cut in it for her head. I'm stifling my giggles.

I feel like I'm trying to saw through rope as I gradually inch along the dreadlocks with my scissors. My hand is going to mutiny if I keep sawing like this. Finally, there is a neat pile of little snakes on the ground and a lot less hair on her head.

"How does it look?" she asks. I pause, probably too long. "How short is it?" she squeaks. At least her arms are pinned down by the garbage bag, so she can't swat me ... or touch her hair.

I'm assessing, but honestly, I don't think I did too badly. "It's a little past your shoulders, and it's a pretty straight cut." Actually, some of the dreadlocks are starting to unwind, so I'm hoping the combing process won't be too bad. That's why she's covered in plastic. I'm about to unleash a ridiculous amount of conditioner on her hair and start picking out the tangles.

Her shoulders relax under the trash bag, and she exhales a long breath. "Okay, good. I don't think the combing part will be that bad because they did interlocking on my hair."

"Yeah, it's already unraveling a bit. Almost like a braid." I massage the bottom of one of the dreadlocks with my thumb and forefinger, and it opens up. "We will see how it goes."

I squirt conditioner into my palm, and a bit splashes up my arm and on the trash bag cape. "I should have brought my lab goggles." We both giggle.

"You don't wear those in the shower? And to bed? I would think you'd have an extra pair in your suitcase whenever you travel."

"I usually sing them a lullaby before I leave the lab so they can sleep until I return and sing them the 'I'm back' song." I massage the conditioner into some of the dreadlocks at the bottom. The heavy smell of lavender permeates the air as I start combing. I'm relieved that the hair I'm tackling loosens easily.

"That got weirder than I was expecting." Saoirse crosses her legs in the opposite direction. "Did you let Colin know that you'll be out of commission all morning? I wouldn't want him to think that you're ignoring him."

A smile spreads across my face before I can stop it. "Yeah. I did. He said he'll call me later." And my tummy does a little dance in anticipation, which is totally corny, but I'm here for it. We've been texting a lot the last couple days since our cheesecake experience, and I'm smiling just thinking about it.

"It seems like you've been staring at your phone all week. It's pretty cute." I can hear the smile in her voice.

"Thanks. I'm happy. We will see how things go." Hopefully this guy isn't a secret spy like the last one. "I'm not sure I should be picking guys for myself after Derek, so I'm glad you and Anthony had already signed off on him before we met."

"And Colin will be thrilled that the bar is so low that all you really hope is that he's not a felon."

I cough out a laugh. "Secret spy."

"Oh, so not a mafia hitman?" Saoirse chuckles.

"I think the jury is still out."

"Have you heard from Derek lately?" she asks. "Not that you want to. I was just curious if he's still bothering you."

"Nothing since that weird video of the patio behind the fish lab that he's working on."

"I never did get to see that. Can I watch while you're working on me?"

"Sure." I wipe a hand on a towel and pop the video up on my phone. She sticks a hand out from under the trash bag and then watches the video, frowning. "Oops." I see her scramble to catch the phone as it slips from her hand, and she manages to get a hold, accidentally cranking the volume up all the way.

"Nice catch." I slide the comb through the bottom portion of the next dreadlock, untangling it without too much trouble.

"Do you hear that?" She tips the phone toward me, and I wipe my hand and take it back. After a moment, I shake my head, confused. "It sounds like there's a water feature. Maybe a fountain or a waterfall nearby. I wonder how fancy the facility is."

Huh, weird. "Well, it doesn't matter," I say, "because I'm not even going to respond to the text, let alone think about working there."

"That's the spirit! You know the lab will open again soon. As long as they aren't talking about closing or stopping your salary, I wouldn't worry about it."

"Dan actually told us at our Thursday meeting," I begin, "that they expect the cleanup and investigation to take one more week, so it looks like a few more days of unplanned vacation."

With the new places to pitch, though, I've been on a roll. I managed to hit a lot of organizations that want to connect high school and college kids with scientists, as well as some groups that help those with disabilities who want to go into the sciences. A couple have already emailed me back with interest.

I'm excited, and it's added a little layer of something interesting to work now. I know this is something I'm passionate about. I hope to keep this going once we're back onsite, maybe even get my lab mates interested. At least a couple would probably like to do more philanthropic work.

I find myself smiling again. "But you're right. And I'm not as worried now."

"Did you ever hear back about Kendra?"

This is the strange part. Dan had said on Tuesday evening that he would speak to Dr. Burgess about Kendra's odd requests, but I haven't heard back from him about it. "I don't know anything new. I haven't heard from Kendra either, though, so that's good."

"Right. As long as she hasn't said anything, you're good. I think Dan has your back on this."

"I do too." I step back to survey my work and am pleased. Her hair from the ears up is twisted on top of her head in a claw, and the rest is hanging almost completely tangle free. It looks like she just crawled out of the woods, but that's nothing that a good wash and an oil treatment ... or maybe five ... can't fix. She's scheduled for that oil treatment and a cut tomorrow to see how damaged it is, so she should be in good shape by the end of the weekend.

"Do you miss your apartment?" she asks.

I pause for a moment, and the question hangs heavily in the air. Honestly, I don't know. "Sometimes I miss having my space and my things, but I'm really enjoying being here. I love being back with my partner in crime." I give her plastic-clad shoulders a squeeze. "We're looking good back here, by the way." I open the claw and pull down the next layer of dreadlocks to work on.

"Nice. Thanks. I'm glad you're here too. And not just because you're doing my hair." We both laugh. "Let's make it a habit to hang out now. I promise I won't ghost you again."

"You better not! I will be the worst maid of honor ever if you do!" She asked me on Wednesday, and of course, I said *yes*. They haven't picked a date, but they know they want it small, simple, local, and with their closest friends and family. It's weird and wonderful to count myself in that number again!

Around lunchtime, Saoirse's hair is completely detangled. It's fuzzy and uneven, but it's done. "You're not going to win a beauty pageant like this, but it's a start."

Saoirse runs her hand over her frizzy head and laughs. "Anthony is going to flip. He's never seen me like this."

"How long have you had dreadlocks?"

"About a year and a half. I had them done soon after I donated my kidney. I met Anthony a few weeks later when he talked his aunt into letting him thank me in person. I agreed to have lunch with him at Sprouts, and the rest is history."

Sprouts is a pretty earthy lunch spot that I'm not sure I would want to eat at. Everyone says it's good, but it's vegan and has a lot of weird stuff on the menu. "That's brave of him." I laugh.

"I figured I would have a good meal even if I didn't enjoy his company. As you can tell, it went pretty well." She stretches her arm out and pretends to admire her ring as the sunlight dances off of the tanzanite, flashing little purple stars across the ground. Okay, she probably *actually* admired the ring.

I swat at her. "Go shower. I'll make lunch, and then maybe we can go for a hike."

"That sounds good." Saoirse heads inside with the scissors and chair, while I follow with everything else. Mission accomplished, and somehow, a crime averted.

We make a Persian herb and chickpea stew and add grilled chicken because I think it would be great. It's an odd recipe, but Saoirse swears it's good. After a couple weeks eating her way, I'm cool with trying it. It definitely took some baby steps though.

She actually says she loves the addition of the chicken chunks. But food prep and cleanup from our late lunch take a lot longer than I thought. Plus, we decided to take some lazy time and play with Saoirse's new hair, which is so hard to get used to. The dreadlocks added a lot of volume that her natural hair just doesn't have. I end up drying her hair for her and curling it with a brush. Yeah, I know we're just going hiking, but we're not in a rush. I didn't do too badly with the cut, but it definitely needs cleaned up. And the oil treatment, of course, to smooth the frizzies.

Using a big round brush helps tame it a bit, but she still ends up with a ponytail and a baseball hat.

Around four p.m., we finally hop in her car and head toward Snoqualmie for our hike. It really has been a perfect day so far, where I haven't focused on any of the confusion on my life at all. It's so nice to be back with my favorite cousin.

I assume the hike will be just as peaceful, but I never could have predicted what would happen.

Chapter Twenty-Six

Even though the woods around the Snoqualmie River is the same place as it was a couple weeks ago, though maybe greener from the new growth this spring, I can't help but feel like it's not the same place I thought it was.

The beauty of nature surrounding us is marred by the memory of that podcast Libby was talking about. By the murder of Everett Vernon. Even though we know he wasn't actually murdered in the house—like the podcast said he was—it's still creepy here.

The memories of Everett and Gloria seem to be here with us in the chill April wood, making hushed sounds around every bend, like we're chasing their specters. The leaves whisper again, but today it sounds like something else entirely.

I still haven't told Saoirse about the dream I had, and this would be a horrible time to do it, so naturally, I bring it up. "I had a bizarre-o dream about Gloria Brennan earlier this week."

"Oh?"

I fill her in on the details, and she grins at me. "That's creepy. I love that Colin was there to lead you through the woods and help you at the party."

"How do you know *he* was leading me through the woods? And can you stop cooing when you say his name? I'm not twelve."

"It's just so cute though!" She skips a couple steps, and her new ponytail bobs with the movement. "It's a cool dream regardless of who was guiding you through the woods."

I realize we're heading down the hill toward the bend where Cedarbrook will come into sight, and Saoirse must too. She slows her steps and looks around her like she's hunting for something, just as I'm slowing down with apprehension.

"Where were you in the dream?" she asks.

I look around for landmarks, but that part of the dream is a little hazy: more *generic-forest* than *this-spot-right-here*. "Not so much on the path. Just tromping through the woods. And we came up right in front of the house." I shield my eyes as I walk through an area where the sun peeks through the branches. "Like down there, closer to the river." I point toward where the river is rushing through the valley. We can just see glimpses of it between the trees. "Then we walked around the side of the house to get to the back patio."

Nerves start tickling my stomach as I recall the feel of the dream and how real it was. The food, the lights, the NPCs. Colin's hand in mine. At least there was something comforting about that.

We come around the bend and see the imposing brownstone. It seems to be lurking rather than standing stately and proper like the last time we saw it. Again, everything has changed. And nothing.

I stop in the middle of the path and stare at the house, trying to keep my gaze from drifting to that top right window. Or was it the left? The one where Everett was in the story that his granddaughter told to keep people away. I shiver and keep going.

"Creepy, right?" Saoirse says.

"Yeah. There's just something fragile and off about it now. Like the house has been tainted for me. When we were little, it was fun to believe that it was haunted. Now, between the lie about it being haunted and the fact that we know how Everett's life ended ... plus what Colin said about Chuck's life afterward. It's just all too strange."

"Maybe we shouldn't have come this way."

"I was thinking the same thing." I stop again, but this time, it's because I see that black sedan parked behind the house again, beside a tanker truck. "That's strange." I squint and peer through the trees. "I think that's Derek's car."

Saoirse stops to look, even though she wouldn't have known his car from anyone else's. She gently touches my arm. "Hey, I don't think this is healthy. It really could be anyone's car. Don't automatically assume it's his." She shrugs.

"I'm not fixating on him or anything. It's really his car."

"There are tons of black sedans around."

"But this one has the muddy boot print sticker in the back window and the license plate that supports an organization. I can't see which one, but his plate is for Mt. Rainier National Park. I doubt there are many black sedans with support license plates and a boot print sticker."

Saoirse frowns. "That's true. Maybe he has a reason to be here." She looks back at the path ahead of us. "Let's just go before he comes out and bothers you."

"Good point."

As we turn back to the path, Saoirse catches her shoe on a root and stumbles. She throws her arms out and smashes into the ground with a loud "Ugh!"

I squat beside her and help her sit up. "You okay?"

She flexes her hands and stretches her legs. "My knees and arms hurt a little, but I think I'm good. Just a little muddy." Both her hands and her knees are dirty from the moist path.

"Let's stop in the restroom and clean up."

A few minutes down the path is a picnic pavilion with a restroom, so we go inside to wipe Saoirse off. Luckily, this is one with paper towels instead of hand driers, so we use them to scrub some of the mud from her fuchsia leggings. The white sweatshirt is a lost cause, but it's not as dirty. Or as wet.

Soon, we head back to the trail to the parking lot. When we get to the car a short time later, I realize I'm starving.

"There is a great gyro place nearby. Clean ingredients. Locally sourced. You'll love it."

"I'm sure I will," I say with absolutely zero snark.

Five minutes down the road, we enter Little Athens, where other hikers and campers are enjoying an evening meal. Even with Saoirse being muddy, we don't stand out too much with this crowd.

It's a cute little place, decorated all Greek and kitschy. The gyros are delicious, and we split a huge Greek salad, too. Definitely a great end to a great day.

"Here's to new beginnings," I say. I raise my Styrofoam cup of water to clank against Saoirse's when her face goes pale. "What's up?"

"Oh my God, I think I left my ring in the restroom at the park."

I look at her hand like it might actually be there, and she can't see it. Nope. No ring. "Shoot." Panic zings through my gut. I wish I could fix this for her.

"I'm sorry, but we need to get back there now." She starts packing up the remainder of her salad. I jam the last bite of my gyro in my mouth and close my salad box too.

"Let's go."

We're both pretty quiet in the car. I know there's nothing I can say to ease her worry or make her feel less stupid. She's only had the ring a couple days. She's not used to it, so I'm not surprised she forgot it. But it's still an engagement ring, and I'm sure she feels totally irresponsible having left it in the bathroom.

We park in the dimly lit lot and jog to the pavilion with the restroom. Saoirse beelines to the sink where we washed up, but it's not on the soap holder where she put it.

"Maybe it fell off?" I suggest.

She bends down and shines her phone light on the grimy ground. After a few tense seconds, she announces, "Found it!"

We both laugh with relief as we leave the building. "Glad that's over."

"No kidding. I was completely freaked out. I've never lost something so expensive before." She leans against a tree and shakes her head, staring at her hand like the sheer will of her eye power will keep the ring on her hand.

"At least you have it now. Let's head back to the house so you can change."

We've only taken a few steps down the path when I hear someone talking in the woods. Instinctively, I glance back in the direction of Cedarbrook House. The sun is setting, and I can see lights on inside, shining through the trees like beacons in the dark.

"Hang on. I just want to see ..." I walk back down the path till the house is in full view, and Saoirse follows. Soon, I spot people outside talking on the stone patio. I can barely hear their voices over the sound of the river flowing in the valley behind the house. The black car is still there, along with the tanker. Two men and a woman are having what appears to be a serious conversation, and I watch them for a moment.

"Ready to go?" Saoirse nudges. "It'll be dark out soon."

"I just need to ... I want to see ..." I start down through the woods, staying behind trees as I approach. Saoirse takes a few cautious steps to follow me and then pauses.

As I get closer, I can see the scene illuminated by the yard light. I was right. The car has plates that support Mt. Rainier National Park—definitely Derek's. Also, he's standing right there in the back yard, hands in his pockets, talking to the other two people.

In my brain, I'm making big black marks with a sharpie all over his face.

Then, the woman turns her head to cough, and I stagger back a step in shock. It's Kendra. From the lab. *What is she doing there?*

And why is Derek there with her?

Chapter Twenty-Seven

This keeps getting weirder. I turn and creep back to Saoirse.

"Well?" she asks.

"It's his car. And Kendra is there too."

"*Kendra*? From your lab? They know each other?"

I frown. They must be connected independently of me. I certainly don't hang out with her. "I guess." Taking long strides down the path, I head toward the car. "Let's get out of here."

Saoirse scurries to catch up to me, and we make it back to the parking lot as the sun is dipping low in the red-streaked sky. I see a ranger walking through the lot and wave pleasantly. He touches his hat and waves at us as we hop in Saoirse's car.

"Good thing we're leaving. He was probably about to close the gate."

Saoirse fires up the engine, and we bump down the gravel path toward the park exit. As we approach the main road, I glance back and see lights coming through the woods. "Look over there." I gesture toward a lane farther down the main road that I had never noticed before. "I wonder if that goes to Cedarbrook House." It's flanked by a huge stone entrance with lions on either side, so it's a solid guess.

"Huh." Saoirse suddenly kicks the car in reverse, backing up about thirty feet, and flicks the lights off. We're shrouded in darkness.

"What are you doing?" I whisper. For no reason. It's a rule that you whisper in the dark, right?

"I'm curious ..."

Soon, the tanker truck rumbles down the rest of that lane and onto the main road, passing us. It seems to be heading back toward town. Saoirse flicks on her lights and follows.

"Why would a tanker truck be at Cedarbrook?" Saoirse wonders aloud.

"That *is* weird. Maybe they deliver natural gas?"

"I think there would be a tank somewhere. I didn't see one."

"Orange juice?" I snort.

"Maybe the new owner is throwing an enormous housewarming party with mimosas."

"That sounds like fun to me. Unless Derek is there."

"Bummer about that, right?" Saoirse says. After a few minutes of tailing the tanker from a distance, she flips on her signal to follow it down another road.

"Where are we going?" I'm suddenly very leery of being out in the middle of nowhere at night.

"I want to see where this truck is going. And I haven't been out here before, so adventure."

"Lovely."

Soon, I realize that we aren't in the wilderness, *per se*, but rather in a small town outside of Seattle that I've never had a reason to visit. Luckily, it isn't a little hollow with a dead-end street and dilapidated housing because that's how horror movies start. We see a sign announcing that we have entered Emmeline, a cute town with a quaint main street and lots of homes nearby. We keep our distance, so it doesn't look like we're following the truck, but I'm still nervous.

"I just realized something." Saoirse slows at a stop sign. "That video Derek sent was shot behind Cedarbrook."

"Whaaaaat?"

"Watch it again."

I pull out my phone and open his texts. The video plays, and I note the surroundings. The patio stone is the same. "That makes sense now. The burbling we hear in the video is the river, not a fountain. I could hear it when I was watching Derek and Kendra talking."

"Heads up." The tanker has pulled over, so Saoirse drives past it and parks down the street away from the street lamps. "That building was Sacred Waters Sushi. I wonder what the tanker is doing there. The restaurant doesn't look like it's open."

A couple other restaurants nearby *are* open, along with a bar, a shake place, and a salon. We hop out of the car and walk slowly down the street like we're going to enter one of the restaurants. I pause by the menu board outside and pretend to glance at my phone. "The guy got out of the truck. He's going down the alley."

A black car drives down the road, and I avert my eyes. "Nooo." I whisper.

"Crap, I think that's Derek," Saoirse says. "Same sticker. He's pulling in behind the tanker.

I keep my head turned so Derek doesn't realize it's me, but he never met Saoirse, so she acts as our eyes. She pulls out her phone and texts Anthony while we're standing there, pointing at the screen as a gesture for me to read it.

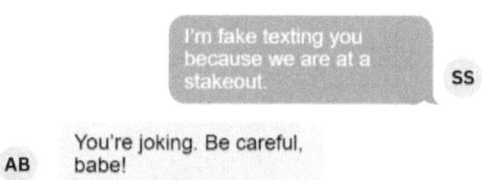

She looks at me and grins.

"If we're at a stakeout, shouldn't we be in the car or in the bushes or somewhere less conspicuous?" I ask, and she returns a smirk. I'm concerned that we can only look at a menu board so long before someone will think we're loitering. Is that an arrestable offense? Regardless, we don't need the cops here.

Or maybe we do?

"Should we call the cops?" I finally ask.

"About what?"

I shrug. "Good point. Let's just go get a shake or something." I cross the street and walk past the sushi place, casually glancing down the alley. The tanker is backing up toward a building at the back, but we pass so fast that I can't see anything else.

The shake place is surprisingly bougie, and the pricing reflects that. I order a Raspberry Chocolate Ganache that makes my wallet cry, while Saoirse gleefully orders a Vegan Madagascar Vanilla without even blinking. These are small shakes in the middle of nowhere. They're making a killing!

I head out to the porch to sit with Saoirse while we figure out the next step.

"So worth the investment." She slurps her shake.

"Shouldn't you be quiet at a stakeout?"

"Are there rules?" We both nervously laugh way too loud because we're just wired this way, and I again feel a surge of love for my long-lost cousin.

"Okay, rule one," I get serious, "we have to be quieter." I hear an engine roar down the block and glance in that direction. "See, we may not have heard that if we were being loud."

Saoirse rolls her eyes. "Okay, I just want to see what they are doing. If there is orange juice in that truck, I'm wildly curious about the reason."

"Good point." I stand and tip my head toward the alley a couple buildings down in the wrong direction. "Explore?"

"Sure. I have pepper spray." Saoirse shakes her keychain at me and winks, and we stroll around the building, still sipping our shakes.

The alley winds past a garage to connect with a residential street, but we duck behind a dumpster near the sushi place. Together, Saoirse and I squat and peer around the side, diesel fumes wafting our way.

I can barely see long concrete tubs positioned in a row up a slight hill. They look almost like railroad cars, but not as tall. Derek and the other man from Cedarbrook are engrossed in conversation, looking at a clipboard. The tanker is parked near the first concrete tub, and a long hose protrudes from the back, stretching across the grassy area and dunking into the tub. We can hear sloshing as something is being poured into the tub from the tanker.

"If that's orange juice, some frat house placed an enormous jungle juice order," Saoirse says.

"No kidding ..." The setup is so familiar, but I can't put my finger on why. Something from years ago, but it feels recent, like a memory someone brought up. Maybe a picture I saw? *What looks like this?*

"What do you think they're doing? For real."

"I'm clueless."

"Well, what do we know? The fish lab that Derek was trying to get you to work at is at Cedarbrook, and the tanker came from Cedarbrook. Maybe this is something they worked on at the lab?"

"What would they work on and then bring out in the middle of nowhere to dump in a concrete tub?"

"After they leave, maybe we can go over and look at it."

I scour the area with my gaze until I spot it. There's a camera on the back of the sushi place pointed straight at the concrete tubs. Figures. "That won't work." I point at the camera. "Plus, I don't want to try scaling that fence."

"Good point." Saoirse slouches to a seated position, leaning against the dumpster. She sips her shake again. "This is fantastic, by the way."

"We'll have to remember this for the next time we want to spend college tuition on a treat."

Saoirse snorts, and we immediately look at each other with bug eyes. She mouths "sorry."

I hear a clanking noise and turn back to the action in time to see Derek and the other man moving the hose to the next tub. "Do we want to sit here and wait on them?" Saoirse shakes her head. "Let's go back to the car."

We end up talking for a while in the car as we wait to see if Derek or the tanker leave. It's a good half hour, so our bougie shakes are gone, and we're starting to wilt. I'm about to suggest that we head out when I hear an engine roar. Soon, the tanker squeezes back down the alleyway and onto the main street.

I do a double-take as it pulls out because I have a clear view of the side of the truck for the first time this evening: Clemons's Liquid Transport.

Chapter Twenty-Eight

I'm pretty sure those are the same tankers that deliver frack water to the ridge for Parsons & Brewster Geological to examine. *Are they delivering frack water to the sushi place?* That doesn't make any sense.

I notice a sticker—actually a huge honkin' sticker that you can't miss—that says "Biological Safe" on the side of the truck, so it's not frack water. But what are they carrying that would need to be safe for the environment?

Saoirse interrupts my thoughts. "Do you want to follow the truck again?"

I frown. We're already in an area we don't know well, and it's dark out. Probably not the best time to be those *meddling kids* from *Scooby Doo*. What we already did was risky enough. "No, I think this is enough." I honestly don't know what to do next because we have a bunch of puzzle pieces that don't fit together, and I want to make them fit. I need to talk this out. "So, Kendra and Derek know each other. The lab that Derek is funding for the sushi place is at Cedarbrook, somehow. The same trucking company that brings frack water to the Plateau where my lab is also just brought some liquid to tanks behind the sushi place."

"We don't know what's in the tanks or how it all fits together," Saoirse adds.

"Right."

She chuckles softly. "Want to scale the fence and find out?" She does a silly dance that tells me she has a story. "One time when I was traveling with Parallax, we accidentally ended up on government property because we were all drunk after a show and scaled a fence, just assuming it was someone's yard, but it was like a Department of Energy lab or something."

"Oh my God, *what*?!"

"Those were the days ..." Saoirse laughs, and I give her a stern look. "I'm so kidding. I'd never go back to ... the partying. It really happened though. None of us got caught, thankfully."

I shake my head. "Okay, focus. I'm still deciding if we should call the cops. What next?"

"I think we need to get closer to those tanks without actually ... hey, wait a minute."

The streetlamp illuminates a figure emerging from the alley beside Sacred Waters Sushi. It's Derek. He's on his phone, and he's just standing there talking all normal like he's not doing anything wrong. *Maybe he's not doing anything wrong?* I feel like something is off though.

Saoirse puts a finger to her lip and lowers her window a few inches. We can hear him talking, but none of the words are clear. Our eyes meet as we both frown. Darnit!

"Scoot down in the seat. I have an idea." She grabs her empty shake cup and mine and then climbs out of the car. Next, she opens the back door and starts rummaging around. She gathers empty water bottles and some other debris from the floor.

"Oh," I whisper when I realize what's up. There is a trash can about fifteen feet from where Derek is standing, and it's the only one near our car. She can get closer without being too obvious.

My phone starts ringing, and the screen shows her name. I turn it on and give her a weird look, but she doesn't pay attention. Then realization dawns. Instinctively, I hit the record button on my phone and wait as she walks toward the can.

Soon, Derek's voice drifts through the speaker. "—are good. Swimming around like usual. This stuff better work." A pause. "Kendra got the remaining info while you were out of town. Just brought the computer home from work and—." His voice is muffled, and then I hear the sound of some trash being dropped into the can. "—turns out we didn't need Lacey after all. Kendra can take it back on Monday with no one being the wiser since she's one of the few allowed onsite."

I freeze. Didn't need me for what?

"Kendra seemed to know what she was doing. She said it's been awhile, but she knows her way around a lab." *What?! Kendra?!* "We got all the chemicals she needed, and she mixed it." Then a pause, muffled sounds. "Do you need help?"

I peek over the seat and see that Saoirse has dropped some of her trash on the ground, evidently to stay near Derek longer and hear the convo.

"I'm good. Thanks though!" I hear a little scuffle as she's gathering the trash and dumping it, but thankfully, Derek ignores her and returns to his call.

"—knows a guy who was willing to help for a little extra cash, and he works for Clemons's so he had access to the truck. A lot has happened since you left town." Pause. "Okay, later."

A moment after, Saoirse climbs into the car and starts it. "I think we heard some interesting stuff there."

"I can't believe we lucked into that." My head is still swimming with the fact that I was a piece of this plot at all. I'm actually not even sure now that Derek was dating me because he liked me or because he needed me to work in their lab. It sure felt real at the time, but ... I don't know what to make of all this! My throat is so tight I can barely speak. "It sounds like Kendra took one of the computers from our lab to get info that she then used for something in the lab at Cedarbrook."

"Yeah, it sounds like a bunch of shady stuff." Saoirse starts the car and turns onto the road back toward town. "And I'm glad you're not dating him anymore."

I'm frantically trying to cram puzzle pieces together now. How does this all fit together? Why did Kendra need that info for the fish lab? What's the connection with Derek funding Sacred Waters Sushi?

Ugh.

"Want music? Or are you thinking?"

"Thinking." What would that tanker have brought from the lab to the tubs behind the sushi place? And why are there tubs here? It might help if we were here in the daylight to actually see what it looks like.

"Do you think the tubs are for a raised garden or something?" I ask. "Maybe they're raising plants there?" I'm spitballing here, but maybe it will lead us somewhere.

"Plants for what?"

"Maybe it's just pretty? Or vegetables? Like they needed some sort of chemical mix to start the plants and then they add soil on top and ... do something special?" Probably not my best assembly of facts.

"Have you ever grown a plant in your life? That's not how it works."

"I killed a windowsill herb garden once."

"That tracks."

"Hey!"

Saoirse gives me the side-eye. "Just so you know, plants don't usually swim."

Dead silence fills the car and echoes in my head. The seatbelt pulls across my shoulder with as I suddenly sit up straighter. *Swim.* "Oh my god. They're raising fish."

"How do you 'raise fish'?"

"Like a fish farm." Suddenly, all that has happened the past few days floods back into my brain. The chemical leak closing the lab. Gloria Brennan yelling at me not to bring the fish inside Cedarbrook. Kendra begging us for the test results. Plus, a special memory tucked away from a college ichthyology class. "That's a fish farm behind the sushi place. They're raising salmon."

Saoirse throws one hand out like she doesn't get it, so I explain. "The row of troughs are on a slight incline so the water runs in at the top and exits near the bottom of the first trough, entering the second trough at the top, and so on down the hill. Fish farm."

Even in the darkness, I can see Saoirse's mental lightbulb turn on. "And salmon are used in sushi. It makes perfect sense." She nods.

I'm not sure what they needed our results for, since they were related to wild and not farm-raised salmon, but they must have used the information to make something in the lab at Cedarbrook that they needed for the fish farm.

I should have paid more attention to that part of the class, but of course, I never thought I would need information about a fish farm because I *didn't plan on farming fish*.

Irony.

Strange that I never suspected that I would date someone who was involved in a plot to control everyone's minds by making them eat sushi with microchips in it. Okay, maybe that's a stretch. But fish and microchips? Come on.

Or something like that.

Man, my life has taken a weird turn. We're quiet for a moment as we wind through the streets by her house.

"That's pretty wild," she finally says. "So what should we do?"

I ponder this as we pull in the driveway. "Actually, I want to talk to Dan and Dr. Burgess first. I think this is lab business before it's a legal matter. They'll have to move fast since Kendra is returning the computer on Monday."

"Sounds good to me. You call Dan. I'll go shower," Saoirse holds her muddy sleeves out, and I grimace, recalling that she's been in those crusty clothes for a while because of our "stakeout."

I can't believe the turn today took.

Chapter
Twenty-Nine

As soon as we're inside, I tap Dan's name on my phone and wait while it rings. For the first time since we started tailing that tanker, I realize that my heart is thudding away in my chest. Adrenaline is making me shaky, so I pace to help wear off the effects.

In four counts, hold four counts, out four counts, hold four counts ...

"Yellow."

I dump the entire story on my unsuspecting lab lead and am greeted with silence at the end of the tale. I bite my lip while I wait on his response.

"Lacey, please don't go back out there. I wish you had called the cops instead."

I let out a dry laugh. "And they would have done something if I told them I saw a tanker truck leave

Cedarbrook and park behind a sushi restaurant? It doesn't sound like anything they would look into."

"Good point." Dan sighs. "I'll call Cliff. Can you email me the recording?"

I tap on my screen. "Done."

"You know I don't like repeating myself," Dan begins, "but I'll say it again. Be careful. Don't go back out there. After I talk to Cliff, we will have a conversation with the police."

"Thanks, Dan." I breathe a sigh of relief and finally sink into the couch.

"I'll let the team know how things turn out. Stay safe."

When I get off the phone, I have this overwhelming guilt that I should text everyone and fill them in, but then they'll just be sitting around wondering what's up like I am.

Telling them that my ex was involved in the whole scheme will be fun. Bile tingles the bottom of my esophagus as I realize that I'm going to feel like a complete idiot for this.

How am I supposed to trust my instincts if they led me to date someone like Derek? And did he date me because I was involved with the lab? Did he like me at all? Because I liked him. I hoped things would work ... Ugh. Just ugh. Good thing I already hated him before I heard that phone call because now I'm boiling mad at the idea of being used.

Worse yet, will my coworkers think that I'm an idiot and not trust me with our work? Maybe they won't listen to me when I suggest something.

I really thought that I would gain confidence with the wrap up of our first big project, but this has been the exact opposite. I feel just as scared and naïve as I did when I was presenting my master's thesis. Like I was part of the big leagues but just barely. And undeserving.

This sucks.

Just then, my phone pings because an email has landed, and I tip it up to see if it's something from Dan, which I know would be really fast, but time has done all kinds of strange warpy things today, and I don't feel like anything is really real.

Alanna@prsymposium.com has emailed me. *Parasitic Research Symposium?*

My stomach drops. Now? On a Saturday night? Not judging, since I was just spying on my ex on a Saturday night, but this is a weird time to be emailing people professionally. Of course, I have to read it. I can't bear to wait till later to see if they rejected me. Or worse …

Dr. Sturm,

Your paper for the Parasitic Research Symposium has been accepted for a panel presentation on the effects of chemicals on fishes in saltwater habitats. Please submit your headshot and a two-hundred-word bio [...]

Wow, so let's go with "worse." I was accepted. How do I feel about this? I don't think I can even process it right now. The event is five months away. I have time to deal. I sink into the dining room chair and put my elbows on the table, head in my hands. My heart rate is coming down, but now, I feel worn out. It's all too much. A couple tears splatter onto the wooden table, leaving little puddles.

Saoirse steps into the kitchen just then, toweling her hair. "What did Dan say?"

I sniff, brief her, and then let her know about the email I just got.

"That's great news!" She grabs my shoulders and shakes me. "Why are you frowning?"

"Is it though?" I turn to face her. "After the whole stakeout with Derek thing, I just lost the last little bit of confidence I had."

Saoirse gives me a serious look. "Yeah, he's a real dirt-bag. I don't care how good you said he smells." She sits down at the table and grabs my hands. With a sigh, she continues. "You don't get it, do you? You are my absolutely brilliant cousin. You're a salmon scientist who just finished an incredibly cool project that you joined in the *middle* of the darn project. Like, walked in and said, 'I'll catch up. Don't worry about me,' and then kicked some ass."

I have to smile because she's trying to make me feel better, and honestly, it's working ... a bit.

"On top of that, you're basically a super spy because you walked out on what you thought was a great relationship when you thought the guy was doing something fishy." She points at me, and I point back because

I see what she did there. "*And*, you just solved a huge mystery, which has revealed nefarious behavior, thus protecting the lab, which I know you care about."

"I didn't figure it *all* out." Another realization pings me in the head. "Oh! That's probably what happened to the missing petri dishes though." *It wasn't my fault.* "Now that I think about it, maybe Kendra took them. I'm just not sure why she was after our information."

"It will all come out. You got the major part though."

"True."

"Your lab partners will be really proud of you. I'd be honored to work with someone who did what you did."

I'm not gonna cry again. Okay, I am because, damn, that was so touching. And to think that we ever thought *all those things* about each other. This is friendship right here. Saoirse really is my soul sister.

"I'm glad I have you, girl." I wrap my arms around her, and she squeezes me back hard.

"We need to chill now. Movie?"

"Movie." I take a quick shower while she picks, and I'm pleasantly surprised to come back to vegan hot chocolate ("I made it with coconut sugar!") and cozy blankets, along with a goofy Christmas rom-com called *You Sleigh Me*.

"Everything will work itself out. Let's just relax," Saoirse says. We stretch out on the couches and chill.

Chapter Thirty

T he next morning, Saoirse's stylist Amber has opened up a special spot for her so she can get a trim and oil treatment. Since she hasn't had her hair cut in a couple years, Saoirse sweetened the pot with an offer to make some updates to Amber's salon's website for free, and it was incentive enough for Amber to come in on a day off.

We enter a peaceful room painted white with gold and teal accents that makes me feel like I've stumbled upon an oasis. Calm yoga-type music drifts through the speakers, and Amber, a tiny, curvy woman with long purple hair and a hoop in her nose, escorts Saoirse to the wash station, chattering about how excited she is to get her hands on Saoirse's gorgeous hair again.

I relax into one of the firm velvety couches and just breathe for like five minutes. I feel pretty calm: it's hard not to in here. It's mostly because I've been pushing everything out of my brain with a *not my job, not in my control* plow. Colin was right. Focus on what you can. I need a lot of work on that, though.

Speaking of Colin ... a text lights up my phone ... fine, and my face.

> Good morning! I was thinking of you. I reached out to Chuck, and we're grabbing lunch today. It will be nice to catch up! I really missed our conversations, so I'm glad to reconnect.
> Thanks for reminding me of this. I appreciate it.

I can't help the smile spreading even wider across my face like cream cheese on a bagel. I text him back.

> Aw, that's great! I'm happy to hear that! Where are you guys going?

> Nowhere fancy, just Harvest Kitchen. It's his favorite. And they have awesome pancakes, so I really don't mind, lol!

> Yes! They have a cinnamon roll one in the fall that's amazing.

He responds with the drooling emoji and a lip-licking emoji, and I know that he gets me. I drool, too, when I see those pancakes. So good!

A couple minutes go by, and my phone buzzes again.

CH
> I was wondering what you're up to on Tuesday. I'd like to take you out for dinner.

I wrinkle my eyebrows. What's up with everything happening on Tuesday? Bummer!

> I would love that, but I'm helping my sister Fallon on Tuesday. I'm giving a presentation and then staying at her place for dinner. I won't be back till late.

Now I get to play the three dots game. Waiting, waiting, waiting … Pop! He's busy the rest of the week but asks about the weekend, and I quickly reply.

> I'm pretty open. What works for you?

CH
> Is Saturday good?

> That works!

CH
> I'll call you when I get back in town so we can finalize plans.

> Perfect! Looking forward to it! Enjoy your lunch!

CH
> Thanks! I'm sure I will.

He sends me a gif of Cookie Monster shoveling a plateful of cookies into his mouth, and I have to laugh.

Now I want Harvest Kitchen pancakes, but I can't suggest that Saoirse and I go there because that would be weird and stalker-y.

I chuckle and glance back at Saoirse for a moment. Amber is coating her hair with a mixture and working it through. I'm assuming it's the oil.

The memory of our talk the other night drifts through my head. I had admitted that I'm glad Saoirse and Anthony already vetted Colin, so I know he's okay for me to date. That's the weird thing about dating. There isn't a list of referrals, no five-star reviews. Just a gut feeling that this is okay.

And it's not always okay, right? Sometimes women get tricked into narcissistic relationships or whatever that was with Derek. What if he never really cared for me and was just using me because he thought I would help with his project? That really hurts.

Maybe I got out before I saw the really bad stuff, if there was more.

Derek never met my friends or family, so I don't even have a backup to say, "We never really liked him." No one to check in with about my gut feeling that I should leave. I had to just trust that. And that's really scary. I hate feeling like I'm an adult and paying my own taxes and stuff but then I also can't figure out if someone is going to be a creep when I meet them.

For all I know, Colin has something weird in his basement and is just really good at appearing normal.

I can trust Saoirse, though, right? She seems like she's got it all together now. Well, except for what she still needs to work out about Toby. But we all have some-thing that affects the way we view the world, and some of it will be there for us to crack our elbows on when we get too close to it and walk into it.

Our worldview is based on our experiences, so I for-give her for that blip, and I'm here to help her get through it one step at a time. But does she know Colin well enough to know what's sitting around ready to hit his funny bone? People keep stuff tucked away all the time.

I'm working myself into a frenzy again, and I'm sup-posed to be sitting here enjoying the Zen of this beauti-ful salon.

But the question remains: what skeletons are hidden in Colin's closet? Is he too perfect? He designs artificial hearts, is a talented musician, happens to be gorgeous, and is shockingly taller than me. I didn't know they made them like that.

I need to get out of my own head. Colin is great. I don't think I would have been dreaming about him half my life if this wasn't a good thing. Of course, there is that theory that people come into our lives for a reason, to teach us a lesson. I think there's something in a song from *Wicked* about that.

Geez, enough, Lacey!

I open my phone to distract myself and check my work email. *There's one from Dan.*

I swallow and mentally push my stomach down out of my throat because I'm completely freaked out about opening this. It came through about five minutes ago.

As my finger is hovering over the email to open it, a text from Dan comes through on Twyla's group chat.

> Check your email.

Yeesh. I tap the email and skim. Special meeting, Thursday at Monroasters, private room. "Don't respond to any emails or phone calls from Kendra. I'll explain on Thursday," I read aloud.

I wonder if anyone else got a phone call since I was supposedly third on her call list. Then my stomach drops. I hope Dan had let Violet and Luke know that they shouldn't send anything to Kendra if she asks, right after she called me the other day, when I got that funny feeling and called Dan. Eh. They would probably know not to and put her in her place without Dan saying anything.

Now I'm wondering if she called me *specifically* because she thought I would be easy to manipulate. My head whirls with this thought. *What do people really think of me?*

So much for getting out of my head.

Maybe social media is a safer option. Some cat videos sound calm and benign about now.

I reply to Dan so he knows I saw the email and open MyCircle to see what's up in other people's heads. Yeah, sounds totally safe and not like the dumpster fire with beer puke and a dead skunk that social media is known for.

I have all my sisters listed as favorites, so I get to see their stuff first. Safe. Home. Love. I scroll down farther and see a picture Saoirse posted of us hiking at Snoqualmie yesterday. We're at the overlook that we love, tree-covered hills in the background, the river far below. A beautiful clump of bleeding heart has been blooming there as far back as I can remember, and it blossomed early this year, as captured in the photo.

Both of us are radiantly happy. No makeup, messy hair and baseball hats, sweatshirts. She had captioned it, "Cousins and best friends." Pure bliss—we had no idea what we were about to do that evening. I sigh.

I click on the friend requests button and see that I have two. The first one is from an older man who is supposedly a divorced colonel in the United States Army. His profile picture shows him smiling smugly in his uniform with the U.S. flag in the background. I click on the page just for laughs. All his "friends" are women my age, roughly thirty of them, and his pictures are all of him "volunteering" for different causes or talking to important people while wearing his uniform. *Wait, how many arms does he have?* No doubt he wore out his AI app doing these. Block and delete.

The other request is from Libby. Aw, of course! She *is* friends with Saoirse, plus I enjoyed talking to her. Accept!

I scroll through her page and see lots of pics of her and Ray from their day out yesterday walking around at an outdoor market, having dinner, the biggest sugar cookie I've ever seen (like the size of her face), and finally them kissing. So cute.

I see pictures of her family, Ray's cat, several of her performing at Riff's ... and then I see that she shared the podcast about Cedarbrook.

The caption says, "This was a great podcast about a legendary local home that you can see from the trail in Snoqualmie, so you've probably walked right past it. Turns out the info isn't true about the murder, but it's still so good! I love creepy stories! Check it out!"

I notice that this episode of the Thirteen podcast is titled "Granddaughter of Actress Speaks about Grandfather's Murder and Legacy House in Seattle." Definitely a clickbait title, but it's not wrong. Just the info she gave in the podcast isn't right. I glance at the show image and do a double-take.

"That can't be ..." The picture shows a man with wild wavy hair and glasses along with a woman who looks distinctly familiar. A feeling of dread washes over me as I click the image. I'm taken to a page where the image appears much larger at the top and a button is available to start the podcast. Below the picture of the woman on the image, confirming my dismay, is her name, "Kendra Glass."

"Kendra is Gloria Brennan's granddaughter?" I actually whisper this aloud. "That's why she's hanging out at Cedarbrook. It's hers."

That makes me feel a little sick. My chest gets tight as I think about this.

Now I know why the lab is there. It's convenient for her to do whatever work she needs to do, *and* it's pretty secluded. I'll have to let Dan know that when he talks to Dr. Burgess, they should confirm that Kendra's address has changed to Cedarbrook. I wonder what they will find there. I'm kind of curious about the lab, but again, not curious enough to reach out to Derek again.

Also, I really hate him now. Not just the *mostly hate* that I had before. What an awful guy.

At the wash sink, Saoirse is laughing about something that Amber said and my heart squeezes a little, knowing that I love seeing her happy and that I almost missed this chance by stubbornly pushing away my dad's suggestion for years that we reconnect. *Almost missed being with my soul sister.*

Another thought pierces my heart, though, and it makes me want to turn off my phone and become a nun. This means that Kendra's dad is Chuck. He was an only child, so there's no other way that Kendra could be Gloria Brennan's granddaughter.

And this means that I am the direct reason why the granddaughter of someone who Colin respects so much is probably going to jail.

I'm so embarrassed by this that I can feel the heat in my face working its way down my neck to my spring sweater.

How can I go out with Colin knowing all of this? Will he be upset? We've just met, so his loyalty will obviously be with Chuck. Will Chuck be mad at me?

Nun is looking better and better by the minute. As long as they have a lab. I could be the next Gregor Mendel, except at a convent.

Should I tell Colin what I just figured out? The plastic seat squeaks as I shift uncomfortably, staring at my phone. I realize that I may not be able to have what I want, that maybe I should trust my gut one more time and back away, that maybe that feeling isn't my gut but my head, my flight or fight response. The pain as those little tendrils start to retract from my heart is too much right now. Should I just choose flight and avoid the pain of a conversation that could end badly?

Chapter Thirty-One

F allon is standing at the front of her eighth-grade history classroom, ready to announce me. "I'm really excited to introduce this special guest to you today."

Meanwhile, I'm looking across the cluster of a couple dozen desks and the range of facial expressions from excited to meh. The excited ones are up front, and I have to remember that these are the ones I'm here for. "This is my sister, Dr. Lacey Sturm, from the Northwestern Laboratory of Biological Sciences in Seattle."

I tell myself it can only get easier from here. "Hi, I'm happy to be here to talk about my career." That's fine. It's all going to be fine. "I'm a salmon scientist. I have the pleasure of studying gut bacteria in *Oncorhynchus nerka* or sockeye salmon. I brought a couple tools I use to examine specimens, and you guys can check them out once we finish talking. One is a microscope, which you've probably seen before. And the other is a petri dish with growth medium and bacteria from a salmon's gut in it."

When our lab shut down, the samples were moved to a secure refrigerator at another facility. We were lucky. Dan gave me several to bring to the school, all with various amounts of different gut bacteria, so the kids could see what they look like. I have them spread out on the table, plus some slides we prepped for the microscope.

"The growth medium acts sort of like the yolk in an egg. It has water, salts, a sugar like glucose, and some other things that help the bacteria grow and multiply. Then, we can study how they operate.

"Some of our testing, though, involves looking at live fish and seeing how they function with and without certain bacteria. This study has gone on for decades. So we've been able to note changes over time. That helps us see what bacteria are essential for certain processes *and* what bacteria are surviving the changes to our environment. Or which ones are not."

Some of them already have the glazed look, but some near the front look riveted. Yeah!

I hit all the bullet points of my career talk, covering some of the more interesting parts of my life as a scientist, avoiding talk about the lab being closed right now, and wrapping up with what I think are some interesting facts about different sorts of research careers available to them. "Questions?"

Hands go up all over the room, and Fallon steps close to me, likely in case I need help sorting through and getting to everyone. I point at a boy in the second row and nod.

"Do you like doing the research or writing up your papers more?"

Easy one. I respond, "I love the research part more, but I don't mind writing up the papers because I know that it helps other people learn from what I've been doing."

I take a couple more softball questions before a girl at the back of the room asks, "Do you ever feel guilty killing the fish?"

Maybe this isn't going to be so easy after all. I flash back to that dream where I stood over a fish on the lab table, holding a ketchup-bloody scalpel. "You know, that's a hard question. I don't think most scientists ever feel guilty, exactly, about the fish that we are examining because we aren't the ones killing them ourselves. We have someone who stocks the labs and brings us dead fish. It's rare that we actually work with a fish that's dead, too, since most of our study is on the bacteria. I think this is another instance where you have to think about why you're working with a dead animal and what the results are going to be."

She's frowning, and I can't tell if it's thoughtful or disapproving, so I continue. "Let me give you this example. If you have to kill a fish every once in a while to study it so you know what is happening internally, you might be gathering information that could save hundreds or even thousands of other animals. I know it's sad that the fish I might be examining had to die, but it would be even sadder if all those animals died because I didn't get to do a thorough experiment. Does that make sense?"

The girl nods and turns to whisper something to her friend. My heart sinks. You can't win them all. Only four more presentations to go.

At the end of the day, I join Fallon at her house, along with her husband and kids. As we prep dinner, I replay the day in my head. Definitely the hardest presentation I'll ever give—kids don't pull punches.

"You did well, you know?" Fallon is using a huge wooden spoon and fork to mix up a salad and dressing in a giant bowl.

"It actually wasn't as bad as I thought." I'm prepping garlic bread to toast in the oven, committing an *infamia* by sprinkling it gently with garlic powder. Shhh.

"Those kids are tough, and you handled every one of their questions. Maybe it will be good practice for what's to come."

"I'm sure it is." I actually don't feel as nervous about all the conferences I pitched now. Older kids who are serious about the sciences are bound to be curious and excited to be there, and the adults at the science conferences will be fine. They're just as nervous and excited as I'll be. I hope. "If get into the conferences I pitched and don't make a fool of myself in front of the kids, I'm good."

My phone buzzes, and I see that Colin has texted to see how the "sacrifice" went, as he put it. I flip the phone over, intending to get to it later. Guilt rises in my throat as I recall how happy he was after his lunch with Chuck. I can't tell him what I know. I just can't.

Fallon raises her eyebrows at me and then turns back to give the sauce another stir. "Huh."

"It's nothing."

"Okay."

I let a slow breath out through my nose.

She taps the spoon and sets it on the spoon rest. "It's strange to finally know the end of the Cedarbrook story after all these years."

I offer a wan smile. I know she's not thinking about the same part of the story that I am. "Yeah. It's sad Everett died the way he did, but I'm glad his wife didn't do it. That put a big damper on her legacy. I'm glad she's cleared."

"I can't imagine what she went through being accused. It's no wonder she and her son hid away in the woods."

Colin's story about the photograph and Gloria Brennan's sad smile haunts me as I slide the tray into the oven. "It's good she's cleared, but her legacy still feels a little dark." I fill her in, and she frowns.

"Oh, Lacey ... that's terrible." Setting plates on the table, Fallon is quiet for a moment. "Do you ever feel like places have memory?"

"It's not something I've thought about." I shrug.

"Remember when we used to talk about Cedarbrook, and I was obsessed with its history?" I hum in response, not willing to admit how much it scared me when she talked about Everett's death back then. She continues. "That's not the only piece of its history, a story that isn't true. There was love and laughter there. You told me about it yourself."

"Yeah, Colin said Chuck used to bring lost and lonely animals there to care for." I pause, thinking back to a strange vision that flickers across my memory. "I had a dream about a party there, and Gloria Brennan was talking to me. She was upset, even though everyone else seemed to be enjoying themselves. Except her. And I think she was trying to send me a message. But that's a different story." I brief her on the dream.

"I see." Fallon walks over to the living room where the boys are playing and Annabel, my niece, is reading a book for English class. "You guys wash up. Dad should be home in a minute." When she turns back to me, she's smiling. "Maybe the good memories there will outshine the bad ones. Whatever your ex and your boss were doing there is just a tiny blip on the timeline of that place Keep that in mind. In the grand scheme of things, I think that Cedarbrook will bounce back."

I glance at my phone and force myself to pick it up. When I open Colin's text, though, the certainty I felt a moment ago fizzles as guilt overtakes me again.

With a deep breath, I chicken out. I let him know that today went well and that I'll tell him about it when I see him. He wishes me a good night, and I wish him safe travels.

But the guilt pounding in my temples feels like it might crack my skull open if I don't get this out.

> Actually, do you have some time to talk later? Can I call you?

My breathing goes shallow as I bend to look into the oven so Fallon won't see me unraveling. My eyes burn from holding back tears. "One sec," I say, dashing down the hall to the guest room. *Breathe, Lacey. Breathe.* In four, hold four ... I open the phone again and type.

> I just wanted to tell you about something that I found out today. Please don't be mad at me. It's about Chuck Vernon's granddaughter. I just found out who she was, and I feel so horrible because I'm the one who reported what she was doing. It was so weird. She's my boss. And everything she did was all illegal, don't get me wrong. I just feel awful that I had anything to do with it. I know how much you respect Chuck, and I'm sorry.

I wait. I watch for the dots. Nothing. Oh God, he hates me. I've ruined his mentor's life, and now he hates me.

Chapter Thirty-Two

Our staff meeting on Thursday feels like a warped *déjà vu* as Dan asks me to repeat everything I told him on the phone Saturday night.

Violet stays quiet, Twyla keeps uttering a surprised "well I never," and Luke high-fives me for the stakeout. It feels like a hollow victory, though, with our boss likely going to jail—along with my ex—and the fact that we now have to go back to work under some weird circumstances. I imagine the entire staff of the Plateau will feel odd coming in for a while.

The nice part of the meeting is that we get to share the places that have accepted our research, and one of them is mine. "I'll be attending the Parasitic Research Symposium this fall to present on gut bacteria." This gets genuine joy from everyone in the room.

Twyla throws her arms around me. "I am so proud of you!"

When the celebration calms down, Dan clears his throat. "Lacey, I was approached by the Association of Deaf and Hard of Hearing Scientists, who said they loved your proposal. They were wondering about partnering with us in the future for a project."

I place a hand over my heart and stare at Dan in shock. They hadn't emailed me back, and it had only been a few days since I approached them. "I'm so happy to hear that." I explain my connection and why I reached out to them, and even Luke looks a little teary eyed.

Maybe I've got this after all.

As I walk back to Saoirse's, I pull out my phone, wishing I could text Colin about my little victory. Still nothing from him. It's been two days, and he hasn't even said that he doesn't want to talk. Just … nothing. So much for that.

***

On Friday, the Plateau is declared safe. That evening, everything feels somber as I drive the twenty minutes back to my apartment with Saoirse following in her car. I asked her to come so she can check out my place, hang out, and then head home later, but it already feels eerily lonely without her riding shotgun beside me.

I get stuck at a light and look around at the houses while I wait. It's the same little neighborhood full of adorable bungalows that we drove through on our way to Libby's apartment, when I met all of Anthony's friends. I spot the house I once imagined belonged to two people in love.

Just a short time ago, I had fantasized about hosting barbeques with Derek in his back yard, popping open a beer with some friends. Corn hole set up nearby. Someone's dog barking as he chases somebody's kids around. Me heading in to grab the ketchup, and Derek asking me if I would also grab the cake when I come back out. It's pineapple upside down cake, just like in that dream. Except it's the wrong house. It's not Cedarbrook or Derek's house ... where is my brain going with this.

And why am I thinking about that felon?! I shake my head to erase the image (like I'm an Etch-a-sketch or something) and gaze back at the house. My heart hums like a guitar being strummed as a new vision flickers across my imagination.

I see the house out my driver's side window. The sweet little front porch and homey shutters, all gray with white trim and exposed beams on the porch. My eye catches again on the bleeding hearts flanking the porch with their flourish of red blooms. I picture myself sitting on that swing while Colin—or someone like him—plays guitar on the stoop.

He sings a song I've never heard before about *being home in someone's arms as a storm whips around us, but he's finally found ... his dream girl.*

A car beeps, and I realize that my light is green. Oops.

As my daydream vanishes like smoke, I spot the for sale sign in the yard and sigh. I'm sure some happy couple will scoop it up and fill the house with love.

Continuing through the neighborhood, I glance at my phone to check the next turn and remember that I have yet to tell Colin about how giving that presentation at Fallon's school on Tuesday went. I guess he doesn't want to know anymore.

I had a couple calls with Dan and Dr. Burgess today. I had to confirm some of the details for them to press charges against Kendra and Derek. They're both in a world of trouble, by the way. I've been surprisingly popular this week with the work crowd thanks to my mad sleuthing skills.

Turning onto Exploration Drive and entering the Plateau, I have the weirdest feeling that I've been here before, but it's not really the same place. It's different from when you go on a vacation and come back. It's been too long. And something has shifted in the land or the buildings. Or me. The way I feel here is different. It's like I can feel the hurt—the betrayal—that the lab feels, from someone trusted to be there and do what they did. Nefarious activities always do that to a place. Or so I'm assuming.

It's like when we were in high school and some of Saoirse's friends broke into a student teacher's car and stole their collection of CDs. I felt like some of my innocence was taken that day because, before that, I didn't believe that people *I knew* would steal.

I know that's naïve, but it was like a piece of the little dream that we all have of living in a perfect snow globe shattered with that act. Like the glass around us was cracking, letting in reality. Forcing adulthood upon us. One by one, over the years, all the parts of the snow globe fell away, revealing the harsher world adults know. Where we are aware of hurts far beyond stealing something that can be replaced. Dreams and lives and hopes shattered with it. Betrayals and cheating and ... disease and death.

A large part of the globe fell away when I went through my treatments. And another when Rona wouldn't reply to my calls and emails.

What Kendra did chipped away another piece of the snow globe—proof that big crimes don't just happen far away. It's right here beside me, beside us all, with the people we know. And it's a strange kind of hurt when it's someone you know, even if you don't like them.

We finally park in the garage, and I meet Saoirse at her car, since she's in the visitor's section on the main floor. The garage has that same slightly damp concrete smell, the same flickering fluorescent light by the elevator on the ground floor. The same concrete planters flanking the walkway to the rest of the Plateau. And yet, it's different.

It feels ... no longer mine.

The realization makes my stomach sink.

I give Saoirse a weak smile, and she helps me take my meager luggage and a few bags of groceries we grabbed this afternoon into the elevator and to the fourth floor.

There's my door, 4L, with its cheerful spring wreath. A plastic song sparrow sits on a cluster of flowers, welcoming me. My cousin is beside me, trailing my little suitcase behind her, and just being a calm presence in this chaos. Her post-dreadlocks hair is now smooth and straight, shoulder-length, making her look even more peaceful. "This is it." I try to sound perky, but everything is so weird right now.

I'm greeted by the strange smell of all the tenants before me when I open the door—because I wasn't here to make my mark, to leave the scents of the natural cleaner I use for my countertops, hairspray, and pad Thai takeout. The scents of me and home.

As the ghosts of tenants past remind me this is borrowed space, I move through the living room to light a cherry blossom candle and diffuse the weird otherness here, while Saoirse takes off her shoes. "This is home!" I say it again with forced cheer.

"I love it." She says it sincerely and then admires the photos on the sideboard of my sisters and their families, my parents, me with some friends I see on occasion, my lab crew at Los Amigos Cantina. All memories I treasure. Her face grows somber, and she puts her hand on her heart, sweeping the row of photos with her gaze. And at that moment, something inside of me catches. The only photos I saw at Saoirse's house were of her with Aunt Mindy or Anthony.

Awareness floods in: *She needs me.* Not in a "feeling sorry" kind of way, but in that support and love kind of way that only your bestie can provide. For spreading your wings. For giving her roots. It's time to make her world so full of love that it spills over into photographic moments too.

I approach her, and just as I'm about to open my mouth, Saoirse grins at me, full of joy. "Show me around?"

"Yes!" It's a quick tour, but we wander through the bedroom, bath, spare bedroom, and kitchen so she can see my lack of style choices, my temporary placement of whatever I've been schlepping around from place to place for a decade, from dorms to apartments. It wasn't obvious before, but I haven't truly made this place my home base. The whole aesthetic says, "This is good for now," rather than, "Let's sink our roots into the soil."

And that might be a harsher reality to accept than the lack of pictures at Saoirse's.

I've been living a nomadic life and not really putting my mark on anything. It comes back to that question I asked the other day. *Who are you, Lacey?* Over the past few weeks, that's changed, I've changed. And I'm starting to find my footing, make my mark with the search for places that I want to share my work with, and maybe, just maybe, with a more permanent footprint where I call home.

I'm not saying I need to knock holes in the walls, but maybe I could at least pick a paint color.

"I'll have to add that pic of us hiking to the table." I gesture at the collection of framed photos.

"I need to do the same." Saoirse smiles. Looks like it's a good start.

We end up fixing the weird smell in the apartment with some pad Thai, which blends pretty well with the cherry blossom candle. I imagine the scents from the years of tenants soaking into the walls here, like layers of paint or rings on a tree, some thicker, some thinner, all important marks of time passed in this place.

It hasn't even been a year, so my ring would be small, but not insubstantial. In my own life, it's been an important ring. A ring of freedom and following dreams. A ring of climbing to the top of my academic goals and jumping to the next ladder like a trapeze artist, ready to climb some more.

As I carry dishes back to the kitchen, my eye snags on one of the pictures in the collection. It's from our childhood, all my sisters, me, and little Rona. It was from a time when we got ice cream from the truck that spun through our neighborhood.

We knew when we heard "Pop Goes the Weasel" that it was our time, and we would all race across the yard, the dry grass scratching our legs as our flip-flops clopped away in the summer sun, leading us toward the prize. Rhiannon would organize our order, present it to the guy in the truck while tapping on our heads to count us each off of the list. Then she would pay the man with a crisp twenty my dad had left for that very thing.

We were five and five, eight, eleven, fifteen, and seventeen. It was Rhiannon's last summer at home before she tasted the freedom of the wide-open world, went off to school and left us with a weird feeling that a piece was missing. Having Rhiannon in charge for the summer was great. It was the first year our parents let us stay home without a nanny. Rona and I were ready to start our own adventure in kindergarten, soon to be gap-toothed, mature little wonderers.

I remember scraping my knee as we ran for the truck the day of the picture, and Rhiannon paused to ask Fallon to help me while she handled the order and the rest of her bustling siblings. Fallon babied me, as usual, kissing my booboo. She got me a rainbow Band-Aid while Rona hugged the hurt away by squeezing me too hard. I'm sure we looked like the wild bunch of the neighborhood, but God, there was so much love.

In the picture, I'm eating my favorite, a cone with chocolate coating over the ice cream, and Rona and I have our arms around each other, cheesing so hard. I remember our neighbor, Mrs. Dorsey, stepping out on the porch as she always did when the ice cream truck came, a silent sentinel, likely making sure none of our brood ran into the road in our excitement. She was a sweet woman. She's the one who snapped the picture of us lined up on the stone wall by our house and gave it to my mom later that week when she had the film developed. I stole it and kept it in my room. Then it went with me to college. Then here.

I've never been without a little piece of them all and the feel of ease and joy from having ice cream with the best sisters, and my Rona sister.

I gaze at my younger self, the scattering of tiny freckles that never grew much in number, the auburn braids, that rainbow Band-Aid, and the happiest grin, the smile of a little girl who had no idea the struggle she would go through just over a decade later, the loss of innocence and friendship. The fear and wavering hope. That little girl would experience so much in the next two decades to get here, and I think she would be proud of me.

Even with the slightly higher chance of health issues from working in a lab—there's always a risk that a scientist will touch a chemical and get burned or breathe in a chemical and damage their lungs—I was dedicated to what I wanted. Even my vacillating faith in my path in recent days couldn't deny that I truly do love what I do, that I may even be *meant* to do this work and help others find the work that they love in scientific fields too. My passion for environmental research and fascination with salmon has continued to push me in this direction, encouraging me to pursue my desires, despite the voice that grows tinier and tinier that says I should be careful.

Little Lacey would indeed be proud.

Together, Saoirse and I rinse the plates, load the dishwasher, and pack away the leftovers. Then, we return to the living room to hang out.

"I have something fun for us tonight," Saoirse says. She reaches into her purse and pulls out a deck of cards.

"Uno?" I joke. I actually have our Uno cards from back in the day, tucked into my game cabinet, but it doesn't look like that's what she has.

She chuckles. "Nah, but I think you'll get a kick out of this." She holds up the pack so I can see that they're Tarot cards. "I just wrapped up a client's website, and she sent me a deck that she had designed for her business as a thank you. I thought it would be fun to see what's next down the pike for you."

I have to laugh. "We don't want it to be a mystery? I don't know how I'll handle anything other than, 'Life will be calm and normal for the next couple years. Just coast and enjoy yourself.'"

She echoes what Colin said to me recently by replying, "You know life isn't meant to be easy, right?" She raises her eyebrows and admires the cards as she shuffles them. "These are really nice." She presents the stack to me. "Knock on the deck."

"Is it going to reply with, 'Who's there?'"

"Just knock. Geez!"

I knock, she shuffles again, and I choose three cards. She places them face up on the coffee table as she says, "Where you've been, where you are, and what you need to know."

I follow her gaze, but I only see that the deck is pretty.

"Huh," she says, and I imagine three dots floating across a phone screen as I wait for her to tell me what the pretty pictures mean.

"Anything good? Lottery numbers?" That would be handy in case we go back to that shake place from the stakeout.

She actually sticks her tongue out at me. "So, the first one, the Eight of Wands, indicates a journey. In this case, I think it's both a journey of personal growth and a physical journey, since you had to leave your 'homeland,' your own place, and go somewhere else for the inner journey to happen. Kinda like when people go to a sacred place searching for something. Except you didn't have a choice and didn't realize you were looking for something at all."

"You just called your house a sacred place."

She ignores me. "The second one, where you are now, is Death."

"Lovely. I'm so glad we picked this over Uno."

"Hush. It's not actual death."

"Oh, pretend death is so much better."

"It means that something has ended for you and something new is beginning," she says. "You are experiencing that now because of the journey you went through. The end of your past relationship. The end of having Kendra as your boss—"

"Ha!"

Saoirse gives me the side-eye. "—the end of feeling like you're not enough for what you do. At least, I hope that part is over."

"Is it ever truly over?"

Another look. "Anyway. Lots of things ending and new things beginning, maybe even with your soul-mate." She says it all singsongy, but I'm not biting. Tears sting my eyes again. I haven't told Saoirse that he's ghosted me.

I press down my feelings with a firm breath and ask, "What's the next card?"

Saoirse smiles. "I think you can figure this one out ..."

The card is half immersed in a huge golden sun, and a woman is dancing with abandon, her arms in the air, gazing up at the sky, and I hear the introductory chords to "Here Comes the Sun" in my head. The card says, "The Sun," on it. I mean, obviously. "Does it mean that it's not going to rain this weekend?"

This time, she swats at me across the table. "It's a good thing. It means joy and success, happiness and love, and my favorite ... 'manifesting your dreams.'" She pauses to waggle her eyebrows at me, and I take the opportunity to swat back. She dodges, and her new sleek lob floats around her delicate face. "It means that you can expect to find success now that you are through your journey. I think it's wonderful. It's exactly what you would want. A happy ending."

I frown. Maybe happiness is *in the cards* for me. I have to chuckle at the jokes in my head. "Sounds good ... in theory."

"No 'in theory.'" She gathers the cards and stacks them with the rest of the deck. "Just good."

Regardless of whether the cards are real or a silly game, maybe I can chill on the overthinking, at least for one night, so we can hang out.

We decide to play Uno for a bit and catch the next episode of Jocelyn Bloom's *Braving Borders*, a travel show we love. Tonight's show is supposed to take place in Paris, and neither of us have been. Maybe someday...

Right after I turn on the TV, though, both of our phones buzz with an update on the news app. As I'm setting up the show, I hear Saoirse gasp.

I grimace, not sure what to expect, my mind racing through all the disasters that could possibly hit on a Friday night. "What happened?"

"It's the report on all the shenanigans at NLBS."

My head spins as I come back to the reality that there was an actual crime committed where I work. Do I really want to break out of my happy haven and find out all the details? I did get The Sun card, so maybe it's safe? Though one of the other cards was "Death." Eh, let's roll the dice. I know it's not my fault, so that makes it a little less scary. "Want to pull up the clip on the app and stream to the TV?"

Saoirse nods and pokes at her phone for a moment. Soon, a video of a reporter appears. She's standing in the parking lot where all three research buildings are visible behind her.

Her voice comes through the speakers. "I'm standing on the site of the Exploration Research Plateau. Earlier this month, a leak triggered sensors here, signaling that the air and groundwater contained an unsafe level of multiple chemicals. All three buildings were shut down, and the associated apartment building was evacuated.

"An investigation has been underway onsite to determine the cause of the leak, but perhaps the more interesting story happened offsite."

I swallow hard, a gross feeling twisting in my stomach that she's about to mention my name. "Oh shit," I whisper.

"An employee at Exploration Research Plateau spotted a tanker truck at Cedarbrook House, the former

home of actress Gloria Brennan, located near Snoqualmie National Forest, where they were hiking."

The screen flashes to video of a Clemons's Liquid
Transport tanker parked outside Cedarbrook and pans
as Kendra is perp-walked in handcuffs to a police car.

The reporter continues speaking in the background.
"It was discovered that the tankers were transport-
ing river water to Cedarbrook, where a local scientist,
fifty-three-year-old Dr. Kendra Glass, the granddaughter of Gloria Brennan, added a homemade sludge of
salmon gut bacteria stolen from a lab at the Plateau. The
tanker then carried the bacteria sludge and river water to a fish farm located behind nearby Sacred Waters
Sushi, where it was dumped into the water and ingested
by the farmed salmon. The restaurant, originally set to
open in September, boasted that it would serve sushi
that mimics the taste of fresh-caught salmon as closely
as possible.

"Numerous containers of salmon eggs that belonged
to the same lab were also discovered at Cedarbrook.
They had been kept in a controlled generator-pow-
ered environment while the lab was shut down and the
power off, but disappeared, presumably taken by Glass,
as she had access to the building. Security footage is
unavailable due to the electricity being off at the time."

Then, to my surprise, Twyla appears on the screen
with a microphone thrust near her face. She looks cool
and poised as she explains why this is important. "One
of the reasons that farmed fish and wild-caught fish
don't taste the same is because they have different gut

bacteria assisting with food processing. That bacteria is determined partly by the mother's gut bacteria and partly from what the fish is ingesting. Once the slurry of river water and bacteria sludge was poured into the tanks, the fish living there would ingest the same bacteria that wild-caught salmon have in their gut.

"The wild-caught eggs from our lab would start out with much of the same gut bacteria as their mothers. Farming fish from those eggs and feeding them the bacteria sludge would give you a near match in gut bacteria. It's over-simplifying things to say that this would accurately produce the same taste as a wild-caught fish, but it would theoretically be close."

I'm absolutely floored by all of this. What a complicated scheme! My eyes meet Saoirse's, and we both just shake our heads. Amazing.

The reporter comes back on the screen and continues with the story. "Derek Flynn, one of the investors in the project, had been quoted in a recent newspaper article, saying that he had high hopes for this new *ethical* farming method that was under development for Sacred Waters."

I snort loudly. "Ethical my butt."

Saoirse cackles. "Seriously. What part of that is ethical?"

"Further investigation revealed that the original leak at the lab was from a Clemons's Liquid Transport tanker full of fracking sludge delivered to Parsons & Brewster for testing by the geological group. Camera footage from several days before the leak allegedly shows Glass thrusting what appears to be a screwdriver into a rusted spot on the underside of the tanker, causing the leak.

"Over the next week, the tanker remained parked near the dumpsters, spilling sludge near an underground spring and eventually setting off the air and ground sensors. During the investigation since the leak, though, it was determined that all compounds present in the sludge were benign to humans and the environment, regardless of whether they were present in the water or air."

I smile. I already knew that part, obviously, since I'm back in my living room.

"Glad it all turned out okay." Saoirse squeezes my knee.

"Key researchers at NLBS were tipped off, though, when Glass made several requests for copies of results from their recent work, since she was unable to access printed copies in the lab herself or electronic copies on her own computer."

"Are you a 'key researcher'?" Saoirse asks.

I smile smugly. "Of course."

The reporter continues. "Glass and officials with Clemons's Liquid Transport were unavailable for comment."

As the reporter cuts to commercial, I lean back on the couch. That's it. The whole story. It's all figured out. How crazy is all of that?

And if the money Derek had was really for a researcher, was he paying Kendra? How much money would someone need to sacrifice their integrity and put their livelihood in danger? Not to mention risking jail time! Does everyone have a price. Does money really corrupt people so badly that they will do anything for it?

Being Gloria Brennan's granddaughter—the child of her only child—you'd think she'd have access to money if she needed it. How sad. And this is Ms. Brennan's legacy ...

But it's over. We go back to work on Monday, and the whole crazy adventure will be like it never happened. As the entire universe and my life as I know it quake through my body, I look around at my gray apartment, at my photos, at my cousin. *Like it never happened.*

No. Things change for the better, even if life takes a ridiculous path to get there.

Chapter Thirty-Three

Saturday morning, I'm jolted awake, but I'm not sure why. I feel weird, looking around at my old bedroom, the gray walls, the comforter from Rhiannon. A Klimt poster that I love above my bed. A terrible painting of a forest with a rainbow that I did at a paint and sip party—is that what they call them?—after graduation on another wall. A set of hooks beside the door hung with necklaces, purses, and belts, cluttered but loved. I'm here again, wrapped in the warmth of my comforts, but it's uncomfortable after weeks at Saoirse's house. Her home.

My stomach is still taking dance lessons from my nerves as my last text to Colin washes over me again. He knows that I know, and he didn't answer. Didn't say a word. I wonder if he happened to find out right when

I was texting him. It didn't seem weird until I asked to call him, and then nothing for days.

I'm kicking myself, but it's not something I had any control over. I didn't commit the crimes. Kendra did. Maybe he considers hanging out with me to be a conflict of interest now. His loyalties would lie with his old mentor, right?

I feel so bad for Chuck, too. I can't imagine what it's like to find out that your daughter has been carrying out illegal activities right there in your family home. That's betrayal on a different level. He grew up there. I imagine it stings.

I crawl from bed and pull open the blinds. My apartment is in the back of the building, so I see the grassy yard available for the residents, the pool that isn't open yet, the gazebo and fire pit, all waiting for spring to fade into summer. A couple moms in sweatshirts are talking while their kids run on the playset. A man is walking his dog on the trail. Life goes on.

Do I let it keep swirling around me? Or do I move forward?

Determination surges through my veins, and on a whim, I check the internet for a phone number, dial, leave a message of interest. My gaze sweeps the gray walls again. Roots are on my mind.

To cement this new idea sprouting in an unlikely place, a feeling near the base of my spine of permanence, comfort, anchoring, I throw on joggers and a tee with a comic book drawing of a woman in a lab coat, holding two beakers, saying, "I have all the solutions." If I didn't laugh at the science jokes, who would?

I make a protein shake and realize that Saoirse wouldn't approve of its ingredients. And she would be right. I can fix that later. Then, I get down to task. I haven't been here in three weeks, and this place is gross with dust. After I've wiped down everything in the apartment, including the trim and the light fixtures, I start on the bathroom. I don't think the tub has ever been so clean!

Taking a break sounds good, so I decide to sort my closet and dresser. It's kinda disturbing how much stuff I have that I haven't worn in a couple years. My style has changed, and my lifestyle has changed, which makes sense now that I'm a "young professional." I fill a garbage bag with clothes and a couple pairs of shoes that are still usable to donate to a local domestic violence shelter that Violet said is always looking for help.

I bring the bag to the living room and set it beside the door. It's too quiet in here, so I flip on *Braving Borders* and let it play in the background. Then, I pull the cardboard box from a recent online order and sit beside the bookcase in the living room. I sort out half the books as ones I'm ready to release. Books from my childhood that I don't care about, textbooks from school that are probably already outdated, novels that people thought I would like that I didn't. Why did I lug these around? What was I holding onto?

Do I need all this crap to feel like I'm home? Like I belong? Like I'm successful because my bookshelves are full?

I can't think of anything else to sort through, so I set the box by the door, too, and grab the vacuum.

Cleaning is perking me up a bit, especially knowing that others will benefit from the purge, especially at the shelter. Plus, I'm enjoying hearing Jocelyn, the host of *Braving Borders*, as she and her boyfriend Adrian are trying real strudel in a little shop somewhere in Bavaria. Maybe I need to add this to my someday-vacation list.

I lug the vacuum to the end of the hall and start with the office/guest room, moving toward the living room on the opposite end of the apartment. When I vacuum, I always picture the floors as repulsive, and I'm making them un-repulsive with the vacuum, almost like they are changing color, like a video game of some sort. It's like I leave each room with it feeling squeaky clean, and I love it.

When I finally finish the living room, I'm famished, so I take a few minutes to grill chicken and make a salad for lunch. Good thing Saoirse thought about groceries yesterday or I wouldn't have any. I feel strikingly gross but accomplished while I eat. I'm back in my home, it's clean ... now what?

It still has that "not mine" feel. But maybe my phone call earlier will fix that. Oh, and I thought of a couple things to order that will make it feel a little homier, a little more mine. I'd love a painting in an actual frame to hang above my couch, for example, instead of a poster held to the wall with putty.

I grab my phone on my way to the shower and see that I have a bunch of notifications, mostly from social media.

I also missed a phone call.

When I click on the phone app, though, I see that the caller was Colin. And he left a voicemail. *Geez, do I want to listen?* My chest tightens as I waver with my finger over the play button, but I can't make myself hit it. I don't want it to hurt more than it already does.

I decide to wait, so I climb in the shower and take my time, using face scrub and foot scrub, and all the fancy soaps and scouring devices I have in there. I shave. Twice. I slowly towel off, sort through my body sprays and select one that smells like green apples and tea. I pick another pair of joggers and a long-sleeve cotton shirt to hang out in. Then I decide to dry my hair and curl it, like I'm going somewhere special. Because it's good to practice. Even though I just did this the other day. You know, practice-y practice for the sake of … wasting time.

Once I'm curled, though, I really can't keep fighting myself. Unless I paint my nails? No, I want to know what he said, but I also *don't* want to know. I haven't heard from him since I sent that text telling him about Kendra on Tuesday. Why bother even calling me when he hasn't texted all week?

Finally, I sit down on the couch, hold my breath, and press play.

"Hey Lacey, I'm not sure where to start. I'm so sorry about this week." I hear him sigh and picture him running a hand through his hair. "Right after I said 'goodnight' on Tuesday, my phone started an update, so I didn't look at it till I was ready for bed, and then I couldn't get it to go past the 'hello' screen. I restarted it and plugged it in, but it wouldn't move, so I had to use an old travel alarm clock to wake me up on Wednesday."

I actually cough out a laugh here because, wow, he has an old travel alarm clock just in case? Way to be a responsible adult.

He laughs too. "How's that for being a responsible adult?"

Oh my God.

"And I actually forgot my phone here when I left for my flight, which reversed my responsible adult points. It's been plugged in on my nightstand since Tuesday night. Then my flight was delayed, so I've been at the airport since yesterday afternoon without a phone. Yes, I slept in the airport. So I had no way to call and let you or anyone else know what was going on. I just got back like twenty minutes ago. I got the phone to start, and your last couple messages came in." He breathes out hard. "I had no idea you wanted to talk to me. I feel so bad. I hope everything is okay. I didn't ghost you for our date. I just couldn't call or text. I feel like an idiot, and you probably already made plans for tonight."

Well, he's wrong on that count, just me and ma' pjs over here.

"Anyway, it's too late to expect you to accommodate me, so let's just plan another night for dinner, if you can forgive me, and—"

Beeeeeep.

No! There's a second message, though, so I check that.

"It cut me off. Anyway, let's plan another night for dinner. I hope you can forgive my mistake. And I did see your text about Chuck." I suck in a nervous breath, and he continues. "It's okay. That's not your fault. Please don't worry about it."

I melt into the couch in relief and put a hand to my heart. Why would I think that something like that would bother him anyway? *Of course* it's not my fault. Geez, Lacey, so silly.

"I'm going to get some sleep, maybe head over to Riff's later and support the gang. If you aren't busy, I'd love it if you stop by. I hope you have a good night. I'll try you again tomorrow."

I set the phone down, my order of new crap for the apartment completely forgotten. *I'm such an idiot.* I can't help but burst into laughter again. Flopping down on the couch, I feel my anxieties melting away. He's not mad. He screwed up too, though it's an easy mistake to make.

I've never been more relieved to hear that someone's phone updated.

He's probably trying to nap now, so I don't want to call and disturb him. I decide to read a book instead and pace around my apartment waiting on the *other* call, the one I was actually expecting.

Finally, I decide to quickly call Saoirse to let her know what's going on.

"Sorry, what?" is how she responds to my story.

"Crazy, right?" I know it's crazy, but I need some confirmation.

"Too funny." Saoirse clears her throat. "So, I actually don't have plans tonight. I was going to stay in and relax, but *since you got an invite to Riff's ...*"

"Would you like to join me?" I'm getting giddy at this point, and I may need someone to let the helium out of my head later.

"I would love to!"

The minutes creep by the rest of the day, and I suddenly feel like a high schooler trying to pick out an outfit. Green? Blue? Purple? Yellow? *God, Lacey, just put clothes on. You've worn clothes before, right?*

I finally settle on a teal long-sleeve dress. It's flowy and flattering. Oh, except Morgan told me it's the same color as a mallard's head. Do I want that?

Do guys even think about these things?

I add a brown belt and knee-high boots and decide to try enjoying myself instead of overthinking.

Maybe.

The phone rings, and it's finally the call I was waiting for. I make an appointment for Monday evening and make a note in my calendar to stop at the bank at lunch on Monday.

Then, in front of the bathroom mirror, I'm suddenly incapable of selecting lipstick either. I put on a bold red, but then I think it's too showy and obvious, like I'm trying too hard. So I wipe it off and go with a coral. But it's evening, so I reapply the red.

I give up.

Chapter Thirty-Four

Finally, Saoirse rescues me by texting that she's downstairs. I run down to meet her, and we head to Riff's.

When I walk in, I discreetly look for Colin but I don't see him. "I guess he's not here yet," I tell Saoirse.

"No worries," she says. We find a table near the back, since the whole place is full, and place our order. Cheese fries. Hell yeah. And a couple drinks.

"Your hair is really cute," I say.

"Thank you!" She puffs the bottom with her hand. "I figured out how to curl it without looking like a clown, and I feel like it's a major accomplishment."

I laugh. "It looks great. I honestly loved the dreadlocks, but this really suits you."

Saoirse grins and dunks a fry into the cheese. "God this is good."

As we chatter, I glance around a couple more times, just to make sure that I don't miss Colin, but it's almost show time, and he's still not here. People are packing in, and it's barely standing room only.

Saoirse grabs my hand. "It's okay. Maybe he's running late. He'll see us. We're hard to miss."

That's when I realize that we are seated right under one of the lights, and it's reflecting off of Saoirse's hair, making her look like a moon goddess. "Huh."

"You're pretty lit up over there, too, *Red*." She smirks.

I roll my eyes. "I really hate being called that."

"Own it," she responds with a wink. "You've got some great hair too."

A smile plays about my lips as I adjust my leather jacket on the back of the chair in an effort to peer behind me without being obvious. Still no Colin. Then the lights on the stage flicker to life, and everyone bursts into applause.

When the musicians take the stage, I realize why Colin wasn't in the audience. He's walking toward the pianos with Anthony and Wes. "I guess Colin is playing tonight," I say. I'm a little bummed. Not that I don't want to hear him perform. It means that I need to wait a little longer to talk to him.

"Oh." Saoirse cocks her head to the side, perplexed. "I thought Libby was playing tonight." She opens her phone and fires off a text. "I'll see what's up. In the meantime, let's just enjoy the show."

Tonight, they open with Guns n' Roses' "Welcome to the Jungle," featuring Wes's tenor vocals, and the place is shaking with enthusiasm. So many people are singing along that you can likely hear it outside. I can feel my chest vibrating.

We spend the next couple songs eating and yell-talking over the music, and I finally start to relax. Saoirse's phone lights up, and when she checks it, she says, "Aw. Libs is sick. She said she texted Colin a bit ago, and he agreed to sit in for her."

"Tell her I hope she feels better." I jam another fry in my mouth and chew thoughtfully as I listen to the gentlemen on stage playing "Bartender."

The server stops by our table to check on refills and asks if we want to make any requests. She has a stack of papers for audience members to fill in their song.

I start to shake my head *no*, but then I stop. Would it be funny...? "Actually, yeah. I do." I take a paper and jot down a song. I trusted my gut. It popped into my head, so it's probably a good idea, right? At least, I think that's what Colin had said.

When the server leaves, Saoirse turns to me. "What did you request?"

Suddenly, I'm embarrassed, and my face grows hot. Maybe that was stupid. No one is going to like that song. The guys won't play it. "Oh, don't worry about it."

Saoirse throws her hands out. "What?! You don't get to do that. Tell me the song. It can't be that embarrassing or you wouldn't have asked for it."

"It's, uh, a private joke."

"Oh. You guys have private jokes, do you?" Saoirse waggles her eyebrows at me, and I shrink in my seat.

"I shouldn't have written that."

Playfully, she punches my arm. "Nah. I'm sure he will love your joke." She turns back to the stage. Then she mutters, "It's a shame I can't be in on it though."

A couple more songs, and Colin reaches for the pile to see what they should play next. He reads a few slips of paper, discards them, and comes to a stop, frowning like he's thinking. Sitting up straighter, he peers at the audience, scouring the crowd. It seems like his eyes rest on me, and he grins.

Ah, he's reading mine. He knows I'm here. I raise my arm a little and give a wave to acknowledge him.

He looks at Anthony and Wes and tips his head to the audience. They clearly know what that means because they both nod. Standing, Colin walks to the stand where his guitar is, scoops it up, and heads to the front of the stage.

"A bit of an unusual request here tonight ..." he begins, and I die a slow and painful death from my face catching on fire.

Saoirse grins big at me, and I sink lower and lower in the chair. The problem with being five foot eleven, though, is that you can't go very far when you're trying to hide. I'm all angles and limbs, poking down under our little table, and I suddenly feel like a giant in a kids' play land.

"A friend of mine asked for 'Daphne,' a beautiful instrumental song that means a lot to me." He pauses for a breath of time. "But I'm not going to play it."

I know I'm at the back of the room, and no one is *actually* looking at me, but I feel like the weight of every eye in here is on me. *Oh no.* Is he upset that I requested that? I just wanted him to know that I'm here.

"Instead, I wanted to share something that I've been working on for years. It's a song about ... well, it's a song about what all songs are about, falling in love. I kept hearing the melody in my head and never was able to pull the whole thing together. Till recently." He clears his throat and strikes a chord. "I hope you like it."

The people in the audience are sharing looks of surprise, but they don't look upset. It's bound to be good entertainment, even if it breaks the rules of the piano bar a little. I wrap my hands around my rum and coke, the condensation running down my fingertips, and try to relax.

The tech spotlights Colin as he strums the opening, and the entire room grows still. It reminds me of Lifehouse's *You and Me*, but it's different. Then, his warm baritone pours through the speakers.

I've scoffed at meant-to-be, and I've laughed at fate
I stumbled through maybes and no-thank-you'd second dates
But a feeling in my heart, a vision in my brain
Drove me on, drove me insane

So I put my head down, a steady path through my work
I don't need anything, so why does this hurt
But a recent vision brought memories back to me

And knocked me to my knees

"This is beautiful," Saoirse whispers.

"Yeah ..." I breathe. I'm mesmerized, and it seems that everyone else in the room is too. It feels like the little pieces of glass from my snow globe—the one where everything is perfect—are starting to meld back together, like we're all enchanted.

He strums harder, tipping the guitar up, and I know instinctively that the chorus is coming.

After I've searched for what seems like forever
Interference from angels has brought us together
I'm home in her arms as a storm whips us around
And now, I've finally found ... my dream girl

"Oh." My mouth forms the word, but I don't dare breathe it aloud or I'll break the spell, break into a thousand pieces, break the fragile snow globe. A realization washes over me as those little tendrils inside my abdomen wrap back around my heart, my lungs, my soul, and whatever other pieces of me are welcoming to them.

I suppose I was right to trust my gut and write that single word on that slip of paper after all.

Saoirse, however, can't contain her emotions anymore. She grabs my hand and squeezes so hard that *she* starts crying. "He wrote a song for you," she says.

I wrinkle my eyebrows, ever the one to ruin everything with logic. "But ... he said he started writing it years ago. That he just completed it recently. It's not for me. It's just, you know, about life, about falling in love, as he said." I glance at Saoirse, and she looks less than amused. "We've all fallen in love before, so he was probably just writing about his experience from having gone through—"

Saoirse gets up in my face and puts her hands on my shoulders. "You know, I love you to death, but you are seriously irritating."

"What? That's what he said it's about."

She releases me and shakes her head at the poor idiot she's stuck hanging out with. "Girl, he's your soul. mate." She emphasizes the syllables like she's banging them into my head with a hammer. "He didn't need to *know* you to write the song. He ... good grief, I'm ruining the moment. Just shut up and listen. This is for you, hon." She pats me on the arm, and we both turn back to the stage.

Tears well in my eyes as Colin loops back to the chorus, and I'm wondering what angels brought us together. Divine? Earthly? I wouldn't have known he existed if I hadn't called Saoirse.

Or would I?

From the stage comes the last line of the song. *I've finally found ... my dream girl.*

It's all there. I bite my lip. Placing my hand on my heart, I feel it beating in rhythm to the song as Colin plays the last few chords, slowing into a final strum.

The place erupts into exuberant applause, and I'm right there with them, slamming my palms together so hard that they tingle. To be fair, though, I'm buzzing all over. I lean toward Saoirse. She's right. "I think that's confirmation he likes me," I say, sounding like a silly kid with a crush. She flutters her eyelids and looks away, and we both laugh.

"You're a goof," she says, pretending to backhand me.

The lights on the stage dim, and the applause finally starts to die away as the musicians pause for a break at the halfway point in their set.

The awareness that he's probably coming over here washes over me like a cold sweat. Actually, it *is* a cold sweat. My palms are wet, and I just hope there isn't a mark on my dress from—

"You paying attention?" Saoirse asks.

I look where she is looking, and Colin hasn't even bothered to go backstage with the guys to circle back through the door by the stage that leads to the floor. He sets his guitar down, hops off the stage, and makes a beeline for the back of the room.

For me?

"Go get 'em, tiger." Saoirse stands and abandons me, her little pink dress weaving through the tables toward the stage door, likely to say *hi* to Anthony. I follow with my eyes for a moment and then turn back toward where Colin is making his way through the crowd with deter-mination, watched by every person in the room.

Nervousness and ego are twin butterflies keeping me rooted in place as they flutter throughout my body. I've been talking to him for a couple weeks, but I suddenly find my brain devoid of things to say, while simultaneously, my whole body is sparking with the fact that *the song was for me*, and this absolutely gorgeous man is pushing his way through a crowded room to see me.

Me.

Our gaze locks and remains so as he finishes the last few steps to my table. I'm standing there biting my lip, eyes wide with all those weird emotions because ... wow.

"Hey," he says softly.

"Hey," I manage. *Me Jane. Ugh.*

Colin takes my hand, looks down at it, back at my eyes. I gaze into his, which are fire and ice, sun and moon, dirt and stars—everything that ever was and will be.

Epilogue

S *ix months later ...*

   I clear my throat and adjust the microphone.
Home stretch ...

   "As a newer member of the research team, my great-
est challenges didn't come from the lab table. They
came from inside." I can't believe that I'm talking about
this, but this is what I felt like I should pitch when my
lab group sat down with the team from The Association
of Deaf and Hard of Hearing Scientists Symposium, and
I took the "trust your gut" advice again. So here I am:
standing at a podium, just a few months after our research has wrapped up, on young scientist's day at the
event.

   My face heats as I realize that my closing remarks
force me to open up to a room full of bright-eyed high
school kids about—gasp—my feelings. Everyone in the
room is staring at me. The fluorescent lighting is over-

whelmingly bright. Like a nuclear explosion. And I can hear it humming somewhere off to the left.

I don't know how Fallon talks to noob humans every day without spontaneously combusting from cringe. *Is that how the kids say it?*

I remind myself, though, that these kids *want* to be here. They *want* to be scientists. Most of them are actually listening. And that's a little scary.

My eyes come to rest on the single friendly face at the back of the room. He nods and smiles, just like he has every time I've looked at him during the talk. I'm so grateful. Though it makes my already thudding heart do a summersault in my chest. I inhale for four, exhale for four, trying to regain my footing.

I lift my hands again to continue signing with my discussion. "It's funny to think that people like us are at the top of our classes, pushing ourselves to be the best, acing our tests, applying for every advanced placement and next step that we can. Goal after goal after goal. And yet, we continue to think that we aren't enough.

"Sometime, that comes from thinking we need to hit just one more goal, win one more award, get a nod from the right person. Sometimes, it comes from our body's protective response to someone else trying to knock us down, even if it's casual or seems like it could be a joke. But what it really comes down to is that we always innately feel like we aren't enough. Despite the accolades. Despite promotions. Despite the 'attaboys' ... *and 'attagirls.'* That gremlin is inside of us, and it's imposter syndrome.

"Everything I told you about my research today is what I experienced in the lab among a group of the most supportive colleagues anyone could ask for. I consider them mentors and friends." I leave off the part about Kendra knocking me down mentally and stealing from us. Not giving my energy to that. "I was nervous around them, fearing that they might think I'm an idiot or that I would take forever to catch up on a project that's been going on for over a decade. Thankfully, they were welcoming and kind, giving me the chance to not only catch up but carve my own place in the team.

"But when I started reaching out to groups about the work we had completed, even when I asked to stand up here and speak to you guys—*yeah, I'm doing this voluntarily*" —that got a knowing chuckle from the crowd—"I was scared I would fail. I was scared that I would get questions I didn't know the answer to. Or that someone would disagree with my work for whatever reason. Our heads are *great* at inventing reasons we'll fail.

"If there's anything I can leave you with today, it's not a greater knowledge of the changing levels of gut bacteria in *Oncorhynchus nerka* and how this indicates environmental change in Puget Sound. Though, if you leave with that, you get cool points in my book." Another chuckle from the room. Made 'em laugh twice! "What I'd really like you to leave here with is the knowledge that you are amazing as you are, and that you can do hard things, but you'll have to do them scared.

"This is the first conference I've presented at as a professional, and I was definitely scared. No amount of evidence that I could do this made me feel like I could succeed. I've presented as a graduate student and defended my thesis to my committee, which was absolutely the most nerve-wracking moment of my life by the way. But my brain has continuously moved the goal post. There has to be one more thing that will finally make me feel ready, right?"

I look around the room, and I can feel them nodding in agreement. Even my single supporter at the back of the room has a tight-lipped smile and is nodding.

"If I actually listened to myself, I wouldn't be up here. I wouldn't get to share my experience with you, and you wouldn't have gotten this little glimpse into the world of what it's really like to be a *noob* scientist." One of the kids signs "noob" to the person beside them, and they both stifle a laugh.

"You can't take a pill for imposter syndrome. You can't get over it like you would the flu. You just have to follow your heart and trust that it's leading you in the right direction. Then you grow, and you get to level up and do another hard thing. Eventually, you'll have done so many hard things that the first one seems like nothing. At least, that's the way I hope it will be." I have to give the group a wry smile here. No one really knows.

"I recently discovered a quote by author Tallulah Carney that has become an absolute favorite of mine. *Even when the odds are against us, we must still pursue what's in our hearts and sets our souls on fire.* I hope that every one of you in here can do just that and that you take one step at a time toward your goals without fear of failing, but with the knowledge that we will fail sometimes, and it makes us stronger.

"The world doesn't need more people who are fearless. It needs more people willing to step forward anyway, despite their fears, because they know what they want. And they deserve to go for it. Because when we live our dreams, it gives others the courage to also live theirs. And that makes the world a better place for us all. Thank you."

I touch my fingertips to my chin and then tip them toward the audience as I sign the last phrase. My eyes flicker quickly around the room when I realize that it's quiet, and I'm done. *What did I just do?*

In reality, it's the longest quarter second of my life as the adrenaline is still flowing, and my heart is pounding in my throat, but everyone starts clapping. I even see smiles.

At the back of the room, Colin mouths, "You did it!" and whoops. But it's not over yet.

The moderator approaches the podium now. "Does anyone have questions?" A couple dozen hands raise, and I prepare to respond to who knows what. Like I can actually prepare. This has to be one of the biggest fears a researcher has. What if they ask something I can't answer?

***

"You did great." Colin wraps his arms around me in a quick hug.

As much as I'd like to smooch him and cuddle him and make goo-goo eyes, there are tons of budding scientists around, and PDA is a no-no. Instead, I smile and allow him to envelop me, drinking in the feeling. He smells like pine needles, sandalwood, and fresh air, which has moved up the scale above cinnamon rolls as my favorite smell.

"You did pretty great yourself!" I respond. "I think the kids enjoyed not only your talk on improving biocompatibility with artificial hearts but also the fact that you brought models they could mess with."

"Agreed. They definitely got some mileage out of those." Colin smiles smugly. "I'll have to remember them for my next talk."

"Fallon will appreciate that." I'm really excited that Fallon invited Colin to come to the school and present about artificial hearts, and exCorde, the company he works for, was more than thrilled to send him there. They're big on educating the public and especially outreach to middle and high schools.

We finally get to Colin's SUV and load our materials in the back. I didn't bring much, but he has a box full of hearts. Which sounds kinda cute, like he's schlepping around his valentines. "Should we stop at the house and drop these off first?" I ask, pointing at the box.

"They can stay in the car," Colin answers. "Besides, ever since you got that place, it's hard to drag you out once you get home. I'm not risking you wanting to stay home all weekend."

"True ..." I can't help it. My house is adorable. This spring, I put a bid on that cute little home with the bleeding hearts on either side of the front door, the one that looks like a great place for a couple, and I actually bought it. Me. I bought a house. I put down roots of my own. Even stranger, Saoirse has been helping me decorate. And Colin has a drawer full of stuff there ... maybe more than one drawer.

I peel off my suit jacket and swap my heels for sneakers. "Ah, better." Then I hop in the car.

We hit the road and turn onto I-90, heading east toward Snoqualmie. I'm excited for the weekend that Colin has planned ... whatever it is he has planned. It will be wonderful to relax after the last couple days of attending the conference.

I enjoyed the sessions on both days, especially Colin's, but being one of the last speakers on the last day meant that I had to sit through everyone else's "perfect" talks and freak out that I was going to destroy the audience with my stupidity.

As I said, our brains are great at making us feel horrible. Seeing evidence that I can present like that helps, a little, but you know ...

Glad I did it, but glad it's over.

"So when are you going to tell me where we're going?" I'm actually glad I had the distraction of the conference for the last couple days because I cannot get him to even drop a hint of what's going on this weekend.

He told me to bring my fishing pole and appropriate clothes, but I'm tossing around whether I should be nervous. It's October. Surely, we aren't going camping. Are we? I didn't see a tent or anything in the back that would make me think that. So I hope not. It's not super cold out right now, but I don't want to be cold and soggy while I sleep.

"You'll just have to see …" He leans back and drives with one arm flopped over the wheel like he's some stud.

"I could smack you," I deadpan. No hints? Nothing? Gah.

Colin barks out a laugh. "Would you just let me surprise you for once, control freak?"

"As someone who grew up with four older sisters, surprises aren't exactly my favorite." I spent all of second grade believing that someone lived in my basement because my sisters took turns hiding down there and making startling noises while another sister would walk past the top of the stairs with me. Do you ever wonder if kids from big families need therapy because of each other? Yes. Yes they do.

"You'll like this one," he says.

"Mmm," I grunt. God, he's amazing. Even if I don't like surprises, he planned a surprise *for me*. Eeee!

My phone buzzes, and I pull it from my purse. It's the group chat that Twyla started way back in April, going crazy with little balloons and party poppers. I scroll up because I must have missed something while I was at the conference.

"Wow—Twyla is the permanent lab coordinator. That's awesome," I say, so Colin knows what's up. I type a quick "congrats" in the chat and can't help the giant grin that spreads across my face.

Dan had been asked if he would like to be the interim lab coordinator after Kendra was arrested back in April, but he passed. He said that his career was winding down, and he was happy where he was with only five years till retirement. Maybe less, he hinted. He wanted someone else to get the opportunity, and he suggested that they talk to Twyla, who accepted right away.

"Good for her," Colin says. "I think she'll do a great job."

I love that Colin likes my lab partners and knows them well enough to say that. I could barely contain my excitement when I brought him with me back in May to meet them at one of our "family nights" at Los Amigos Cantina. I'm sure I looked like a dingbat walking in there drooling over Colin, clutching his hand in mine as if he might try to escape like a rogue toddler. The lab crew got it though, and they said they were happy for me. Everyone seemed to like him.

We veer off the main road and down a street that I know heads to one of the parking areas by the trail. I give Colin the side-eye, but he doesn't notice because, um, he's driving. Maybe he wants to hike first? I'm getting kinda hungry, so I'm glad I packed some jerky. Saoirse found me an organic chicken and pineapple jerky that is surprisingly good. I've been taking her advice on food, and I like it. Trying new things ... who'd have thunk it?

I dig in my purse and pull out two of them. "Want one?" I ask.

Colin glances my way and shakes his head. "Nah, we'll eat soon. Don't worry about it."

"I have a tube of cookie dough in here too."

"Lacey, seriously?" Colin can't help but laugh at this because I'm absolutely hilarious. And weird. But I don't care. He likes my brand of weird. "I'll feed you soon," he adds.

I look around us. The hills are thinly swathed in gold and red as the trees do their autumn finale. There are exactly zero signs of civilization, but I know some roads out here lead to little towns I don't know about, like that one Saoirse and I found a few months ago as we followed a tanker truck to find a fish farm behind a sushi restaurant. "*Soon* like how soon?"

Chuckling, Colin puts his hand on mine and squeezes. "Soon. Really. Put the jerky away."

We pass the entrance to the park, and my stomach does a funny little dance. Where is he taking me? "This is a really elaborate plot for a murder."

He sighs.

Then, we turn onto the most unlikely road, the one that leads to Cedarbrook House. I smile questioningly at him, but again, he's focused on the road. I can be patient for two minutes, I suppose.

Tick. Tock.

The tires make that slick sound from running over fallen leaves as we trudge slowly up the gravel drive, and there, in the clearing, is the beautiful giant that is Cedarbrook. The bold yellows and oranges dull into the warm chocolate tones of the cedars surrounding the lovely brownstone. She's changed again—no longer a stiff, unwelcoming matron, Cedarbrook feels open and free, almost calling to us through the trees, like a wild maiden. You know, like the way people were in the 1970s. Or maybe like Belle running through that field in *Beauty in the Beast* saying she wants adventure.

Anyway, Colin parks and turns to me. "Here ya go." He gestures toward the house.

I look around for a moment. There's the patio where Gloria Brennan hosted her parties, where her granddaughter forged a bond with criminals to steal from my lab and profit from it and where so many memories happened in between. Ahead, over the hill, the river pours on, never-ending in its chase to the sea. The ground here is littered with a carpet of golds and oranges and browns, and the husky gray sky above stretches on forever, the clouds like wisps of smoke from an extinguished fire. It feels like a magical land where anything can happen.

"What are we doing here?" I'm still a little nervous that Colin is taking me camping, though it's a lovely place to do it.

He smiles, shakes a keyring at me, and steps out of the car.

I'm still stuck in that not-quite-sure-what's-happening zone, but I have an idea. But it's ridiculous. *Does Colin have the keys to Cedarbrook?* When I step out of the car, I shrug at him. "You're enjoying this, aren't you?"

In response, he cups my chin, kisses me, and heads for the back door. "We're staying here tonight. Chuck suggested I give you a nice weekend away here, and I couldn't say *no*."

My jaw drops because *oh my God*. I've dreamed of this since I was a little kid. "You mean I get to see inside?"

We both laugh, and Colin answers, "Unless you want to sleep out here."

I grab him and kiss him so hard that I almost knock him into a wall.

"If I knew you'd like it so much, I would have brought you here months ago." He kisses me on the forehead and smiles down at me. Then, he unlocks the door, and we press inside. "The downstairs renovation isn't complete, but the upstairs is ready."

When he flicks on the light, I'm delighted to see that the kitchen and dining area are done because, hello, I'm famished.

The kitchen is modern, of course, but the décor in both rooms is reminiscent of the 1940s, right down to the floor to ceiling built-ins filled with books on the far wall. Pale blue walls are welcoming and will likely give it an open, airy look in the daylight.

"There's a baby grand in the living room, too," Colin says. "It's covered right now, since they're remodeling in there."

I can see what I assume is the piano through the plastic sheet hung between the dining room and the rest of the main floor. "I'm sure you're itching to play it." I pat his arm playfully and head for the refrigerator. Hashtag priorities.

"Let's change first." He grabs my arm and pulls me up the stairs to a big room at the end of the hall. Like the rest of the house, it's baby blue, and the king-size bed has a white eyelet lace comforter. He tosses the bag on the bed, and I go for my pjs. "Not yet," he says. So we both slip on jeans, tees, and fleece, though I'm not sure why.

"Seems a little overdressed for hanging out alone in an empty house," I mutter. But he winks at me and guides me back downstairs.

Automatically, I jog back toward the fridge, but Colin grabs my arm.

"Geez, hang on a sec," he says, so I pause.

"What?"

A moment later, there's a knock at the door, and I'm delighted to see it's a delivery that smells like dinner.

Colin slips the driver a tip and takes the bag. "There's a seafood place about ten minutes from here. Chuck was telling me about it."

"You had me at *seafood*."

Colin scoops another bag out of the fridge and motions for me to follow.

I start to, but I pause by a huge photograph on the wall. There's a woman in a green party dress. It has a sheen like a quick fish darting through the shallows.

Her hair is set in victory rolls, and she has a warm closed mouth smile that just touches her huge brown doe eyes. Beside her is a man in a spiffy suit, his arm wrapped around her waist and his other hand resting on the shoulder of a boy in short pants, also dressed up. He looks to be around four or five.

My breath catches. This must be the whole family, Gloria and Everett and "good ole Chuck." Together and happy, before that tragedy struck. I can almost hear the strains from a song coming from the patio, like the party in my dream. This was supposed to be their home, where they grew old together, and instead, it had to become a place of healing.

I touch the glass on instinct, and I think it feels warm. Maybe. Surely that's my mind playing tricks on me. A single tear slips down my cheek. At least they had this photo together to remember their joy, and to watch over those who come to Cedarbrook in the future, to make more wonderful memories.

I feel a gentle hand on my arm and turn—but no one is there. Again, I hear a whisper, like the trees saying *shhh shhh* in the breeze, but this time, it sounds more like *thank you.*

"You're welcome," I murmur.

Quickly, I catch up to Colin at the car, where he hands me the bags and pulls out our fishing gear and a blanket.

"I think I know where this is going ..." I take a couple steps and then stop. "Jackets first?"

"Oh, right." He grabs those too.

As we're standing there by the brownstone patio, the Edison bulbs flicker on around us like dozens of fireflies.

"Ohhh." It's enchanting. "This really will be perfect for Saoirse and Anthony's wedding."

"I'm glad Chuck suggested it."

A moment later, we're walking down a path toward the river. Just as we reach the perfect flat spot on the bank, the gray skies finally clear, and we're greeted with a gorgeous view of the sun dipping lower in the sky. I feel a piece of the snow globe above us lock into place again, showing off with colors that mimic the hue of the leaves.

I spread out the blanket and set our dinner down while Colin sets up our fishing poles. I open the other bag and am delighted to find plastic forks and two cold beers. "What did you pick for dinner?" I say as I pluck a Styrofoam container from the bag and open it. *Be still my heart.* "Seafood linguini? You shouldn't have."

"Chuck says it will be the best damn seafood linguini I've had in my life."

A ridiculous flashback from a few months ago zigzags through my brain, and I snort laugh. "Oh no. But maybe close."

Colin cocks an eyebrow at me and flops down on the blanket. "Well, I'll have to try your favorite sometime, but for now, I'm pretty excited about this one." We click our plastic forks together and dig in.

Oh. my. God. "This is perfect," I coo.

Colin murmurs something through a bite, and we both leave each other alone with our joy.

After a few minutes of delighted munching, Colin pops open our beers and hands me one. "A toast to Lacey and her first conference as *Dr. Sturm*. You did a fantastic job, and I'm so proud of you."

I smile and clink my bottle against his. "A toast to the man with the fire in his eyes, who kicked ass talking about artificial hearts today ... and stole my very real one." For the full effect, I make a silly face and place my hand over the cavern where my pilfered heart once lain.

"You're so corny." He leans over and pecks me on the lips.

"You love it." I wink. I actually don't feel weird about winking at him now.

When we finish our dinner a few minutes later, Colin and I cast our lines into the water and get quiet. I watch our lines, calmly caught in the current. Some leaves pass in the water. It's so relaxing that I could fall asleep, now that I've come back down from that two-day adrenaline high. I scoot closer to Colin and tip my head against his shoulder. He kisses my hair and wraps an arm around me.

In the flawless stillness of the sunset woods, Colin clears his throat and whispers. "Ever have a weird dream that felt important? Like it was a message or ... something?" I feel him speaking as much as I hear it, the warm baritone vibrating through his chest.

I hum in response. Staring into the woods across from us, as I listen to the *shhh shhh* of the trees telling secrets, as I breathe in the scent of cedar and pine needles and perfection, I'm transported far away to a time when I wondered exactly who was visiting my dreams and why. It feels fuzzy, like another lifetime, like I'm watching a movie. As I'm drifting, I feel a warmth from deep inside of me as the tendrils wrap themselves around everything, my soul, my dreams. As they wind and bind, as they grow strong and hum with delight like the last chord of a love song.

After a moment, Colin sits up a little and looks at me, no doubt to see if I fell asleep. "You okay?" A breeze rushes through the trees, feeling like a friendly reminder of my journey to this moment.

"Yeah," I whisper. I tip my head up to look back at Colin, with a deep knowing of all that is being said in that moment without words. "I'm good."

Author's Note

The idea for *Good in Theory* started when I recalled something a chemistry professor said over twenty years ago. The memory floated into my head as I was thinking how cool it would be to write a story about a female scientist.

My professor was actually fun and candid with us. One day she started talking about how everyone has a price. I don't remember what triggered the conversation, but it was funny to think about. How much would someone have to pay you to quit your job? Would it have to be enough to set up a lab in your basement so you could keep doing what you love and not really get paid for it? She might have been talking about winning the lottery, but whatever the trigger, that idea stayed with me. And it became a major driver for this book.

Then, the rest of the story came at me in layers, and the last one that dropped into my head almost didn't get to be part of it!

When I first set out to tell the story of a scientist who was thrown back into her cousin's world after a decade of estrangement, I meant to entwine that storyline and the one where something sinister was happening at the lab. But, for a few years, I had also wanted to write about someone who dreamed about her soulmate and then actually met him.

I had read a post where a friend said that she had experienced the dreaming part but hadn't met him in real life yet. It was like he kept coming to her and saying *hi* in her dreams, but then never showed up in person. Of course, I was intrigued by this and wanted the happy ending for her, so I decided to give it to Lacey.

Once I had the main plot of the book laid out, I played with the soulmate idea until I finally felt like it would work. The final result was a story that I was so excited to write because it not only had that "trudging into the unknown" quality with the lab story and the reconnection with her cousin, but it also had the beautiful rush of new romance.

And, funny enough, some of my favorite scenes to write were about Colin playing his guitar. I grew up as a musician, playing trumpet in marching band, clear through college, so I loved being able to describe the way the music feels and how a room changes with a live performance. It gives me chills!

I have so many people to thank for making this book possible!

First, Kayla Komondor was so open with her experience as an early-career scientist, and I loved that I got to talk to her and ask the deep questions I needed to be able to really dive into Lacey's character. I knew a bit of the behind the scenes stuff, having worked as a writer at a lab for eight years and holding a biology degree (that's where I learned about the fish stuff), but I didn't know what it really felt like to put on that white coat and step into this world dominated by men. Thank you, Kayla, for sharing all the good and the not-so-good with me!

Stephanie Samolovitch, who founded and runs Young Adult Survivors United, thanks for grabbing coffee with me that one random day in the spring! After that, Lacey started nudging me about her personal journey with cancer, which hadn't clicked until you were so open with me about your own experiences. Thank you!

My writing group—Em S. A'cor, Ann Howley, Sarah McKnight, and J.V. Hilliard, all incredibly talented authors—made writing this book absolutely delightful and fulfilling! I grew as a writer because of you guys and also loved getting feedback as I went through the writing process. It was a unique experience with this book! Thank you for all your wisdom and praise for me work! I especially loved getting notes with all the little "lols" and "hahas" in the margin. That made my day!

When I did my undergrad in biology (dual major with English), my professor Dr. Joseph Marshall taught me two things that I'll never forget. First, sometimes it's better to know where to find the right info rather than knowing all the info. And second, how to build a fish farm. That second piece was knowledge I never thought I would use! Thanks, Dr. Marshall!

Thanks to my daughters, London and Talia, for helping me name some of the characters and give me ideas! They provided the names for the lab crew and Lacey's ex and his friend. And thanks to my husband, Matt, for understanding that I may need to go spend hours at my desk hallucinating a story while you handle everything beyond the closed door. Your support makes my books possible!

Thank you, Allison, for your work editing my book! As always, you did a fantastic job! I couldn't do it without you!

And to my friends and fans, thank you for your support and for reading my work! Hearing your love for my characters and the hot water I love to put them in really makes a difference! I appreciate you! If you have a moment, I would love a review on Amazon and/or Goodreads. Thank you!

Discussion Questions

1. What would you have done if you walked in on your significant other and their friend stuffing money in a bag? Would you walk out immediately? Let them explain?

2. One of Lacey's biggest fears is not knowing the answers. Do you think that is a common fear among professionals? What about in your own life?

3. Cheese fries are Lacey's favorite comfort food, one that brings back memories of spending time with her best friend, her cousin. What does that for you?

4. Lacey wonders about what made Kendra the

way she is. How do you think the environment she works in has shaped Lacey?

5. Do you have any special skills that aren't related to what you do every day that would make your life that much more interesting if you could combine them? Lacey does this with her ability to sign and her work with the lab.

6. Is there a rational explanation for why Lacey was having dreams about a mysterious man?

7. What do you think life was like for "good ole" Chuck Vernon after finding out that his granddaughter was using his home to commit a crime? How would he cope?

8. Would you feel comfortable staying with a friend you hadn't seen for ten years in an emergency? Or would you have opted for the hotel?

9. Lacey compares her world to a snow globe with pieces breaking off or reassembling based on the destruction of her innocence and the rebuilding of hope. What has happened in your life recently that would repair pieces of your snow globe?

10. Did you suspect that Kendra was Chuck's granddaughter?

11. How would you feel about someone writing a song for you and performing it live to a crowd?

12. If you were whisked away for a weekend, what would be perfection for you?

Ashes and Other Inheritances

A hundred-year-old journal and an old flame might *not*
be the strangest parts of
Morgan's story of
Ashes and Other Inheritances
Keep reading for an excerpt from
Cori Wamsley's next novel.

Chapter One

Some people say that life is a bowl of cherries, and they would be right in some respects. There are definitely pits. And a variety of sweet and sour moments.

But they miss the mark because that you are literally comparing life to something that was once living and has been plucked from the living thing that nurtured it. It begins dying the moment that it becomes valuable to us. And if you don't eat the fruit, it rots.

Morbid, but *seize the freaking day*, right?

So I do. I always have. I've always sought the most flavorful, big moments. The moments that make us feel like we're truly living. The moments that leave us breathless because *that was a rush* ... or *we almost got caught* ... or *I just defined another epoch of living*.

I'm not an adrenaline junkie. But I love to feel alive.

"This is so close to perfection ..." I mutter to myself. I'm in Castel Gandolfo, a gorgeous town in Italy, south of Rome, with the man of my dreams. As in, he's in my dreams and not here in Italy with me physically.

I'm dreaming about him right now, as I'm gazing at the pristine lake from the porch of the villa, the sun angling off of the water, making it sparkle. I sip my cappuccino and let the flavor wash over me. Real Italian cappuccino, the bitterness of the roast mingling with sugary sweetness. Thinking about how wonderful it would be if he were here. But we broke up months ago. We had to.

I get this funny sinking feeling in my belly. Dread? Loneliness? A missed opportunity for joy? Or maybe it's something else. Something that doesn't feel like missing him so much as missing... something I haven't found yet.

Maybe I should have invited him to escape with me anyway. Just to see what he would say.

Unfortunately, this impulse hits when I'm halfway across the world from Mr. Gorgeous. I should have invited him to join me, and I am kicking myself for not thinking about it before.

Anyone have a time machine?

"You remind me of a painting." Interrupting my musings, Signore Zangari joins me on the porch and leans against the railing of his lovely home. I've been lucky enough to stay here in a guest room while working on the project on the adjacent lot.

"Oh, I do?" I smile thoughtfully at my host, raising my eyebrows. "I didn't realize I was so picturesque."

He laughs. "No, you remind me of an *actual* painting. *Tè e Fantasticheria.*"

"What does that mean?"

"Tea and Reverie."

"Beautiful." I sip my coffee.

He gestures to me and then out at our gorgeous view. "It's a painting of a woman standing on a porch and looking at Lago Albano, painted somewhere in this area well over a hundred years ago. It's quite famous in the region." Pulling out his phone, he calls up the image and shows me. A woman in the foreground gazes dreamily at the lake in the distance, a porcelain cup in her hand. Her hair hangs loosely around her shoulders and her blue-green dress sweeps to the right, as if she just entered the frame.

I glance from the painting to my coffee cup to the lake and back. "I don't see a resemblance."

Again, he chuckles. "You have the same faraway look. Like you are thinking of something magical that we can't see."

Now it's my turn to laugh. "You're reading my mind." We smile at each other, sip our drinks, and gaze back at the lake. But I refrain from telling him about my daydreams. They are like a delicious little burrito wrapped up in my mind, warm and welcoming. Or should it be a ravioli, since we're in Italy? "Is this painting at the papal palace? I'd love to see it while I'm here."

"Sadly, it has been missing for over a hundred years. There are rumors that it was smuggled to America." He points at his phone again. "This image was created from the artist's original sketches by someone who saw the painting and redid it by memory. That's all we have now." He points at the description on the Lazio Museum, Rome's website. "This painting is in Roma," he confirms.

"That's a shame." How sad that a piece of history went missing.

A beat later, Signore Zangari nods toward the worksite near the villa. "Progress is good, yes?"

"Yes, Baker & Willow will be pleased," I agree, pausing to inhale the aroma of my coffee. "Kenzi and I both are. And everything is on budget." I flew in to check the progress on the event center project being managed by the architectural firm I run finance for.

"We were certainly lucky that Kenzi attended our dig." He smiles. "Ottavia and I are so happy."

Signore Z wanted to open an event venue on their property, but as you would expect in the region around Rome, the ground was riddled with artifacts. In this case, a chunk of a house. He had to stop excavating and bring in a team to check it out.

Kenzi is one of our architects and had happened to volunteer for the archaeological dig at the Zangari villa. She struck a chord with Signore Z. By the time the dig wrapped up, Kenzi had inadvertently talked him into incorporating the beautiful ancient building into the new design. He and his wife, Ottavia, pitched her for the project. When all was said and done, Baker & Willow ended up taking it on, with Kenzi leading the whole thing.

Kenzi has flown out here several times to ensure that her design is coming to fruition properly, and as luck would have it, Baker & Willow decided to send me over before the next phase starts.

I didn't complain! A week in Italy in the fall—or, well, any time of year—is *fantastico*!

Smiling at Signore Z, I add, "I negotiated with a couple of the local vendors for different aspects of the project. We're getting tile from Caltagirone, which so perfectly coordinates with the ruins."

"I'm impressed. The most beautiful tile always comes from that city." He puts his hands in his pockets and smiles. "Baker & Willow has been spectacular. Only a few more months."

I nod, turning back to the lake. "I'm going to miss this place." I drape my carnation pink cashmere sweater over my arm and glance at my suitcases. Nico will be around with the car any minute to take me to my hotel. "Glad I get a day in town to explore before I head to Rome." And I'm thankful that the magic doesn't end here, today.

"You need to see the papal palace," Signore Z says. "I think you'll enjoy the gardens there." I did rather love the gardens at the villa, so he's probably right. I spent so much time sitting on a bench in the shade of the lemon trees crunching numbers that I will always associate the smell of lemons with spreadsheets.

A black sedan pulls into the drive, and I wrap the older man in a big hug. It's not very businesslike, but everyone from Baker & Willow stays at his villa when we visit the site, so I feel like I'm leaving my uncle. I'll miss the big family-style dinners in the villa's dining room ... and someone else cooking for me for three meals a day. "I hope to be back again before we wrap up. You and Signora Z have been so kind, and you have such a beautiful home!"

"Ciao! We hope you come back, too." With a sly smile, he slips a long, narrow box into my open tote bag, and I just *know* that it's a gorgeous pair of handmade Italian loafers from his company, Pelletteria Zangari.

"Oh!" I want to rip into the box like it's my birthday. "Thank you!"

He laughs easily. "Wait till you get to your room." Then Nico loads my bags and whisks me down the road to Lago Albano Albergo, my hotel.

Once I unpack in my room—and try on the chocolate brown loafers; YES!—I decide to sit on the balcony and enjoy the sunshine and an afternoon breeze: *il dolce far niente*. There really is so much sweetness in doing nothing! I pull out my crochet hook and work on another coffee cup koozie to drop off at the shop by my house. I've been selling them there for a couple years, and they're always a hit.

The air is fragrant, like there is a bakery nearby, and I make a note to check on that for the morning. The sky is Tiffany blue, and the view from the balcony shows me the entire town down into the valley. Catching myself halfway through an enormous exhale of pure bliss, I realize something: I'm on vacation alone in gorgeous Castel Gandolfo, Italy, and I'm sitting on my balcony crocheting? Maybe this is every little old lady's dream, and I'm just living it out a little early.

A lot early. Thirty-five is the new eighty-five, right?

And that's my cue to leave. Gotta grab life's sweet cherries.

About the Author

Cori Wamsley is a sweet romance author, writing coach, and publishing consultant who specializes in emotional-arc storytelling and character-driven fiction. Her novels explore identity, healing, and the courage it takes to begin again, blending heartfelt relationships with themes of personal transformation.

As the founder of Aurora Corialis Publishing, she helps authors develop clear, compelling narratives and build sustainable writing careers. With a background in editing, coaching, and small-press publishing, Cori brings a holistic understanding of both craft and industry to her work. She is the author of Ashes and Other Inheritances, Exactly What It Looks Like, and several earlier titles. Cori lives in Pennsylvania with her family, where she continues to write stories that invite readers into emotional clarity, hope, and connection.

Follow Cori on Instagram, Threads, or TikTok @cori-wamsley_author.

Learn more at www.coriwamsley.com.

Cori Wamsley's Books

For more sweet romances with humor and heart, check out Cori's other books!

Want the Music?

This is the playlist for *Good in Theory*!
It features all the songs from the book ... except
"Daphne."

For "Daphne," you'll need to go here:
https://bit.ly/3WqzuCP